NANBERRY
Black Brother White

D1304727

Jackie French

NANBERRY

Black Brother White

📚 Angus&Robertson
An imprint of HarperCollins*Publishers*

Angus&Robertson
An imprint of HarperCollins*Publishers*, Australia

First published in Australia in 2011
by HarperCollins*Publishers* Australia Pty Limited
ABN 36 009 913 517
harpercollins.com.au

HarperCollins*Publishers*
Level 13, 201 Elizabeth Street, Sydney NSW 2000, Australia
31 View Road, Glenfield, Auckland 0627, New Zealand
A 53, Sector 57, Noida, UP, India
77–85 Fulham Palace Road, London W6 8JB, United Kingdom
2 Bloor Street East, 20th floor, Toronto, Ontario M4W 1A8, Canada
10 East 53rd Street, New York NY 10022, USA

National Library of Australia Cataloguing-in-Publication entry:

French, Jackie.
    Nanberry : black brother white / Jackie French.
    ISBN: 978 0 7322 9022 1 (pbk.)
    For children.
    Australia—Social conditions—19th century—Juvenile fiction.
A823.3

Cover design by Jane Waterhouse, HarperCollins Design Studio
Cover images: Aboriginal boy © Penny Tweedie/Corbis; View of Sydney Cove by
    Dixson Galleries, State Library of NSW, Call number: DG 60; leaves and possum
    from shutterstock.com
Typeset in Sabon 10/14pt by Letter Spaced
Printed and bound in Australia by Griffin Press
50gsm Bulky News used by HarperCollins*Publishers* is a natural, recyclable product
made from wood grown in sustainable plantation forests. The manufacturing processes
conform to the environmental regulations in the country of origin, New Zealand.

5   4   3   2   11   12   13   14

*To the extraordinary people in this book, and
to all those who helped me find their stories.*

*Also to the children of the Wallaga
Lake Community, with love.*

Prologue

NANBERRY

WARRANE (SYDNEY COVE), THE TIME OF MANY
FISH AND FEASTS (26 JANUARY 1788)

The harbour was emu-berry blue, the ripples playing with the sun. The breeze smelt of smoke and cooking fish. Nanberry waded in till the water tickled his waist, felt the sandy mud between his toes, then took a deep breath and dived down.

It was a new world. Light drifted in gold shivers from above. Nanberry wriggled like a fish, turning so he could see the surface of the water. He loved this most of all: how in one instant you could change from air to sea.

At last his lungs began to ache. He pushed himself into the daylight in one strong sweep.

One of the girls yelled at him from the shore — his sister, Yagali, catching a ball of twisted twigs and feathers as one of the others threw it to her. 'Hey, you with empty hands! Where are the dainya?' The other girls laughed. Behind them the stream trickled between the trees and mud flats to join the waves.

Nanberry grinned. Who needed dainya, the mud oysters? The women had been out in their low-slung canoes, hauling in fish with nets and lines. Colbee had speared a giant waragul, a mackerel, too.

The girls went back to their game. Nanberry began to wade to shore.

'Maigul!' Stranger!

Nanberry turned to see where Yagali pointed.

For a second he thought he dreamt. His eight years had been full of familiar things. The warriors and old women knew all that was important in the world. But no one had ever spoken of anything like this!

Massive canoes surged across the water. They looked like whales that had learnt how to swim on top of the sea. Giant skins flapped on tall spears jutting from their middles.

How did canoes move with no paddles? Had the spirit ancestors made them?

The girls ran for the trees. Their ball lay abandoned in the sand. But Nanberry stayed, his toes in the mud and sea, his eyes straining to capture every detail of the big canoes.

'Nanberry! Guwi!' Nanberry, come here!

Colbee strode towards him. Colbee was his mother's brother, a warrior. You obeyed when a warrior called you, especially if he was your mother's brother. Nanberry splashed back to the shore, then turned once more to stare at the strange canoes.

'Into the trees,' yelled Colbee. He pointed to the women and children standing still and almost invisible next to the tree trunks.

This time Nanberry didn't move. 'What are they? Are they ghost canoes?'

'I don't know. But others have seen things like them before.'

'Who?'

'It is no business for small boys.'

Nanberry still didn't move.

Colbee gave a half-smile. His eyes shifted back to the strange canoes. 'A runner came from the south. A great fleet of murry nowey came to their country. The murry nowey slipped across the line between sea and sky, the land of clouds and ghosts. The murry nowey gathered in the runner's tribe's bay. The creatures on them had white skin, like ghosts, but they looked for water, like men, and hunted with long sticks that went *babooom*.'

The murry nowey were even closer now, gliding across the water.

'Go!' ordered Colbee.

This time Nanberry went.

The warriors strode down to the water, waving their fishing spears, the jagged shell points gleaming in the sun. 'Jiriya! Wari! Wari!' Get away from here!

The big canoes floated straight towards them, as though the warriors were buzzing bees who had no sting. And then the canoes stopped, even though they were still far from the beach. Nanberry stared out between the trees.

He could see people! Men with white faces, their bodies covered in the skins of strange animals, blue and red and brownish grey. Their voices sounded like human voices, not the wind-whispering of ghosts.

Some of the white ghosts glanced over at the warriors. None bothered to answer the challenge, or even call a greeting. It is as though *we* are the ghosts, thought Nanberry. As though they expect us to fade away.

The giant canoes glided on. The warriors yelled a challenge again. The white ghosts laughed, then looked away. Colbee muttered something to the other warriors. They melted back into the trees, urging the women and children to follow. Whatever the white ghosts were going to do next, it was best to stay away.

Life would go on, in its proper seasons, as it always had before. The ghosts would float away.

Only Nanberry lingered, still peering from behind his tree. He had thought he had made himself part of the sea. But these big canoes conquered the waves like the sea eagle controlled the wind. If only he could ride the waves like that. If only he could slip between the wrinkle at the edge of the sea and sky and see the world beyond the blue horizon.

But he was Nanberry. This was his home, and the Cadigal were his people.

The breeze held the scent of strange things now, of memories of a world far away. Nanberry took a last look out at the pale men busy with vast ropes, then ran back to join his family.

Chapter 1

NANBERRY

Tumbalong (the place where food is found, now Darling Harbour), the time of thickest possum fur, smoked fish and fat yams (13 April 1789)

The wind snickered between the trees like an old woman laughing. Nanberry drew closer to the fire as around him the shadows thickened into night. The girls and women sang as they hung today's fish up on the lines to dry in the smoke.

Though the murry nowey had floated away, the white ghosts had not. They had stayed through a whole sky full of seasons.

Nanberry had expected great warriors to come from such extraordinary canoes. But instead they had been poor strange creatures, small and hunched over, with pale, pinched faces.

The white ghosts chopped down trees. They built big huts. They lived in them all year, until they stank. Their women didn't know how to fish and when they gathered oysters they threw away the flesh and kept only the shells.

The white ghosts stole Cadigal canoes and spears. They tried to attack the Cadigal women, though the women had fought them and run off. They had even made the stream a filthy stinking thing. Didn't white-ghost mothers tell their children how important it was to keep the water clean?

How could people be as stupid as these? When they had captured Colbee — maybe so he could show them how to build canoes — it had been easy for him to escape.

Nanberry had heard the white ghosts had kidnapped Arabanoo, a warrior from another clan, and kept him prisoner. But Arabanoo was not Cadigal. He might have his own reasons for staying in the white-ghost camp.

The Cadigal warriors had talked about attacking the white-ghost camp. But they had decided to let them be — for now. The land was big. The white ghosts perched on such a tiny part of it. They hurt it now, but it would recover when they left.

Maybe the white ghosts would simply fade away. How could any people live who knew so little about the simplest things, like hunting food and keeping water clean? It was easy to keep away from the white-ghost camp. Their hunters made more noise than a mob of kookaburras.

Nanberry smiled at the thought of a row of white ghosts, hunched on a branch like the cackling birds.

Auntie grinned at him. 'Are you dreaming of food, boy?'

Nanberry grinned back. He was always hungry these days. He hoped it meant that soon he'd start to grow tall as a man.

Auntie thrust her digging stick into the dirt near the fire, and pushed out a cluster of the sweet yams cooking there. 'Stuff your belly, young one. The rest of us are full of fish.'

Nanberry looked around to check that no one else wanted yams too. This was the best time to eat them — and bungu too — in the blue and gold days before the cold winds came, when animals and roots were fat.

But the men had eaten their fill of the badagarang, the kangaroo, left from yesterday's hunt. The women and children had nibbled freshly caught fish all day, cooking them on tiny fires in their canoes.

There were fewer fish this year, now that the white ghosts hauled up so many in their nets, but there was still plenty if you knew the harbour.

Nanberry picked up a yam and juggled it between his fingers till it grew cool enough to bite into. The outside was crisp from the fire and ash; the inside was hot and sweet and good.

Auntie laughed. 'Look at the boy. He could eat a whale and still want a feast of grass-seed cakes and figs.'

'I think his legs are hollow,' said Yagali.

Nanberry ignored them. Aunties and sisters were best ignored when they laughed at you. He took another yam and bit into its sweetness.

Auntie moaned.

Nanberry's mother looked over from the fish she was hanging up to smoke. 'What's wrong?'

Auntie shook her head. 'I ... I don't know. It was sudden. Like an axe hit my head ...'

Nanberry's mother shared a look with another of the women. She vanished into the shadows, then slipped back, her hands full of leaves. She threw them onto the fire, then put her arms around Auntie. 'Sniff the smoke,' she said soothingly. Then she held out a small, reddish lump of resin. 'Here, it's bloodwood sap. You'll feel better soon.'

Auntie bent towards the fire, shivering. She began to chew the sap. All at once she pushed herself away. 'Hot,' she muttered. 'So hot.'

Nanberry stared, his mouth still full of yam. Auntie had been cold a moment ago. He looked at her more closely. Her skin was as spotted as a leaf when the sweet insects sucked its sap. The spots were white on her dark tummy and chest.

They weren't mosquito bites, or nettle stings. Nanberry had never seen white spots like that. His skin prickled with sudden fear. Were they ghost spots on Auntie's skin?

Auntie moaned again. 'Hot. So hot.'

Nanberry's mother nodded at Yagali. The girl fetched a bark coolamon filled with water and began to splash the liquid on Auntie's body.

'Sleep,' said Nanberry's mother. 'You will feel better after you have slept.'

Auntie began to pant.

—⦿—

The wailing woke him. Nanberry rubbed his face and peered out of the hut. Auntie's body lay in his mother's lap. Her dead eyes stared at the sky. The spots were bigger now: sores that seemed to weep across her body. It was as though the sores were still alive, while Auntie was now dead.

Nanberry began to run towards them. Colbee grabbed his shoulder. 'No,' he barked. 'Stand back.'

Nanberry obeyed. He watched as the women dug a shallow grave and lowered Auntie into it. Around him the warriors had gathered their spears. Now the women loaded themselves with sleeping furs and cloaks, with baskets and hatchets and fishing nets.

It was time to go. You didn't stay where someone had died. You never spoke their name or their spirit might call you to the grave too.

The camp was quiet. Even the kookaburras had stopped their cackling alarm calls to say that humans were near. No one had seen an illness like this, nor any other that killed so quickly.

Nanberry looked at Auntie's grave a last time, the rough soil among the shadows of the leaves.

'Come, boy,' said Colbee. His eyes were dark with shock.

Nanberry picked up his soft bungu-skin rug and his knife. The warriors strode into the trees, carrying their spears. The women and children followed.

They walked towards the sea, away from the stream and from death, further from the white-ghost camp too.

Nanberry was glad.

They hadn't got far when Nanberry's mother stopped. She put Nanberry's baby sister down. She shook her head. 'Hot,' she whispered. 'Hot.'

The baby began to cry. Her face was flushed too. Her eyes looked red, and there was sweat on her skin.

Nanberry's grandfather put down his spears, and stared at the white blisters on his chest. An hour ago his chest had worn only his warrior's scars, and its eagle feather on a string of twisted hair. Now it looked as though an evil hand had decorated it with white clay.

Colbee gazed at the rest of the clan, one by one.

He is looking for the white blisters, thought Nanberry. He is checking to see who might have a fever too. He looked down at his own chest and hands, but they were clear.

Colbee pointed at Yagali. Everyone else stared at her too. Nanberry could see the raised marks of three white blisters just under her chin. Only three, he thought, but there will be more soon.

Yagali gave a cry. She ran to their mother, and put her hands over her face, as though to hide from what was happening.

Colbee muttered with the other warriors. 'We need to go,' he ordered. 'Now. Fast, before the sickness spreads. We leave the sick ones here.'

Colbee's face looked like a rock. That was what made you a warrior — learning to ignore pain so you could keep your people safe.

Colbee was right. Nanberry knew that Colbee was right. This strange illness spread and killed so fast that the whole clan might be dead in a few days if they stayed here.

And yet he couldn't go. He stood still as a grass tree, as the others began to walk away.

'Come, boy!' yelled Colbee.

Nanberry didn't reply. Let Colbee think Nanberry had the sickness too. It was right for his uncle to take the others away. Nanberry wasn't a warrior. If the illness took him he never would be. But it was right for him to stay here, to care for his family. A warrior ignored the pain so he could do what was right.

He watched as the clan turned into shadows among the trees — the friends he had swum with, the Aunties peering back now and then with horror and sympathy — till even the last glimpse of them was gone. And then he knelt to help his family. Already his mother was too weak to stand alone.

He couldn't let them die!

Maybe if he could cool their hot skin the illness would go away. His grandfather seemed to have the same thought. 'To the beach,' he whispered.

Nanberry lifted up his little sister. Her body felt like coals in the fire. His grandfather helped his mother and Yagali stagger towards the waves.

Step after step after step ... his grandfather stumbled as Nanberry's mother and Yagali leant on him. The short walk to the beach seemed like the longest journey they had ever taken.

Nanberry looked down at the baby in his arms. White blisters seeped across her chest.

At last they reached the water. His mother and grandfather and Yagali sat in the cool shallows, with the waves lapping at their knees. His mother put her arms up for her baby. The tiny girl began to cry. Blisters had erupted on his mother's face now too. The spots on his grandfather's chest had turned to weeping sores.

Nanberry tried not to cry as well. He watched his grandfather bend his head and splash water over his hair, over and over as though he might beat the fever with its freshness. His mother lowered the baby onto the wet sand and let the waves run across her body.

Nanberry clenched his fists. The cool water would make them better. It had to! Meanwhile they needed food. If you didn't have food and fresh water you died. He was the only one now with strength to care for them.

He had no spear — only warriors could carry spears, and it would be many summers yet before Nanberry could go through his initiation ceremony and have his front tooth knocked out. But he had seen a bungu tree as they had staggered here: a big tree, with scratches on the trunk showing where the bungu scrambled up every day to sleep in a hollow where a branch had rotted away. The bungu would be so sound asleep it wouldn't wake until it was too late.

You didn't have to be a warrior to catch a bungu, a possum. He could dig yam roots, and roast them on a fire.

Nanberry glanced down at the others. His mother's eyes were shut, but she still held the little girl. Yagali had covered her face again, perhaps so she couldn't see the blisters breaking out across her body. His grandfather muttered, words that made no sense, staring at the waves.

'I won't be long.' Nanberry didn't think they heard him. He ran into the bush.

The bungu tree was where Nanberry remembered it. He wrapped his arms and legs around its trunk, and pushed with his knees many times, till he reached the first branch. He pulled himself up next to the hollow.

Sometimes snakes or lizards slept in holes like this. But the bungu scratches told him this hole was safe. A big bungu would keep snakes away from its home.

Nanberry reached inside. His fingers met soft fur. It didn't have time to struggle before he twisted its neck and pulled it out. Its head hung limply on its body.

Something dropped from the bungu's back onto the leafy ground. Nanberry peered down. It was a baby bungu, perhaps half grown; it had faint dark fur, not the pink skin of a tiny baby. It lay there stunned, its eyes big and black.

Nanberry considered it, as he slid down the tree. There wouldn't be much meat on it. He needed to get back.

He ran through the dappled shade, leaving the baby bungu among the dead bracken and grass.

His family were where he had left them, dozing as the waves lapped around their limbs. It was late afternoon now. The beach was striped with tree shadows.

Nanberry gathered driftwood and dried tussocks, thrown up above the high-tide mark by the last storm. He held the fire bone — a hollow bone with a slow-burning coal inside it — to the dry grass until it flared. He threw on dry branches, then skinned the bungu. He poked a stick through it, then propped the stick up with stones so the meat would cook.

He sat there as the night gathered itself around him.

How could life change so suddenly?

There had always been many hands to share each task, and songs and love and laughter to brighten the work. Now there was only him to care for his family on the beach.

All his life the seasons had come as they were supposed to: the season of the emu pattern high in the night sky, when the fish swam thickly in the harbour; the season of rain when the geebungs and five-corners fruited, and the figs swelled; and the cold days when you knew the shellfish were sweetest, and the kurrajong bark was at its most supple for weaving into baskets or fishing lines — just before the bloodwood sap flowed so the women could soak the lines in it to harden them.

When the sun rose higher it was time to travel up the river to Parramatta, to strip the stringybark sheets to make the new canoes. When the wattle bloomed the fish swam once more in great families, so many that the lines were always heavy.

There was a time for the settling of disputes, and a time to go west to feast on eels, a time when the bees wore fluffy yellow pollen on their legs, when you knew that in another season of moons the nectar would flow sweet and pale green when you poked a stick into the honey trees.

Everything has its time, he thought.

So this was a time of death.

The moon rose. He held meat to his mother's lips. He tried to coax his grandfather to eat. Yagali just shook her head. 'Water,' she whispered.

How could he have forgotten? He hurried to where his mother had dropped her net, and took out two coolamons.

There was no stream near this beach, not even a waterhole, but he'd seen a half-burnt tree, hit by lightning before he was born. There would be rainwater trapped there. He climbed the tree and filled the coolamons, trying not to let the water spill as he climbed down and ran back to the beach. The moonlight was making blue shadows under the trees.

His grandfather gulped the water eagerly, then shivered. 'I'm cold,' he muttered. 'Cold.'

Nanberry felt hope surge through him. Had the cold water driven away the illness? He helped the old man over to the fire, then took the water to his mother. She held the coolamon up to her daughters' lips then she drank too.

The tide had gone out. The waves fell back towards the sea. His mother lay in the wet sand, cradling her baby. Yagali huddled next to her. Nanberry nestled down in the cool sand. His skin burnt like the sun had kissed him.

He slept uneasily, waking every time one of the others cried out in fever dreams. He dreamt that tomorrow the women would be out in their canoes, laughing and singing, the children feasting on the shore while the fish smoked in the fires, to keep for the winter days when the schools no longer gathered so near the shore. Tomorrow he would swim again, in the soft blue water. Nanberry opened his eyes. The light was like a spear. He forced himself to look around.

The sky grew grey, then pink, and a too-bright blue. Yagali had vanished. He struggled to sit up. Why did his body feel like a jellyfish? He peered around frantically, looking for her. Had she run into the bush to find the others, or tried to swim out to cool her body? But even her footprints had been eaten by the waves.

'Gumna?' he cried to his grandfather. 'Wianga?' he called to his mother. But they only muttered, their eyes blank, their minds lost in the land of fever.

He looked down at his hands, his arms, his legs. The white blisters covered his skin.

He forced himself to his feet. He had to fetch fresh water before he grew too ill to move. He had to find Yagali. But his legs had turned to whale blubber. He collapsed onto the sand.

Chapter 2

SURGEON WHITE

You can cure men of many things, thought Surgeon White, as he tramped through the trees with his two convict assistants. But you can't cure stupidity. Below him Cockle Bay gleamed in the sunlight.

New South Wales! The Surgeon snorted.

He'd done what he could. He and Captain Phillip had brought eleven ships and nearly 800 convicts, poor starving wretches, white-faced and weak from prison, halfway across the world, the longest journey a fleet had ever made. Only twenty-four had died — far fewer than if they had remained in prison in England.

It was a miracle. And it was due to him.

As Chief Surgeon he had insisted that the convicts eat fresh food in England, at Tenerife in the Canary Islands, and at Cape Town on the Cape of Good Hope at the southern tip of Africa, the last port before the final seemingly endless voyage across the almost uncharted ocean. Convicts who refused to eat because the fruit juice stung their mouths were whipped.

The day after they had landed in this poor excuse for a country he'd made sure the tents for his laboratory and the sick had been put up. He'd had a garden fenced off to grow fresh vegetables. The poor wretches, swollen with scurvy, their teeth falling out, too weak to stand after so long at sea, needed fresh food, not medicine. And again, he'd had to threaten beatings if they didn't eat.

The Surgeon snorted once more as he pushed away a branch. Stupidity! Most of the convicts only knew the stews and slops and bread of city streets. They thought fresh fruit would kill them.

Well, fresh food had saved their lives. But most convicts and marines were too stupid and too lazy to grow their own.

The tiny colony had been established at Sydney Cove for more than a year now. Time enough to get huts built, gardens planted and harvested, for their sheep and cows and hens to have given birth to more. But what had happened? Surgeon White shook his head.

Most still lived on their rations, the salt meat so hard you couldn't cut it with a knife but had to hold it on a toasting fork over the fire to roast it. Sour flour that was more weevils than grain, dried peas ...

You could count the good men on the fingers of one hand. Governor Phillip, as he now was, wearing himself out with work and worry; Watkin Tench and Captain Waterhouse. The others were as bad as the convicts. Major Ross was a liar and a troublemaker. Even his Assistant Surgeon Balmain refused to give White the respect due to a gentleman of his rank.

I'm lonely, thought the Surgeon. Deep, bone-deep lonely.

The marines refused to guard the convicts or act as magistrates.

They were here in case the French invaded, or the natives attacked. But no such trouble had arisen, so the marines lounged around complaining that they hadn't got their due supply of wine or rum. None of them even lifted a finger to grow corn or cabbages, relying on the convicts assigned to them to do everything from digging their gardens to pulling on their masters' boots.

Few gardens produced enough to feed their owners. Most of the cows had wandered off into the bush. All of which was why Surgeon White was here today, hunting out fresh greens and native fruits to add to the colony's supply of food, trying them himself first in case they were poisonous. Luckily only one lot had been really dangerous, the 'native beans' he had tested last year. He'd had to keep the chamberpot handy for two weeks after he'd eaten those.

Surgeon White looked at the convicts on either side of him. They were browned from the sun, but far too thin. Yet he doubted either of them would bother to eat his share of the wild spinach he'd ordered them to gather today, the samphire, the leaves of the vegetable tree, the native cabbage and sarsaparilla, or even the fish the Surgeon had caught last night. The fools would eat ancient salt pork and weevily flour instead of good fresh fish and spinach.

Well, he made sure the convict patients in his hospital ate properly. They ate or they were whipped!

One of the convicts muttered something to his friend. Surgeon White held up his hand for silence; the men would scare the birds. This land was paradise for a scientist, if good for nothing else. Birds were moving north for winter now. Who knew what he might spy …

The older of the convicts — a wiry wretch, thirty years old perhaps, starved all his life so he looked more like a monkey than a man — pointed silently towards the tussocks.

Surgeon White squinted. A bird?

No, it was an animal; a small one lying on the ground. He gestured to the convicts to stay back, and trod quietly forward.

The tiny creature didn't move.

The Surgeon peered down at the scrap of fluff and bones. It was just a baby o'possum. He'd discovered three new species of o'possum here, but they were too like American o'possums to be worth describing in the book he was writing.

On the other hand, a baby o'possum was small enough to fit in a preserving jar. Someone in England might be interested — if a ship ever came, bringing them fresh stores and taking his letters and specimens home.

He gestured to the smaller convict. 'Put it in the sack with the wild spinach.'

The man nodded. He reached down and picked the creature up. 'Sir ... it's still alive.'

'What?' The Surgeon peered at the o'possum. The tiny beast's heart beat under the long soft fur. It looked much like an adult: the cat-like face, the long tail with its white tip, the front fur white, the back almost black.

Surgeon White shrugged. 'It will be dead by the time we get back. Just put it in the bag, man. We need at least another four sacks of greens if they are to be of any use at the hospital.'

Chapter 3

MARIA

Maria peered into the black pot on the kitchen fire. It held wild duck the Surgeon had shot last dusk, and potatoes from their garden, stewed with turnips and parsnips.

Later she'd add wild greens, like Surgeon White had told her to, and use their flour ration to make fresh soda bread on the hearth, near enough to the coals to cook but not to burn.

She and the Surgeon ate better than anyone in the colony except the Governor, she reckoned.

Gran had taught her to boil a pudding and sew a seam. Then Gran had died. She'd eaten flour and water gruel in the workhouse after that, till the lady came to buy her to be a kitchen maid. But she weren't no 'lady'. She wanted Maria to pick pockets — after she'd lured them into an alley for what Gran called 'Men's Rampaging Lusts'.

All there was to eat was penny stew after that, small bones she were sure was rat.

She were always hungry. Once you'd starved she reckoned that nothing ever made you feel really full. She'd had cold kangaroo meat and hot potatoes for her midday dinner, all she wanted, and Indian maize pudding for breakfast, with oyster pie, and now she were hungry again.

Maria gave the pot another stir. Oh, but it smelt fine. She'd picked the buckshot out of the duck, so the Surgeon wouldn't break a tooth when he ate the meat. The buckshot could be melted down and used again. Surgeon White had told her that buckshot was precious now, till a supply ship could reach them from England — if it ever did.

Starving when she were a child was probably why she still looked a tiny scrap now. She were fifteen years old, but she looked more like ten. That were a good thing. Looking young and helpless had meant the judge back in England had only given her fourteen years instead of sending her to the gallows, to be hanged by the neck till she were dead.

Maria had seen coves kicking and screaming as the noose tightened around their necks after they dropped from the gallows to their deaths. At least she'd been spared that.

There'd only been stale bread in prison, thrown onto the straw for everyone to fight for. The ship had been better — stew and biscuit twice a day, except she'd been too terrified and sick to eat, shivering in the filthy darkness as the water seeped through the wooden ship, holding onto her breath as the great waves tossed it.

But Sydney Cove were better — or Sydney Town as it were starting to be called, though it were a long way from a town yet.

Governor Phillip was a right good 'un. He'd sent the youngest convicts to Norfolk Island, away from the Men's Rampaging Lusts. There were nearly 600 male convicts here, and close to 250 marines, and only 200 girls and women. Sydney Cove weren't a place for a child, or for a woman neither, unless she didn't mind Rampaging Lusts.

It had been good of Governor Phillip to send her to Surgeon White. The Surgeon had no Rampaging Lusts. All he wanted was his food well cooked, his hut kept clean, his uniform mended. And Maria could cook and sew better than any girl in the colony. She liked things clean too.

Port Jackson might well be a prison without bars, and convicts might have to work for whoever they were assigned to, but there were few who'd been lucky enough to be assigned to a man like Surgeon White.

The door opened. She bobbed a curtsey as the Master stepped in, stamping the mud off his boots on the mat. Big Lon followed, casting a sack of wild greens onto the table. He touched his forelock to Surgeon White, then went out.

The Master sat in his chair before the fire. The chair was colony-made, its legs already twisted and out of shape. But it had arms and was comfortable enough. She sat in it, when he were out. It was the only chair they had.

She knelt to take off his boots. She put them outside for Big Lon to clean, then poured water from the hearth pot into his teapot with a handful of the dried sarsaparilla flowers to make the herb tea he liked. The Master wasn't one for getting drunk either. He nodded his thanks, then picked up his notebook.

Nor for talking, she thought, or not to servants any rate.

She opened the bag of wild greens. The samphire was sandy. She'd have to wash it, which meant lugging more water from the stream, unless Big Lon was in earshot. And somehow he were good at not being in earshot whenever there was water or wood to lug. She'd have to —

'Arrk!' She stepped back.

The Master looked up. 'What is it, girl?'

'Something moved, sir. In the sack. A furry beast with big black eyes!'

He looked back at his notebook. 'It's just an o'possum. A baby one.'

'Will it bite?'

He looked interested for the first time. 'I don't know if they bite or not. I thought the creature would have died by now.'

'It didn't feel dead, sir.'

'I'll take a look.' He peered into the sack. Maria looked over his shoulder.

The black eyes stared at her, wide and frightened. It looks a bit like a cat, she thought, all black and white. Gran had a cat like that. It had sat on her lap and purred, while Gran fed her a pile of buttered toast almost up to her knees. She remembered a big rice pudding cooking on the hearth.

A couple of the officers had cats here, but she'd never seen them, only the Governor's dogs following him about. She supposed even if the colony cats had kittens there wouldn't be a cat for the likes of her.

Fool, she told herself. What did she want with a cat? Look out for yourself, that was it.

Surgeon White lifted the o'possum out of the bag. For a moment the tiny creature lay in his hands, then it sat up on its hind legs, holding its paws like tiny hands. It stared right at Maria.

She gave a gasp of fright. It didn't look like a cat at all now.

Surgeon White glanced at her, amused. 'Don't take on, girl,' he said. 'I'll wring its neck and put it with the other specimens. Mr Balmain can preserve it in a jar tomorrow to send to England.' His face darkened at the thought of his rebellious assistant. 'And if Balmain doesn't like the job he can take it up with the Governor.'

The o'possum twitched his whiskers. Maria stared at it. 'Sir —' she began. Suddenly the beast grabbed her with tiny claws. Before she could even scream, it had run up her arm and over her face. She shrieked as it clung onto her hair. 'Get it off me! Help, sir! Help!'

Beside her she heard a strange noise, a spluttering, choking sound.

It was Surgeon White. He was *laughing*. This was stranger than any beast. She had never seen the Surgeon laugh before.

'Sir! Help me!'

Something dripped down her chin. The creature must have scratched her face. She put up her hand. It came down wet, but not red. Yellow ... 'Eeeerk!'

The laughter became chuckles. The Surgeon reached over and pulled at the beast.

'Ow!'

'It's tangled in your hair. I'll have to cut it free.'

'You'll not cut my hair!'

He smiled at her. 'You would rather the beast stayed there all night?'

'No! But not my hair!' Little scrap she might be, but her hair were her one beauty, long and black.

'Well, let's try something else then.' He reached over and took a crust of yesterday's soda bread from the table, dipped it in water and held it to the creature.

She felt the beast wriggle on her head and screamed again. 'Sir!'

'Quietly. You're frightening it.'

'*I'm* frightening *it*?'

'It might be hungry. Let's see ...'

And the weight was gone from her head, leaving a sour stink. She'd have to wash her hair before she slept tonight, and dry it by the fire too, if she didn't want to get cold and catch the consumption. She turned around.

The o'possum sat on the table on its hind legs. Its tiny front paws held the crust, just as if they were hands. As she looked, it bent its head and nibbled. It seemed to like the bread, though every now and then its big dark eyes glanced around suspiciously.

What a waste of precious soda bread. She waited for Surgeon White to wring the little beast's neck. Good riddance to bad rubbish, as Aunt Effie would say.

Surgeon White stared at the animal, absorbed. 'Interesting. I assumed o'possums ate only leaves. See what else it will take,' he ordered.

Maria gaped. It had made a mess in her hair and on her dress and now on her clean scrubbed table. And she was to fuss about and feed it delicacies?

The o'possum finished the crust of bread. It sat there staring with its big black eyes, its mouth open, panting a little.

'Probably thirsty,' said the Surgeon. 'Feed it some water in a spoon. No, sarsaparilla tea.'

'But, sir —' she began. What if the animal climbed up her again? Those claws hurt!

The little creature swayed. It looked as though it might collapse on her table.

Surgeon White scooped it up. It lay still while he put it back with the greens in the sack. He arranged the edges of the sack to give it air, but still keep it dark and covered. 'Keep it warm by the fire,' he ordered. 'I'll tell Big Lon to put a good log on tonight, to keep the house warm till morning. Try feeding it some tea in a spoon before you serve up dinner. I'd like to keep it alive for a few days before I put it in a preserving jar. It's ... interesting.'

Maria tried to keep her expression polite. Now on top of everything else she had an o'possum to look after.

Chapter 4

MARIA

Maria woke when the rooster crowed. She peered at the grey light through the cracks in the storeroom wall. If only she could lie down on her straw-filled pillow, and sleep and sleep ... But only ladies and gentlemen had the luxury of all the sleep they wanted. A servant had to be up before her master, and stay up in case he wanted anything before he went to bed too.

She washed her face quickly, then pulled her dress over the petticoats she slept in. Her shoes were wearing out, so she kept them for Sunday best now, when she went to hear the Reverend Johnson's service. At least no one could see her bare feet under her well-mended hems.

She pulled open the kitchen door quietly, so as not to wake the Master, shoved wood quickly onto the coals to get the fire going again — it was a fearful business lighting it from scratch with tinder, steel and a flint — then peered into the sack.

The o'possum was still asleep. At first she thought that it was dead, but when she touched it with her finger she could feel its heartbeat.

She pulled back. What was she doing, petting a wild beast? A creature that had made a mess in her hair and scratched her? She had no place in her life for pets, and certainly not for a strange animal like this. For all she knew it might wake up later in the night and suck their blood …

And ghosts might rise from the well, and sea monsters eat ships, she scolded herself. Other convicts might whisper of imaginary terrors. Not her.

Almost by itself her finger stretched out, and stroked the beast again.

She could hear the Surgeon's snores from the hut's only other room. It was time to get to work.

More wood on last night's coals; then water in the pot to heat for the Surgeon's tea and for him to wash in. Big Lon was supposed to fetch two buckets full from the Tank Stream twice a day, and milk the goat, as well as tend the garden and fetch and chop the wood, but the good-for-nothing was probably still asleep back in the convict huts.

She scrubbed the hearthstone so it would be clean to bake the soda bread on.

It was baking nicely by the edge of the fire when she carried in the Surgeon's tea. He sipped it sleepily as she lugged in a bucket of warm water, then shut the door to let him dress.

She'd just put boiled eggs and buttered toast before the Master when there was a knock on the door.

She dragged it open — its rope hinges had sagged. Mr Balmain, one of the Assistant Surgeons, stood there.

'Sir,' he said to Surgeon White. The word was respectful, but the way he spoke weren't. Mr Balmain never seemed to realise that Surgeon White was his superior, and a gentleman, and that

Mr Balmain was only an Assistant Surgeon and should show respect.

Surgeon White looked up. 'What's so important that it interrupts my breakfast?'

'Dead natives. Sir.'

Surgeon White took a bite of soda bread. 'If they are dead, Mr Balmain, then they do not need my urgent assistance.'

'It looks like they died of the smallpox.'

'The smallpox!' Surgeon White pushed away his food.

Mr Balmain nodded. 'Some of the work parties yesterday said they'd seen dead Indians in most of the coves.'

'How many?'

'At least twenty, sir. I sent a couple of the men to bring back some bodies.'

Surgeon White shut his eyes briefly, almost as though he were praying. He stood up. 'The smallpox. God in Heaven, what will this cursed land send us next? Is anyone sick in the camp?'

'None reported. Sir,' he added.

The Surgeon nodded. 'Have the bodies put in one of the huts. Tell everyone to stay clear of them — and that means everybody — unless they've been inoculated or survived the pox back in England. I want every man in every work party examined for symptoms each night.'

'Yes, sir.'

Surgeon White shook his head.

Maria watched as he took his coat and hat, and left the hut. She sat down in his chair to finish his breakfast. She wasn't no thief now. But no point wasting good food.

The smallpox. She looked at the faint scar on her hand. Gran had said she'd had the smallpox when she were small. The smallpox had killed her parents, and her uncle too, but she'd survived. You only got it once, they said. If it didn't kill you, then you were safe from it.

How many would die if the smallpox spread through the colony? A third? A half? Her eyes grew wide, imagining the horror; mothers watching their babies die, babies crying as their mothers lay in the grave.

Her face hardened. It wouldn't affect her. She was safe. She was sure Surgeon White would have been inoculated, like all the other doctors. And what if so many convicts and marines did die? All the more rations for the rest of them. She wiped her eyes on the sleeve of her jacket. Stupid, stupid tears.

Maybe so many would die the Indians would attack them, and wipe them out.

She took up her broom, and began to sweep the hard dirt floor as clean as she could make it. Natives might be lurking, and the smallpox and starvation, but at least she could keep her house clean.

Chapter 5

SURGEON WHITE

Cockle Bay Hospital; Sydney Cove; Cockle Bay, 15 April 1789

Surgeon White stood in the hut of mud and cabbage-tree trunks. It was one of the scattered buildings of his hospital. Four dead bodies lay on roughly made benches: two men, a woman, a child. Pustules covered their bodies, crusted black with dried blood and still oozing yellow pus.

Balmain had been right. The smallpox.

The Surgeon closed his eyes for a second.

Had the fleet come all this way, survived so much, just for the colony to be wiped out by plague? Even if only a quarter of the wretches in the colony died, could the rest of them survive, perched on the edge of an unknown continent with natives all around?

'Governor wants you down at the harbour. Now.' It was Balmain again.

The Governor would have said: 'Offer my courtesies to Surgeon White, and ask if he would be able to attend me.' But rebuking Balmain would only make the man even harder to deal with.

The Surgeon gathered his medical bag. It wasn't likely that the Governor wanted him to join one of his expeditions to survey new lands today. He headed down between the convict huts to the harbour.

Governor Phillip was already there, next to a fishing boat, with two men to row it — convicts, for the marines felt it beneath their dignity to row boats. Arabanoo, the gentle native the Governor had captured to see if the warrior might be able to broker a peace between the colonists and the natives, was with the Governor to act as translator.

Arabanoo's peacemaking had been unsuccessful — the natives still speared any stragglers from the camp, or struck them with their axes. But Surgeon White respected Arabanoo. Never had a prisoner had such dignity, such kindness for all. The man was a gentleman, even if he was a native.

Arabanoo knew medicines too. When he'd had a touch of dysentery he had demanded the root of a particular fern. It had worked. White had tried the root on his own patients. It was better than any remedy from England.

The Surgeon nodded politely. 'Good morning, Your Excellency, Arabanoo.'

Governor Phillip looked worried. He always looked worried these days. 'One of the men who was out fishing this morning says there are more sick natives a few coves over. I suggest we look at them ourselves.'

White nodded. 'It will be easier to get an accurate diagnosis if I can examine living patients. But Your Excellency ...' He hesitated.

'You believe it to be the smallpox?'

'Nothing else fits the symptoms,' said the Surgeon frankly.

The Governor looked back at his colony of huts and humpies, convicts and ragged marines, and at the wilderness of trees and ocean around them. Surgeon White could almost see Phillip's thoughts on his sombre face. Home — and any help — was nine months away from them now, nor had they any ship big enough to sail from here or even send for aid. 'Then let us pray.'

The small cove looked deserted. Only the waves moved, back and forth on the muddy sand. It wasn't till they drew nearer that the Surgeon could make out a tiny fire, its smoke spiralling up to the sky. An old man sat next to it. As the Surgeon watched, a boy staggered down the sand to fill a container with water, then crept back to pour it over the old man's head.

The bottom of the boat hit sand. The convict rowers jumped out into the shallow water, and pulled the boat up so that the Governor, the Surgeon and Arabanoo could get out with dry feet.

The Surgeon stared at the boy and the old man by the fire. Their bodies were covered in white blisters. Neither of them seemed to have noticed the boat. Even as he looked the boy sank down onto the sand.

Had the effort of fetching the water been too much for him? Was he dead or sleeping?

A child's body lay nearby, so covered in sand and sores it was impossible to tell at first that she was a baby girl. The Surgeon trod across the sand and bent down to examine her. Dead.

Further up the beach, almost out of sight, a woman lay, her arms outstretched in death, her body swelling. The Surgeon glanced over at Arabanoo. The old man hesitated, still in the boat. He met White's eye, then climbed out and began digging in the sand.

'A grave,' whispered White.

Phillip nodded.

The girl's grave was tiny. Arabanoo hadn't seen the dead woman. The others waited as the translator gently carried the child's body to the grave, placing it in the hole almost as though the child only slept. He covered the girl with grass, then mounded up the sand.

The Surgeon hesitated. Should they bury the woman too? But the old man was still breathing.

The boy gave a tiny moan. He was still alive as well. That decided him.

The Surgeon turned to Governor Phillip. 'We need to get the man and boy to the hospital.'

There was no cure for the smallpox, but at least back at the colony the man and child could be nursed, given food and water. So often, thought Surgeon White, the sick die of thirst or starvation, their friends and family too scared to approach. 'Take them to the boat,' he ordered.

One of the rowers shook his head. 'I ain't touching no one with the smallpox.'

The Surgeon sighed. He and the Governor carried the old man to the boat between them. The Surgeon went back and lifted the boy in his arms.

He was small and light, only eight or nine years old. He muttered something, and nestled closer.

The Surgeon felt something ache deep in his heart. How long had it been since he had held a child in his arms? There were convict brats here, but none had needed the attentions of the Chief Surgeon. If he had been posted to India, or had a job in England, he might have been married now. He'd have children of his own. Instead he was on a distant beach, holding a native boy dying of the smallpox.

The Surgeon bit his lip. He carried his small burden back to the rowing boat.

Chapter 6

NANBERRY

The world had been black, but somehow too bright too. Even dreams hurt.

Someone lifted him. Was it Colbee? They had come back! They would bring sweet water, make the right smoke to send the illness away. Soon he would be well again. Life would be as it had been before ...

Someone said something. At first he thought that it was the sickness that made him not understand. Then he realised.

They were white-ghost words.

He opened his eyes. The world swam as though he was underwater. But he could see a boat: not a canoe, or a big ship, but one of the craft the white ghosts could make surge through the water.

'Has he a chance, Surgeon White?'

'I can't tell, sir. Perhaps, if we can get the fever down.'

The words had no meaning, but the men speaking sounded kind. Suddenly water touched his lips. Cool, wonderful, fresh water.

He wanted to ask questions. Where was his family? How did the white-ghost paddles make the boat glide across the water? But he was too weak. The hands felt kind, and they had given him fresh water.

Nanberry let himself sleep.

Chapter 7

MARIA

Maria trudged along the path to the stores. They were the only brick buildings in the colony, apart from the Governor's house. The roofs were made of proper tiles of baked clay too, unlike the others, thatched with dried reeds, though the tiles were already crumbling.

The Governor had ordered everyone in the colony to have the same rations: so much each for a man, a woman, a child. Major Ross and the marines complained, but the Governor had stood firm.

The marines had shouted even louder when the Governor ordered the rations be reduced again last week: two pounds of salt pork for each man, two and a half pounds of flour — wheat or maize flour, depending on what the stores had most of that week — and two pounds of rice or dried peas and a tiny scoop of rancid butter. Women had two-thirds that amount and children half.

The flour was bitter with weevils; the sacks of rice quivered with the insects that infested it; and the pork was at least two years old — who knew how old it was when it was loaded on the ships?

Maria waited in line to get her rations, and the Master's, trying to avoid the eyes of the men with their thin and filthy faces who'd take a smile as an invitation. Good-for-nothings, she thought. There's food to gather here, and wood in plenty to cook it and water to wash in.

But she still wanted her rations. Flour to make soda bread and the peas for a boiled pease pudding flavoured with salt pork meant a taste of home. She'd wipe the sour butter over the eggshells to keep the eggs fresh for when the hens stopped laying in winter.

There were only a dozen in front of her in the line now; men with shadowed faces, gazing at the Store Master doling out the tiny black lumps of meat, as though they could taste the hard salt pork already; women with thin children clinging to their skirts. She glanced at their hands and then back at their faces. No one had the blisters or sores of the smallpox. No one had even mentioned the sickness this morning.

Perhaps, she thought, only the Surgeon — and the Governor of course — know there's the smallpox in the colony. Fools like these might panic, or use it as an excuse to do even less work.

Didn't they have the chance now to make a new life for themselves? No chains around their ankles — not unless they committed another crime here. They'd been given tools to dig with and seeds to plant, land for huts and gardens, saws and hammers, as well as pots to cook in. But half the tools had been lost or broken, or simply thrown away.

She wrinkled her nose at the stench of the man in front of her. Imagine a cove like him touching you! She'd warrant not one in the line besides her had washed since they'd come ashore.

The convict next to her — a long-limbed, almost toothless man — took his filled pannikin from the Store Master and hurried off.

She held out her wooden bucket and some china cups. The other convicts could get their flour and dried peas and meat all mixed together if they liked. 'Rations for me and for Surgeon White.'

'Aye, I remember. Maria Kent.' The young man ticked off her name and Surgeon White's and ladled out her dried peas. His nails were clean, she noticed. She looked up at his face.

He was only a few years older than her, and his ginger whiskers were tidy — there were no razors for convicts, but most had access to scissors. His hair was trimmed too, and clean.

He grinned at her suddenly. His teeth looked clean as well, strong and white. 'Fellow were here earlier, asking for Surgeon White's rations. But I said as you collected them.'

'Big Lon, I'll warrant.'

The Store Master nodded. 'Big fellow, name of Laurence. I told him to come back with a chit from the Surgeon next time. It's the gallows for stealing food.' He looked at her steadily. 'You want me to put him on a charge?'

She hesitated. Big Lon was a fool, and lazy. He ate as well as she did, so he had no need to cheat the rations. But to see him hanged, dangling there on the gibbet, his tongue swollen ... no, she couldn't do that.

She shook her head. 'I'll give him a rollicking. He won't try it again.'

'You will and all too.' The Store Master looked at her admiringly.

She blushed. Many men had tried to paw her, but she wasn't used to admiration. 'I'd best be off,' she said. 'The Surgeon will be wanting his meal.'

The young man nodded. 'I'm Jack Jackson,' he said. He lifted his cap.

She gave a tiny curtsey, and heard snickers from a woman in the queue behind. Few bothered with good manners here at the end of the world.

'I'm pleased to meet you, Mr Jackson.' She hefted her bucket up and looked down at the meagre contents. It's a pity, she thought, that you can't get a ration for an o'possum. But maybe it had died while she was out …

—✽—

It hadn't.

She gazed down at the tiny creature. It was so deeply asleep it didn't stir as she ran a finger across its long soft fur.

She sighed, and put the stores in a sea chest, where she hoped the o'possum couldn't muck them up, keeping back the peas and flour. The Surgeon liked pease pudding, all boiled in a cloth till it was firm and savoury. He could have some hot tonight when he came in, and take some cold to the hospital tomorrow. She'd need to make fresh soda bread too.

She put more wood on the fire — she liked the fresh smell of wood smoke after London's yellow coal smoke — and mixed the soda bread. The secret of good soda bread was quick making and quick cooking.

The cooked soda bread smelt so good that it was hard not to gulp it all, leaving none for the Surgeon. She was even used to the sour taste of weevils now. She forced herself to take only a third of the bread, spreading the crust with the end of the gravy from last night's stew.

Something rustled on the table. It was the o'possum. It peered up from its sack, big black eyes wide and frightened. Impulsively she dipped a bit of the fresh soda bread into a mug of cold sarsaparilla tea, and handed it to the creature. It took it in both paws, then bent its head, its eyes still on hers, and nibbled it.

The tiny animal looked so silly she had to laugh. Whoever heard of a beast holding its food like that?

The o'possum finished the bread, licked its paws thoughtfully, then abruptly scampered down out of the sack onto the floor and up her skirts onto her lap.

Maria gave a startled squeak, then froze. Would it get into her hair again?

But the o'possum just crouched in her lap, staring up at her, and sniffing with its tiny pink nose. Suddenly it moved. She started to push it away before it could scratch her or clamber further up her dress. But instead it leant over to her hands. Before she knew it a tiny rough tongue licked at her fingers.

She nearly laughed. It was almost like a gentleman kissing a lady's hand. What did the creature think it was doing?

It could smell the fresh bread on her hand, she realised. It was trying to find more crumbs to eat. Well, the remaining bread was too precious to give an o'possum. It could make do with cold potatoes.

She picked it up, carefully, in case it bit her, and put it on the floor. But before she could fetch a potato it clambered up the table and into its sack again.

Who'd have thought it? she thought, a bit breathlessly. Kissed by an o'possum. And she found she was smiling as she swung the broom up to tidy away the cobwebs.

Chapter 8

NANBERRY

THE LAND AND TIME OF SICKNESS

There was a time that was no real time, and no real place. He lay in a hut that was the wrong shape and smell, with no sounds of the sea or trees. Voices barked around him instead, white-ghost voices, white-ghost smells.

Hands washed him with cool water. Hands lifted water to his lips. Sometimes other liquids came in the strange hard coolamons. He drank them too.

He listened for the voice of the man who had brought him here.

'How is the boy doing?'

'Well enough, sir. He ate some fish — even tried to cook it himself on the fire. He might just make it.'

'He's young and strong. The old man?'

'Died last night, sir. Does Yer Honour want to examine him afore we bury the body?'

'I think not.' The voice was tired. 'There is no shortage of bodies to examine now.'

The sounds had meaning. He had to work them out. He had to find out where he was too. Had the white ghosts taken him across the horizon, into the land of ghosts?

A kookaburra laughed. Nanberry relaxed. A ghost land wouldn't have kookaburras. The sickness killed quickly, but he was still alive. Tomorrow I will be well, he thought, as he shut his eyes again. Tomorrow or some other time ...

Chapter 9

SURGEON WHITE

It had been nearly a month since he'd brought the boy and the old man to the hospital. Each day since then the fishermen had reported more sick and dying natives: hundreds of bodies, some in every cove around the harbour.

The Surgeon had ordered that any still alive should be brought to the hospital. But only two had survived long enough to be placed on a bed, another boy and a girl. The boy had died. The girl was still alive. So was the first boy that they had brought in.

Now Surgeon White stood next to Arabanoo on the sand of yet another beach and gazed at the bodies scattered among the lapping waves in the early morning light. Some had been dead for days, their bodies pecked at by the gulls. Others might have died only an hour before.

Arabanoo stood, his hands limply at his sides. 'Bo-ee! Dead!' he cried. 'All dead.'

The Surgeon touched Arabanoo's shoulder gently. What did you say to a man when his whole people died? 'I'm sorry ...' he began.

Arabanoo stared at the ground.

The Surgeon ordered the rowers to take them to the coves nearby, in the desperate hope there might be more survivors. But each beach was dark with bodies.

Arabanoo said nothing. His eyes were full of pain.

At last they headed back to Sydney Cove. The Surgeon watched as one of the convicts led Arabanoo back to the bark hut where he was kept prisoner, then he headed over the stream to the hospital on the west side of the colony.

His heart clenched with fear as he approached the hospital. Would there be convicts with the smallpox waiting for him?

Hospital! Huts of mud and wattle, with dirt floors and bark roofs. No medicines left besides the native remedies he'd learnt from Arabanoo. No help for thousands of fierce, storm-racked miles.

'Well?' he demanded as he stepped into the first hut.

The convict assistant shook his head. 'No smallpox yet, sir.'

'Thank God. What have we got then?'

'Man who chopped his finger off. I put a string around it to stop the bleedin'. Boy with a cut head. Needs stitchin'.'

The Surgeon nodded. Balmain could have, should have, treated them both. But as usual his assistant was nowhere to be seen.

'Bring me a hot iron,' he said curtly. He beckoned to the man in the bloodstained shirt. 'Shut your eyes.'

The man screamed as the end of his finger was touched to the red-hot iron. But the wound would be safe now. The man would die neither of blood loss nor infection.

It took only a minute to stitch the other wound.

'Have the assistants seen to all the patients?' They had five in the hospital just now: a burns case, a spearing, a head wound and an ulcerated foot, as well as a woman with childbirth fever. He doubted she'd live to see the evening, though the others should survive.

'Yes, sir. Chamberpots been emptied, dressings changed and bandages washed, floors swept. Gave 'em all their soup for breakfast too. Just as you ordered, sir.'

He doubted it had been just as he ordered. But there wasn't time just now to check.

At last the Surgeon trudged down to the small isolation hut housing the smallpox cases. The girl, Booroong, had still been breathing when he'd left this morning. Would she be alive now?

She was, curled in sleep, her face to the wall. The boy looked up from his plank bed with frightened eyes. The Surgeon forced himself to smile. A bright lad. He'd already learnt a few English words even though he was sick.

'Good morning, lad. How are you today?' The Surgeon touched his forehead. 'Hot?'

'Good morning.' The boy spoke the words cautiously, as though they might bite him. 'No hot.'

'Good. We'll soon have you up again.' He smiled again, hoping to make the boy smile back.

The boy stared at him, obviously trying to work out what his words meant. Ha! thought the Surgeon. The boy was no fool. Even Arabanoo hadn't learnt as much this quickly.

The Surgeon bent down to the girl and felt her forehead. It was cool again, and she was breathing steadily.

She and the boy would live. Three natives left — two children and Arabanoo — out of how many? thought the Surgeon.

He glanced out the door. The harbour had turned grey. It would be dark soon. He began the long march away from the hospital and convict huts and back again over the Tank Stream, to his own home among the slightly better dwellings of the marines.

Sleep, he thought, as he opened his sagging front door, and dreams of England and green fields ... Out of the corner of his eye, he saw a flicker of white on the harbour.

He turned, and stared, unbelieving. A ship! He shaded his eyes, peering as the sails bobbed against the blue. No, not the supply ship from England they had been longing for, had expected now for over a year. It was the colony's tiny ship *Sirius*, sent to the Cape months before to bring desperately needed flour and seeds for planting.

It had made it back!

'Maria!'

'What is it, sir?' She ran out, looking so scared he had to reassure her. He pointed at the tiny ship in the harbour. 'Sir, are we saved?'

He had to laugh at that. 'Scarcely. She's got supplies for another four months, at most. But at least we'll have seed to plant this spring, and fresh flour instead of weevils. Now what's for dinner?'

'Fish stew, sir, and maize pudding. Sir, about the o'possum ...'

He shook his head, tiredness overcoming him again. 'I don't have time to preserve it tonight. Tomorrow maybe, or the day after ... Now, where is this fish stew?'

Chapter 10

NANBERRY

Nanberry lay without moving on the thing called *bed*. It was
made of wood and set above the ground, with sides on it, like a
giant container for grass seeds. A thing called *pallet* was on top
of it: some strange skin covering filled with bracken. It crunched
when he moved. On the other side of the room Arabanoo sat
next to the girl, Booroong, as she slept.

His world had vanished. 'Dead,' whispered Arabanoo to the
sleeping girl again. 'All the people dead.'

Not just his family, thought Nanberry, but bodies on every
beach.

Everyone dead.

The laughter, the stories, the world. Gone.

Would their ghosts whisper on the wind?

Booroong muttered, half awake. Arabanoo held her tenderly.
He lifted a coolamon of water for her to drink, and stroked her

hair. Booroong and Arabanoo were from the same clan, which was why Arabanoo talked to her, not him. Booroong had fourteen summers. She was a woman now, though when she was brought in she had been wearing a bungu-skin apron to show she wasn't married yet. Nanberry was nothing to a warrior like Arabanoo — even a captive one — not till he was initiated as a man.

But Nanberry could never be a warrior now, unless Arabanoo did the ceremony alone. Nanberry would never be allowed to carry spears, never be able to marry. Would he be a boy forever without the proper rites?

He lifted the pale cloth he was wearing and looked at the sores on his skin. They were starting to form scabs.

He was going to live. Just him and Booroong and Arabanoo. Could a warrior, a boy and a girl re-create a people?

Maybe Arabanoo would marry Booroong. But where could they live? People had died at every beach and every stream. How could they live where their family ghosts must roam?

Suddenly Arabanoo gave a cry. Nanberry sat up, as Arabanoo opened the cloth — his *shirt* — and stared at his own chest.

White blisters puckered the dark skin.

Arabanoo looked at the blisters for a moment, then stood up, and walked to the door. He looked out at the harbour. The empty harbour, thought Nanberry. No women singing in their canoes as they cooked fish for the small children. No warriors on the rocks with spears.

At last Arabanoo had looked enough. He came back into the hut, and sat on the thing called *chair*, as though to wait.

Nanberry hoped the man called *Surgeon* would come again soon. The Surgeon had saved him, and Booroong. Maybe he could save Arabanoo too. For only Arabanoo now knew how to make a warrior.

Chapter 11

SURGEON WHITE

Arabanoo was dying.

The Surgeon sat in the small isolation hut — shoddy, leaking, like every building in this wretched place — and held the old man's hand. Arabanoo muttered in his fever.

The Surgeon had ordered the convict orderlies to place the bed so that the translator could see out the door to the tree-clad harbour, the sunlight streaming down like gold rain into the water. But for the past few hours Arabanoo had been beyond seeing anything. His skin was crusted with pustules and his breath bubbled in his chest.

The Surgeon bit his lip. He had tried every potion he knew: willow bark to bring the fever down, the sap from a red gum tree to open his bowels, even the fern root that Arabanoo had showed him how to use for dysentery. He could cut off a wounded leg and cauterise it with pitch; he could sew up a split head. But against the smallpox he was powerless. If only he had laudanum left, to ease the old man's suffering. And Arabanoo had borne it all with the serenity with which he'd faced his captivity, the gentleness with which he treated all he met, from the most ragged convict child to the Governor. Phillip's plan to use the old man as an ambassador was dying too.

There had still been no smallpox cases among the convicts or marines. But surely they couldn't escape a disease as deadly as this for long.

Further inside the hut the boy, Nanberry, seemed to sleep. Mrs Johnson, the clergyman's wife, had taken the girl, Booroong, to her home to nurse. She would adopt the girl, she said, and try to train her to be a decent servant.

Booroong would be safe with the Johnsons.

'Bado! Bado!' Arabanoo's voice was so weak the Surgeon had to bend to hear his words. At least the old man was conscious again. *Bado* meant water, he knew that much. He held a mug to the man's cracked lips, and watched him sip.

Arabanoo turned his head so he could see Nanberry. He pulled at the Surgeon's hand. His eyes pleaded.

The Surgeon realised what Arabanoo was asking.

'I'll look after the lad. I promise.' He meant it. They had taken so much from this man already: his freedom, his people, and now his life. The least he could do was to make sure the child was safe.

Arabanoo muttered in his fever. The Surgeon gripped his hand again, and the old man grew quiet.

No man should die like this, away from his people.

Surgeon White looked out again at the blue harbour.

He was as lonely as Arabanoo. One could be lonely even with his countrymen around him. Desperately, deeply, and with no end in sight. Who could he share his fears with, here at the end of the world? Only the Governor was in any way a gentleman, and he too was burdened with more than he could stand.

All of the other officers had provided themselves with a woman — or even more than one — poor convict wretches who had no choice but to smile and try to please their masters.

He smiled at the thought of Maria. The girl was safe with him. He at least wouldn't lay hands upon a child.

Back in England you might meet a man to befriend or a woman to be a wife at the next ball or dinner. But here it was the same faces every day.

Suddenly he realised what it might be like to have the boy in his house. A child with a bright, enquiring mind could bring laughter into grim days. Perhaps he knew places where White might discover birds he'd never seen. He could take the lad fishing ...

A lad such as this might be the ambassador the Governor had wanted, one who could learn English properly then translate for the native tribes. It was ironic that the plague should bring him this lad and at the same time destroy any need for an ambassador.

Assistant Surgeon Balmain walked by. White hailed him. 'You, fetch the Governor, if you please.'

'Why?'

'Arabanoo is dying.'

Balmain shrugged. 'You think the Governor will come to a sick native?'

White shut his eyes. 'Yes. He will come.' If he knows in time, he thought. If this fool bothers to go and find him.

At last the old man's hand grew limp. Arabanoo had died without a sound. The Surgeon loosened his grip, then gently closed the ambassador's eyes.

'Bo-ee?' The boy — Nanberry — sat up.

'Yes,' said the Surgeon quietly. 'He's dead.'

The boy frowned. 'Bo-ee ... *dead*?'

'Yes, *bo-ee* means dead.'

'Dead.' The boy lay down, fingering the buttons on his

nightshirt. It was impossible to read the expression on his face. The Surgeon shivered. Strange that one of the first English words he heard a native child say should be *dead*. But that is what we have brought them, he thought. Death.

Now God save the colony from the smallpox.

Chapter 12

NANBERRY

WHITE-GHOST HOSPITAL, THE TIME OF FEAR AND
CONFUSION (18 MAY 1789)

The white ghosts wrapped Arabanoo in a cloth. They carried
him away. They would put him in a hole.

A woman called Mrs Johnson had taken Booroong. It was
hard to tell which white ghosts were men and which were
women, for their clothes covered the most important parts.
Nanberry decided that those who wore long cloth to the ground
were women. The long-skirted ones had no beards, though a few
old ones had moustaches.

Now there was just him in the hut where someone had died.
He forced his mind not to even think the name of the dead man.
Once someone had gone, even someone you loved — especially
one you loved — you did not say his or her name till the stars
had turned over in the sky.

Someone screamed in another building not far away. The scream
went on and on. This place smelt bad, of death and pain and blood.

He had to leave! He had to find a place where no ghosts whispered. Under the trees? But people had died there too …

It didn't matter. He just had to get away from here. He pushed off the blanket, which was rough and scratchy, not soft like bungu fur, and put his feet on the ground. The sores had scabbed over; some of the scabs were even peeling off. But he still had to steady himself with his hand on the wall to stand.

'You, boy! What do you think you're doing?'

It was the man called Surgeon. Nanberry didn't understand the words. To his horror, he felt himself begin to cry. He felt the man's arms about his shoulders. The Surgeon's voice said, 'A hospital is no place for a child.'

He didn't understand. Nanberry tried to find a word the Surgeon would understand. 'Dead. Go. Go.'

'Don't worry. You're coming home with me.' The Surgeon hesitated, then said: 'I am going to adopt you. You have no family, and nor do I. Your new name is Andrew Douglass Keble White. Can you say that?'

'Aggrew Dadabblite,' said Nanberry.

The Surgeon laughed. 'Almost. And you will call me *Father White*. I am your new father now.' He touched his chest and said the name again. 'Father White.'

Nanberry made the sounds carefully. He knew the man was giving him his name. 'Father White.'

'Excellent! Good lad.'

Nanberry felt himself lifted into the man's arms and carried out the door. For a moment all he felt was relief that he was gone from the hut where a man had died. Then amazement took over.

He peered from the man's arms at the harbour. There was one of the murry nowey there again, bobbing on the waves as if it was a giant bark canoe. All around there were huts, and strange things growing, not grass or berry bushes or yams or anything he had ever seen, but tall slim plants in straight lines. What magic had made plants grow in straight lines?

And so many people, wearing filthy clothes that should have been left to rot under a tree. Most of them were hunched over like old men, even though they looked young. Not one had the muscles and shoulders of a warrior. Did the white ghosts cover their bodies because they were ashamed?

At least Father White stood straight. He had a belly too, which meant that he was skilled enough to hunt good food. And he had taken him away from the death hut …

Nanberry shut his eyes. He was tired. Too tired to think, or even look at all the wonders. This man had saved him once, when the fever took his family, and again today, sparing him from the place of Arabanoo's ghost.

It seemed this man would decide what would happen to him now.

Chapter 13

MARIA

Maria stared at the child in the Surgeon's arms.

'But he's a native, sir!'

'I am aware of that.' The Master's voice was tired and curt.

'In my clean house!'

'It is *my* house. He'll sleep in a crib in my room for now. I've ordered Lon to build on a new room. You can have that. We'll move the boy into the storeroom when he's stronger.'

'But he has the smallpox!'

The Surgeon sighed. 'The blisters have scabbed over. He's not infectious now. He just needs care — gentler care than he'll get in that excuse for a hospital. Give him sarsaparilla tea and fish and as much fresh fruit and vegetables as he'll eat.'

The Master and his fresh fruit, she thought. Everyone knew that fresh fruit was bad for you, especially for children.

'If you say so, sir.'

'I do say so.' He strode through the kitchen, the boy still in his arms. She watched as he laid the child tenderly on the hay-stuffed mattress and covered him with a blanket. 'Now, you be a good lad, and Maria will bring you some supper.'

The boy looked up, the whites of his eyes pale in his dark face. 'Su-pper?'

'Supper is food.'

'Food.' The boy nodded. 'Thank you.'

Maria stared. The little savage had said *thank you* clear as a bell. He looked clean too, despite his scabs. But who knew what trouble he'd get into? A native boy and an o'possum …

The o'possum! She turned. 'Sir? Do you want me to keep feeding the o'possum?'

But Surgeon White had gone.

Chapter 14

NANBERRY

He was tired. So many new things: the smells, the white ghosts, the angry woman who had stared at him. He hadn't understood the words, but he knew she didn't like him.

Worse was the knowledge that outside this hut was an empty land: only the white ghosts, the trees, the animals. None of his people left. A land of ghosts. White ghosts, and dead ones.

He tried to shut his mind to ghosts.

The bed here smelt better than the one in the hut where the man had died. There were other smells too. Food smells, strange, but good.

The woman came in. Even her footsteps sounded angry. She was small, but her thick clothes made her look bigger. Why wear so many clothes when the wind was warm?

'Here's your supper.'

Nanberry sat up and took the container from her hand.

'You stupid heathen! You don't drink stew! You use a spoon. Like this, see?'

He watched carefully to try to understand what she meant. This was a new world. He had to learn its rules.

'Spoon.' He lifted it the way she had shown him. The food tasted different from a spoon. But it was good.

'Say thank you.'

'Thank you,' he said cautiously. He held out the empty container.

For the first time she gave an almost-smile. 'Liked that, did you? You won't get better than my stew at Government House. I'll get you another helping, and then I'd better feed that wretched o'possum. What does a fine gentleman like the Surgeon want with an o'possum and a native?'

At last Nanberry lay down, his belly full. He listened to the woman clang and clatter behind the wall. He heard the man called Father White come in. He shut his eyes, pretending to be asleep. He was too tired to try to talk. He was afraid that he might cry again too.

A warrior didn't cry.

He watched Father White take off his clothes and put on a *nightshirt*, then lie in the bed. Father White was fat, as he'd thought.

Father White's clan had good food. But there was no laughter, no singing. Outside he knew the sun had sunk behind the mountains. It felt like his own sun had sunk forever too.

He slept. And then he heard the scream.

Chapter 15

MARIA

The crash woke her. She sat up on her pallet of dried bracken and unwrapped herself from her blanket. The storeroom was in darkness.

She had no candle to light her way in the dark. Only the Governor had any candles left now. The meat from the wild animals in this wretched place was too lean to provide any fat for more, or even to make slush lamps. But she knew where the door was. She fumbled for the opening, then ducked through the cold outside into the warmth of the kitchen.

At least there was light here, a red glow from the fire. She bent and threw on more wood and prodded the coals with the poker. The flames flared. A blob of sap burst into tiny sparks.

She straightened and looked around.

One of her — the Surgeon's — precious china bowls lay shattered on the floor; the cold potatoes it had held were scattered about the room. She stared at it in dismay. There was no way to get another bowl till the next ship came — if it ever did. And even then it mightn't bring crockery.

What had happened? Had that native boy tried to steal it? Would the Surgeon blame her?

Perhaps she could glue the pieces together ... but there was no glue. Not for half the world away.

A shadow moved in the corner of the room. It leapt from the back of the Surgeon's chair onto the table, then perched on the sack, peering at her with its big black eyes.

She grabbed at it. The o'possum leapt once more, over the hearth this time. She heard a scrabble as it tried to climb the chimney, its scream as it burnt its paws. Black and sooty, it fell back to the hearth — her clean scrubbed hearth. Black eyes stared at her again then made a dash and tried to climb the wall.

Even in the firelight she could see the soot across her floor and up the wall.

She bit back a scream, but not soon enough. She heard the Surgeon stir.

'Maria?' He stumbled from his room, his long nightshirt and cap white in the firelight, holding his musket, the one he gave his shooter to hunt with. He peered at her. 'What are you doing, girl? I thought it was thieves.'

The o'possum squeaked and ducked into the sack. The sack gave a wriggle and then was still.

'The beast! The horrid, horrid beast!'

The Surgeon took in the scene, then made a strange sound. It took her a few seconds to realise he was laughing again.

'Oh, child, if you could see your face! Now put the china away where it will be safe.'

Where? she wondered. The kitchen had only a few shelves tacked to its rough cabbage-tree walls, as well as the table, the chair, the hearth. There were no cupboards to keep a wild creature out. She'd have to lug it all into the storeroom with her.

'Sir, will you ... take care of him ... tomorrow?'

She meant wring the beast's neck. Kill it. Put it in one of those big glass jars, like the snakes and the other creatures he had preserved.

'When I have time. There are more important things just now than preserving an o'possum. Pick those bits up, girl, before someone cuts their foot on them.' He shut the door behind him.

The moon had climbed high in the doorway by the time Maria had finished taking the china into her room. She cast a look of dislike at the silent sack.

Soon, she thought. Soon the creature would be gone for good.

Chapter 16

NANBERRY

Father White's hut, the time of strangeness (18 May 1789)

The scream had startled him. But it was only a bungu.

The other sound had reassured him. He hadn't known that white ghosts could laugh. This new life had good food and kindness. There might be laughter too.

His heart still wept. But now it held hope for his new life as well as grief.

Chapter 17

NANBERRY

Nanberry sat on the bed in the storeroom to pull on his new trousers, then stared at his legs. They looked … odd. But he liked them. His trousers smelt like an early morning, not like the clothes most of the white ghosts wore. He liked his shirt too, and his boots. He grinned at the word. It sounded so funny. 'Booooooots.'

Boots made big thuds when he walked, so everyone could hear him coming. That was fun, but he missed the feel of the earth under his feet, as well as his old silent footsteps.

It was strange living in a *house*. He missed the smell of morning when you woke up with the dew about you. He missed sitting by the fire as the air changed from day to night, and all the light left was stars and flames. More than anything he missed his family, his people; he missed knowing who he was and what he would become.

And yet …

His people had left him. They had left him to die; worse, they had died themselves. Nanberry knew that none of it was their fault. Aunties knew the order of things, how things should be done to keep the world straight. Even they had no way of fighting death.

And he had new people now. He was learning to be *English*.

English didn't die of the white sores. English had big boats. True, most English were small and smelly, but others like Father White were big and fat, and not so smelly.

It was good to belong to Father White's clan. Most English did what Father White said, as if he was one of their greatest warriors. Only the man called *Governor Phillip* was greater than Father White, and he and Father White were friends.

Best of all, Father White and the Governor treated him as a man, not a little boy who hadn't been initiated. Father White had taken him fishing in a boat — not the big ship in the harbour, not yet, but in a boat very much larger than any canoe.

Father White smiled at him and said *good lad* when he learnt English words and English ways. Father White answered questions instead of laughing and saying, 'That is not for little boys to know.'

And the food!

He looked around the storeroom. So much food! Chests of sweet *currants* and a vat of something sticky called *wine*. Other chests were nailed tight; and there were sacks of brown things called *potatoes*, dug up from the ground, and of others called *corncobs*. The corn and potatoes grew near the house, for the English knew how to make much food come from a small space, just as they could make big ships and houses.

The corn was the best thing he had ever eaten. Maria boiled the cobs and covered them in *salt* and *butter*, which was a bit smelly but still tasted good. He had eaten twenty cobs yesterday. Father White had laughed, and said he counted as well as he could eat.

But why did the English need to store so much? Every day brought its own food, according to the seasons. As you walked you ate: a few berries here, some greens, the sweet nectar of the blossoms. You roasted yams by the fire at night when the cold wind blew; you feasted when a whale came ashore. This fish in one season; eels in another; frogs to eat after a good rain; and figs in late summer — fat fruit bats when they had been feeding on the figs too.

The whole world was food. Why keep it shut up in here? The door was locked every night, so the small dirty Englishmen didn't steal it. Which meant that Nanberry was locked in too.

He didn't mind. The English camp outside still frightened him, especially at night. The shadows of the houses loomed in a way that tree dapples above you never did. Sometimes men yelled and Maria sniffed and said that they were 'as drunk as lords'.

Nanberry wished there was something he could do for Father White.

He walked carefully in his boots and trousers into the room they called *kitchen*. No, it was *the* kitchen just like *the* table. *The* chair too. He could hear Maria singing softly as she swept the room next door. He wanted to sweep for her, but she had just glared at him when he tried to take the broom.

And then he saw it: a bungu! A fat one, sitting on the table, staring at him with big dark eyes.

Nanberry grinned. He stood, totally still, till the creature relaxed.

And then he sprang.

The bungu shrieked. But Nanberry's hands were about its throat now. One good pull and it would be dead. He could skin it and tan its hide for Father White. They would eat bungu meat, roasted on the fire tonight.

'Stop it! You heathen savage, stop it at once!'

Nanberry stopped. He'd learnt the word *stop*. The bungu wriggled in his hands, and tried to scratch him. He stilled it against his body.

'You put that o'possum down.'

He didn't know the words, but the meaning was clear. Slowly he put the bungu on the table again.

The bungu gave an angry snort, then jumped into a basket. It peered out, chattering at them both.

Nanberry put his hands out to ask Maria, *Why?*

'That is the Master's o'possum!'

'O'possum?' He nodded at the bungu.

'Yes, it's an o'possum. And a messy troublesome brute it is too. You must have woken it with your noise. But it's the Master's, so don't go touching it.'

'Master ... eat o'possum?' He corrected himself: 'Master eat *the* o'possum?'

'Eat it? The very idea! He's going to put it in a bottle and send it to England for wise men to look at.'

None of the words meant anything, but one thing was plain: this bungu was not for eating.

Maria glared at him. 'Now you behave yourself, Andrew.'

Andrew. That meant him.

Nanberry sighed. This new world was strange.

One day soon, he thought, I will be strong again. I will catch a badagarang, a great kangaroo, and give all the meat to Father White. He and Father White would feast together, even Maria perhaps, though she was just a woman.

It would be a better feast than a bungu.

And by then he would really be Andrew, an English boy. Nanberry would be gone.

Chapter 18

MARIA

Maria sat by the firelight and glared at the o'possum, sitting on the top shelf chewing a cold potato.

Why hadn't she let the native boy kill the wretched thing? For two halfpennies she'd do it herself.

But the Surgeon had been good to her. And you couldn't ask a man trying to save the colony from death by fever to waste time preserving his o'possum.

Hss chee. The creature bounded down in front of her. It looked up with those big dark eyes.

'What are you wanting then? Another potato?'

The beast chattered again, almost as though it understood her.

'Potatoes are precious. How about a cob of corn?'

The o'possum gave a squeal. She grinned at herself. Talking to an o'possum! But at least there was no one to hear her. The native lad was outside, helping Lon shuck the corn crop, pulling off the outside leaves to find the big yellow heads inside. How that boy could eat! She'd never seen anyone eat so much corn, cob after cob, and as for fish — he just kept eating till it was gone.

She fished another cob out of the pot, and held it out to the o'possum. It grabbed the offering in its tiny paws, and began to gnaw it. What a waste of good corn. It should be eating leaves ...

She grinned again. She went to the door, shutting it carefully in case the creature escaped, then yelled into the darkness. 'Big Lon?'

'What is it?' The yell came from the hut down the hill.

'Go get leaves for the Master's o'possum.'

Big Lon's lanky form was silhouetted against the hut door. 'And why should I do that? If the Master wants summat he can ask me.'

'Because if you don't I'll tell the Master about how you tried to get his rations as well as your own.'

And you'll be hanged by your neck if the Master decides to charge you with it, she thought. At last Big Lon said sulkily, 'What kind o' leaves?'

'The kind where you found the o'possum.'

'But that be an hour's walk away!'

'Then you'd best start at first light, hadn't you?'

She slipped inside into the warmth again. The o'possum had nearly finished the cob of corn.

I'm just doing my duty, she told herself. If the o'possum were a chicken the Master planned to eat for dinner, she'd have kept it alive till he was ready to wring its neck just the same. It would be dead soon enough, its eyes staring sightlessly at the world from its glass jar.

And she couldn't help a strange ache in her heart as she watched the tiny animal finish its corn.

Chapter 19

SURGEON WHITE

Surgeon White trudged home, the late-afternoon southerly gusting at his heels buffeting the bark huts around him like it planned to flatten them. At least the wind washed away the scents of men and sewage. Stench and death and every sin known to man — that is what they had brought to this land.

It was the colony's second winter. And where were they now? Starving, in bark huts, with death all around them. No word from England in all that time. Had the colony been forgotten? Had each one of them been left to die here at the end of the world?

But one miracle had been granted to them. Somehow only one colonist had been struck down by the plague. And he was an American native, a sailor. No English man, woman or child had caught the disease.

Impossible. Yet it was true.

Surgeon White shook his head. What was this curse, that natives died, and convicts and soldiers were immune?

It was *impossible*.

Surgeon White sighed. So much was impossible here. Animals that hopped and carried their young in pouches; swans that were black instead of white; wood that didn't float, that twisted as it dried.

Where had the disease come from? There had been no outbreak since the Cape, eighteen months before. True, he had brought some bottles of cowpox pus and scabs, to inoculate the settlers in the event of another outbreak. But he knew better than anyone that the seals on his bottles were still intact — and it was unlikely, so many years after leaving England, that they'd be able to infect anyone, even if someone had stolen them.

The French? But they were long gone.

Had Dampier or some other explorer brought it here? Was it a disease the natives had suffered from before? Then why hadn't Arabanoo asked for some native medicine, as he had when he'd had dysentery?

Too many questions and no answers. He needed to sit by his own fire. A hot rum and water, and a good dinner … He opened the door.

A creature stared at him from the table, sitting on its hind legs and holding a crust of cornbread in its paws. It twitched its nose at him, then bent its head to nibble the bread.

'What in the —'

'It's your o'possum, sir.' Maria looked up from turning the cornbread on the hearth. His heart warmed at the sight of her, so neat, so clean, unlike the other convict wretches.

'I'd forgotten it.' Surgeon White stared at the animal. It was almost twice as big as it had been just a few weeks before.

'It's quite tame, sir.'

'Nonsense. I've tried to tame American o'possums back in England. It can't be done.'

'He eats from my fingers, sir …'

He was too tired to bother with an o'possum. It wasn't as though the animal was interesting, like a kangaroo. He'd sketch it tonight, then wring its neck and put it in a preserving jar.

He reached towards the animal.

Gah! squealed the o'possum. It jumped onto the floor, then ran on four legs, out the open door.

Maria ran to the door and stood staring after it. 'You frightened it, sir,' she said, a little sadly.

'Were you hoping to make a pet of it, child?'

She shrugged. 'I have no need of pets.' She turned back to his cornbread.

He watched the girl for a moment. Was she as lonely as he was? What did she have in common with the other women, with their drinking and their swearing? Thank goodness the Governor had assigned her to him.

He would have liked to hug her, but it might be misinterpreted. He didn't want her to think that his interest was anything but fatherly. Fatherly ... Were a convict girl and a native boy as close as he would ever come to having children of his own?

'You can't tame an o'possum,' he repeated gently. 'Where's Andrew?'

'Asleep, sir.'

'Wake him up and ask him to join us for supper.'

'Us, sir?'

'Tonight all three of us will eat together.'

Chapter 20

ANDREW/NANBERRY

SYDNEY COVE, 2 JUNE 1789

'Toast,' said Nanberry, carefully turning the slice of soda bread over above the flames so that it browned on both sides. Outside the kookaburras welcomed the new day.

Father White smiled at him. 'Excellent, Andrew. Now bring it to the breakfast table and put it in the toast rack.'

Maria brought a bowlful of boiled eggs over. She sat next to Father White, a bit uncomfortably, Nanberry thought. He placed the toast in its rack then sat on the other chair. They had three chairs now, one for him and Maria too, even though she was only a woman.

Chair, toast, table, eggs ... He knew so many words now. He was even working out the complicated ways the English put them together.

'Would you like an egg, Andrew?'

Nanberry took an egg. He placed it in the eggcup, just like

Father White did with his, and cut off the top. It was a funny way to eat an egg, yet this was what the English did. It was silly to sit dangling your legs off a *chair* too, instead of comfortably on the ground.

Father White smiled at Maria. 'Are you missing your o'possum, girl?'

She flushed. 'Of course not, sir.'

'If the Governor's cat has kittens I will try to get you one.'

'A cat? Truly, sir?'

'If I can.'

Father White took his hat and coat — freshly brushed by Maria — and opened the hut's door.

The bungu glared up at him from the doorstep. It gave a squeak, then ran inside on all fours and clambered up the table leg. It looked around for its sack of wilted greenery and squeaked again.

Nanberry laughed. Oh, it was good to laugh.

'Maria's friend is back.'

'My friend —' Maria blushed. Nanberry wondered if she had another friend.

'Your o'possum. I think it's looking for its bed.'

'I threw the leaves out and washed the sack. It stank.'

Father White stared at the bungu, no, the *o'possum*. 'Let's see how tame it will become. It's quite fascinating, don't you think?'

'No, sir,' she said frankly.

Father White smiled. 'Get Lon to gather dry leaves for a nest. Find it a basket.'

'On my clean table, sir?' Maria's voice was resigned.

'I'll send a small table up from the hospital. The o'possum's basket can sit on that. Lon can bring fresh leaves for it to eat each day too. But see what other things it will eat.'

'Oh, it will do that, sir.'

'It will be company for you,' Father White said gently. 'What do you think, Andrew? Will it amuse you to have a pet o'possum?'

Nanberry knew the word *pet*, though the idea was strange. A pet was an animal you owned, but didn't eat; you laughed at it, though it could be useful too. The English kept dogs and cats. Like Father White keeps me ...

He thrust the thought away. He was no pet!

'I am Nanberry Buckenau.' The words came before he knew he was going to say them. It was the first time he had used his full name in the colony.

Father White looked puzzled. 'Your name is Andrew now.'

'I am Nanberry.'

Father White shook his head. 'I don't have time to argue with you. You be a good boy, and help Maria and Lon.' He picked up the stick with the silver end that he used to help him walk. It was another English thing, using a stick even when you didn't have a sore leg or foot.

Nanberry watched Father White stride down the dirt lane between the huts. Behind him in the kitchen the bungu — o'possum — chattered, demanding corn.

Nanberry, he thought. I am no pet. I am Nanberry Buckenau. Nanberry.

Chapter 21

SURGEON WHITE

Late winter breezes fluttered a touch of fresh air into the sour stench of the hospital. Surgeon White glanced out his office door as a tiny canoe, almost level with the water, vanished into one of the coves.

Surgeon White found himself smiling.

Only a couple of months ago he'd thought the whole race of natives wiped out. But they were trickling back to the harbour — and they were healthy too. He supposed many had fled inland to escape the infection. There had been no signs of the disease for weeks.

'Sir!' One of the convict porters puffed up the hill towards him.

'What is it?'

'Bad case, sir. Cove got 'is leg crushed under a tree down by the stores. Got 'im in the surgery 'ut.'

Surgeon White nodded. He reached for his surgical apron and his bag of instruments. 'I'll be there directly. Get the iron hot, will you?'

'Yes, sir.'

He heard the young man's screams as he neared the hut. Its bark roof was already half rotted, offering almost no protection from the rain. Army surgeons on the battlefield work under better conditions than I do, thought Surgeon White. At least they could get medicines.

The blood had left a wet trail on the dirt floor. Too much, and bright red, thought the Surgeon. An artery cut …

He looked down at his patient, a skinny lad but so tall he only just fitted on the bench. The youth panted in agony, his eyes wide and terrified, his face sweating. Black hollows under his eyes showed he'd lost a lot of blood already. His trousers were black with it.

He might only have minutes to live.

The Surgeon grabbed a scalpel, slit the trousers and assessed the leg quickly. Bone protruding. Blood pumping. He pressed down on the artery. The pumping stopped. He gestured to one of the convict assistants. 'Press here. Hard. Don't let up.' He bent down and picked up his bone saw.

'No!' This scream was anguish as well as pain. 'Don't cut it off! I can't be a cripple! I can't!'

'The leg is crushed, boy. There's dirt in it, bits of cloth. If it gets infected you won't just lose your leg — you'll be dead.'

'May as well be dead as have only one leg!'

'There's work for a man with a wooden leg …'

'Not here there ain't. I want a farm o' me own one day! Please, sir. Don't cut it off!'

The Surgeon hesitated. 'Very well. But I warn you — if infection sets in I'll have to cut it off anyway. And this is going to hurt.'

'I can take it. I can take anything. Just don't take me leg!'

'I'll do my best then. What's your name?' he added to try to distract the youth while a porter put the iron in the fire.

'Jack Jackson. Work in the stores,' his breath came in panting gasps. 'Seen your housekeeper there.'

'Maria? She's a good girl.'

A year ago the Surgeon could have given Jack laudanum to ease the pain, and got him drunk on gin to boot. But there was none of either left now.

The Surgeon nodded at the three convict porters. They held Jackson down on the bench as Surgeon White wrenched the leg into shape. Jackson howled like a dog. Sweat ran down his face.

The Surgeon strapped thigh and foot to a length of wood, to keep it straight. He reached for the tweezers and extracted every bit of cloth he could find in the wounds.

Now for the great gashes in the leg. He bent and lifted the iron out of the fire with a pair of tongs. It glowed white hot, then red as it began to cool. The Surgeon carefully pressed it for two seconds — no more — to the flesh within each gash in the man's leg.

Jackson screamed, then fainted.

White bit his lip. At least his patient would feel nothing for a while. And maybe, just maybe, he had saved the leg. The hot iron had sealed the wounds and perhaps stopped infection from the dirt too.

White wiped his bloody hands on his apron, then took it off and handed it to his convict assistant. Well, he had done what he could. 'Give him sarsaparilla tea when he wakes up — well boiled, make sure of that. Keep the leg dry. When the flies lay maggots in it, come and tell me, but don't try to wash them out. Understand?'

'Why not, sir?'

Surgeon White nodded. He liked a man who asked questions. Perhaps this one could even be trained to be a surgeon too.

'Maggots eat dead flesh. They stop the wound rotting. Once rot starts you have to cut the whole leg off, fast, before it spreads. But you have to watch maggots carefully, stop them eating into good flesh once they've cleaned the wound, or the wound will just get bigger. You understand?'

'Yes, sir.'

'Good. I'll look at him tonight. But if the wound begins to swell, send me a message at once. I'll need to work fast. If wounds have dirt in them there's a risk of gas gangrene.'

'I've heard of that, sir.'

'Good man. And don't touch the wound if it swells — if you have any cuts on your hands you might get infected too. Then you'll be dead as well.'

'But what about you, sir? Mightn't you get gas gangrene if you touch 'im?'

'It's my job,' said the Surgeon. Typhoid, dysentery, cholera, diphtheria, gas gangrene — a surgeon risked them all.

'Sir?' It was another of the convict porters. 'A message from the Guv'nor. He's sending out an expedition to capture another native to replace Arabanoo. He asked if you'd bring your little native boy down to the harbour to interpret.'

The Surgeon's face brightened at the thought of his adopted son. 'I've never known a child to pick up a language so easily — nor a man. I'll fetch the boy now.'

He put his hat and coat on, and walked swiftly home. The colony needed some way to talk to the natives. He'd heard there'd been an attack on convicts out hunting. Or that was what the men had claimed they'd been doing in the bush. The Surgeon frowned. He wouldn't put it past the wretches here to have been after native women.

He was sure Andrew would be able to translate for the Governor. Perhaps they didn't even need to capture another adult native. Andrew was a brilliant child. He already spoke English almost like a white man — better English than most of the convicts, for he spoke with the Surgeon's own gentleman's accent.

Suddenly the Surgeon realised that the boy still didn't know that any of his people had survived. Maybe he would want to go back to them …

No. How could a lad who had been welcomed into a gentleman's home want to go back to the miserable native life?

He pulled open the door of his hut — it sagged even more since the beginning of winter. 'Maria?'

The girl looked up. The o'possum sat on her lap, nibbling at a bunch of leaves. She dropped it back into its basket, as though embarrassed to be seen petting it. 'Yes, sir?'

'Where's Andrew?'

'Out in the garden, sir. He's pulling up the carrots and eating them, like he's never seen a carrot before.'

'I doubt he has,' said the Surgeon dryly. 'Don't let him eat too many. There'll be no more carrots till the new crop next summer.' He opened the back door. 'Andrew!'

The boy didn't even look up. The Surgeon called again. 'Andrew?'

The boy looked around, then stood up and made his way over to him. He wore his shirt and trousers, but no boots.

'Father White?'

'Come, Andrew, wash your hands and put your boots on.' He spoke slowly and clearly, so the boy could understand each word.

The child looked at him for a moment, a carrot in his hand. 'My name is Nanberry Buckenau,' he said quietly.

'Not this again! Your name is Andrew White.'

'My name is Nanberry.' The child clutched his carrot, as though fearful of his adoptive father's anger, but still determined.

The Surgeon sighed. The lad was too young to realise a good English name would help him. And he had lost so much. Perhaps

79

it was best to let him keep his old name for now. 'Nanberry, then,' he said. 'Nanberry White.'

The boy considered. Suddenly he smiled, his face brightening like the harbour gleamed after a winter. 'Nanberry White!' He held out the carrot to the Surgeon. 'Are you hungry?'

The Surgeon laughed. 'Not for raw carrots, young man. We're going down to the harbour.'

The smile grew wider. For a second White thought that the lad was going to dance in his excitement. 'To go in ship?'

'In a boat. A big boat, not a little fishing boat. But it isn't as big as a ship. A boat is a little ship.'

'In a big boat!' It was as though he had given the lad the crown jewels.

Nanberry stared down at the harbour, the white caps of the waves gleaming in the sunlight. 'Will more ships come soon? Big ships?'

'Yes, of course,' the Surgeon lied. You couldn't tell a child of the fear that no ship would ever come from England, that they had been forgotten, that some idiot in the Admiralty had retired and the whole project had been abandoned, to be found in the files in a decade, too late to send rescue. Perhaps there would never be a ship, or new stores, or gunpowder to keep them safe. And they would vanish into the vastness of this unknown continent. 'Yes,' he said again, almost to reassure himself. 'A big ship will come soon.'

'Father White? May-I-please,' Nanberry made it sound like all one word, 'go on a big ship when a big ship come?'

'Yes, lad. Now put your boots on.'

The boy ducked inside the storeroom, grabbed his boots and thrust his feet into them with no thought of stockings. 'Father White, do we go on the boat to find birds?'

The Surgeon felt a smile spreading across his face. The lad loved bird-watching as much as he did. He had an extraordinary talent for finding the creatures too. He could even stand still for half an hour, while the Surgeon sketched a honeyeater poking its beak into flowers, moving as little as possible so he didn't scare the bird away.

'Not this time, Andrew ... I mean *Nanberry*. The Governor has a job for you to do. An important one.'

The boy looked up at him trustingly. The Surgeon took the small fingers within his own. Black fingers, thin and dark against his own red and white hand.

Yes, he was a good lad. Clever and helpful. But this boy was not his son, not really, just as the girl in there was not his daughter, nor the Governor a friend. Phillip was a good man, but that was, in truth, all they had in common: two good men among a company of villains, trying to do their best. He was alone, cast down to the bottom of the world, away from all that he held dear.

He shut his eyes briefly, and prayed. If a ship came, let it bring not just food, but new orders, new soldiers to guard the colony, a new surgeon and news of a new posting for me. Please, oh Lord, let me go home.

He opened his eyes, and forced a smile again for Andrew ... no, Nanberry. 'Come,' he said. 'The Governor is waiting.'

Chapter 22

NANBERRY

He was in a big boat!

It was bigger than Father White's fishing boat. Six men pulled at things called *oars*, making the boat fly across the water, while he sat with Father White and a man in a red coat.

It was like magic, bouncing up and down so fast through the water. Already they were past two headlands, and heading for a third.

No one had explained where they were going. He didn't care. He was moving faster than a dolphin, faster than a whale!

And then he saw it. Smoke — the small spiral of a cooking fire.

The English didn't make small fires like that.

The sea and sky seemed to whirl around him. It was as though his past life had slapped him in the face. Some of his people were alive!

Maybe Colbee was alive, and the Aunties. Maybe they had left in time, so the sickness hadn't caught them too.

Nanberry clutched the edge of the boat as the rowers changed course, heading towards the fire. He could make out a group of young warriors, fishing spears in their hands. There was no sign of women or children.

Was one of those warriors Colbee, or another man he knew? He felt the blood thump through him as the boat drew closer.

He could see the people's faces now. Disappointment washed through him, like the cold south wind across the harbour. They were strangers, not Cadigal like him. Guringai, perhaps, or Dharug. No, he thought, this far across the harbour they would be Guringai.

But what were Guringai warriors doing on the beach now spring was coming? This was the time everyone went inland along the river to Parramatta, to strip the bark for the next year's canoes. Canoes only lasted one year and the bark was most easily stripped in big pieces after winter rain.

How could the Guringai women fish if there were no new canoes? Had the women and children died? Was that why there were only warriors here? His world had been torn from him once. Now it seemed some of it was being given back to him, but in pieces he couldn't understand.

The boat was near the shore now. Four of the rowers jumped out and dragged it up onto the sand.

The Guringai men stared at the boat without expression. They did not approach.

Father White touched his shoulder. 'Can you talk to them, lad?' Nanberry nodded. The languages around the great harbour were close enough for all the clans to understand. He had learnt Guringai words, as well as Dharug and many others, at the Parramatta feasts too. 'Tell them we are good people,' Father White said slowly. 'Say we give them much food if they come with us.'

Nanberry nodded, despite his confusion.

If some Guringai had survived perhaps some Cadigal had too. Should he leave Father White's to look for them?

But they had left him to die! Did he want to leave the land of boats and houses and wonderful new things? Did he want to leave Father White for a clan who had abandoned him to illness?

'Tell the men to come over here,' urged Father White.

'Guwi!' called Nanberry.

The men glanced at him as though Nanberry was a dung beetle, then looked away.

Nanberry felt a flush heat his body. The men were warriors, with the gap in their teeth from their yulang yirabadjang ceremony. Their noses were pierced with reeds or bones from the nanung ceremony too. Why would warriors like these speak to a little boy? But he was too embarrassed to explain this to Father White.

The warriors began to walk away.

'Wari, wari!' cried Nanberry. Stop!

Two of the warriors halted, the others kept walking. But even those two didn't look at Nanberry directly.

What should he say? He couldn't ask if Colbee and the others were alive. If they were dead their ghosts might haunt him if he spoke their names. Instead he said, 'Do you know if Cadigal are here?'

Neither of the warriors answered. They still didn't look at Nanberry.

'I am Cadigal,' he offered desperately. 'I am Nanberry. Please tell me if any Cadigal are alive!'

The warriors still said nothing.

Nanberry looked back at Father White and the other English. He had to make the warriors listen! 'The white ghosts want you to come with them. They will give you all the food you want. Lots of meat, and fish. They have other foods too. There is bread and corn —'

One of the warriors glanced at him and laughed. 'What do we want with white-ghost food, little boy? We do not talk with little boys like you. Tell the white ghosts to send a man to talk to us. Go and play with the women.'

Nanberry flushed again, glad that Father White didn't understand the warrior's speech. He had seen things these warriors never had. He had ridden in a boat! He had sat on a horse! He knew how to speak the white-ghost — the English — tongue. He could wear boots.

Father White took him hunting and fishing and making pictures of the birds, just as though he was a warrior already.

The warriors were strangers, even if they had the same colour skin as him.

All at once he knew what he wanted to be now. I will be English, he thought. I will forget the ghosts of Cadigal. I will stay with Father White. I will eat corn and sit on chairs. One day I will go in a big ship with sails.

'Just get them natives close enough so we can grab one,' muttered a man in a red coat.

Nanberry forced himself to smile as though a storm wasn't raging inside. He beckoned to the men, and pointed to the boat.

The warrior who had spoken to him laughed. He and his friend turned their backs. They leapt up across the boulders and out of sight.

Would Father White be angry? But Father White patted his shoulder. 'You did your best, lad. That is all any of us can do.'

Nanberry didn't understand all of the words, but he understood their meaning. He sat close to Father White as the boat bounced across the harbour again, forcing himself not to look back towards the beach where the warriors had vanished.

The world he had known was gone, even if some of its people had survived.

Yes, he would be English now.

Chapter 23

NANBERRY

'Come on, lad. You must know more than that.'

Nanberry looked helplessly from the man called Mr Tench to Father White. Mr Tench wanted to know if there were rivers and grasslands beyond the land explored by the colony. But Nanberry didn't have the words to explain how to find them. He'd never even been to the big river to the north, or across the mountains — he'd only heard about those places when the clans met to feast at Parramatta.

But how could he explain all that?

'He's only a lad,' said Father White. 'You can't expect maps from a boy.'

'Natives!' The yell came from down the hill. One of the convict porters puffed towards them. 'Mr Bradley were out fishin', and caught some natives! They're coming in to the harbour now.'

Nanberry followed Father White and Mr Tench as they ran

down to the water. People in smelly trousers and ragged skirts crowded on the shore, staring at the boat skimming towards them.

Father White pushed his way through the rabble, holding Nanberry by the hand. 'Do you know these natives, lad?'

Nanberry gazed at the boat. His heart leapt like a dolphin. Colbee! And he knew the other man too. 'Colbee!' he yelled, dancing up and down in his excitement. 'Bennelong!'

Father White smiled at Mr Tench. 'I would say the boy knows them,' he said dryly.

Nanberry hunted for words to explain. 'Colbee is very big warrior. Great man. Very, very great man. Wollarawarre Bennelong is a ... a man.'

'Not a great warrior?' asked Father White. He looked amused.

Nanberry hardly listened. He had only met Wollarawarre Bennelong a few times.

Colbee! His determination to forget his people vanished in his joy. Some of his clan lived!

The boat was pulled up onto the shore. Guards stepped forward to grab the two dark-skinned men. They were bound by ropes, tight around their hands and legs and bodies. Bennelong looked frightened, but Colbee stared ahead unseeing. His face was scarred.

He has had the smallpox, thought Nanberry. But he survived, like me. 'Colbee! Colbee!' he called.

Colbee glanced at him, then looked away.

Nanberry frowned at his shirt and trousers. He doesn't recognise me, he thought. I have grown too ...

'It's almost as good as a hanging,' said a woman behind him. Her breath was foul and her two teeth were yellow. 'Look at them big savages, naked as the day they was born!'

'Wouldn't do for you, Madge,' said another woman. 'You likes 'em hairy, don't you?'

Both women dissolved into shrieks of laughter.

'Colbee!' cried Nanberry again.

But neither man even glanced around as they were led away.

Father White looked down at Nanberry. 'Come up to the Governor's house,' he said gently. 'You can talk to them there.'

They walked behind the captured men, the crowd yelling in excitement. It was frightening, being in the middle of so many loud people. Nanberry was glad of Father White, solid beside him. Colbee still didn't turn around and see him.

It was good to be inside the Governor's house. So big, room after room. The Governor stood to meet them, with Booroong, dressed in an English skirt and shoes, and Mrs Johnson and the Reverend Johnson too.

Booroong gave a shriek of joy. 'Colbee! Bennelong!' She ran to meet them, her shoes making clapping noises on the wooden floor, then stopped. Neither man even glanced at her.

Booroong crept over to Nanberry. 'Why don't they speak? Why don't they even look at us?'

'I think they are scared,' whispered Nanberry, in their own language.

'Warriors are never scared.'

'Warriors don't show that they are scared.'

'Perhaps they think we're ghosts,' Booroong's voice held despair.

They watched as the two men were led off.

It was morning before he was taken to the hut where Colbee and Bennelong were imprisoned. The door creaked open. Nanberry stared at the two men.

Their fine beards had been shaved off, and their hair too. Nanberry had seen the patients at the hospital shaved — Father

White said it was to get rid of lice, the tiny creatures that made your head itch. The warriors had been dressed in trousers and shirts too. But worse was the big iron ring each had on his leg, tethering him via a rope to a convict.

Nanberry shivered. 'No,' he said to Father White. He pointed to the ropes. You didn't keep warriors penned like eels in a trap.

'They tried to escape last night,' said Father White gently. 'Chewed through their ropes. Luckily savages don't know how to open doors or windows.'

Savages. He had heard the word before but didn't quite know what it meant. Someone who didn't know about doors or windows, he supposed, but it sounded worse than that.

Behind them officers in uniforms crowded in to watch the show.

'Speak to them, boy,' urged Father White. 'You said their names were Colbee and Bennelong?'

'He is Gringgerry Gibba Kenara Colbee of the Cadigal.' Nanberry gave the full name. 'He is my uncle. The other man is Wollarawarre Bennelong of the Wangan people.' He took a deep breath and turned to the two captive men. 'It is me, Nanberry.'

Once again, neither man looked at him. Colbee stared unseeing at the door. Bennelong gazed at the officers.

'Are you using the right language, boy?' asked one of the officers.

'The lad knows his own language,' snapped Father White.

'They ... they do not want to talk to me,' said Nanberry quietly. 'They are angry.' And scared, he thought, but he couldn't say that. They want a warrior to speak to them, one who has had his tooth knocked out, not a boy like me.

He couldn't say that either.

'Never mind, lad,' said Father White. He shrugged. 'We'll give them a few days to settle down.'

Day after day Father White took Nanberry down to the hut to see the prisoners. Sometimes the warriors were still eating — giant platters of fish that they gnawed down to the bones, and wine and bread.

But the men never spoke to the boy.

At last, twelve days after Colbee and Bennelong's capture, Big Lon brought the news at supper.

'The native has escaped!'

'How, man?' demanded Father White.

'They was eatin' their suppers outside when he just plucked off the rope and jumped the fence. He were into the bush afore any could bar him.'

'And the other?'

Big Lon's face broke into a gap-toothed grin. 'Tremblin' like he were waitin' for the lash, he's that scared. Thinks they is goin' to hang him, I reckon.'

Nanberry put down his spoon. He stared at his meat pudding. So it was Colbee who had escaped. Colbee would never show fear like that.

Colbee, free again.

It had hurt to see a great warrior tied by the leg, shamed in front of so many people. But it had hurt more that his uncle hadn't spoken so much as a word to him.

'I reckon that savage will talk to the lad now,' said Big Lon gleefully. 'Now he's alone an' all.'

Bennelong sat on the dirt floor in the hut. His convict keeper stared, bored, out of the window as he held Bennelong's rope.

Bennelong glanced up as the Governor, Mr Tench, Father White and Nanberry came into the room.

'Tell Bennelong he is not to be frightened,' said Governor Phillip.

Nanberry hesitated. How could a boy say that to a warrior? But the Governor was the leader of the colony. *His* leader …

'The Governor — the beanga, father of the colony — says you need not be afraid.'

Bennelong surged to his feet. He struck Nanberry a great swipe across the cheek. Nanberry fell back onto the floor. He bit his lip to stop himself crying out.

'How dare you —' began Father White.

Mr Tench held him back.

Nanberry struggled to his feet again. He wiped the blood from his mouth. 'I am sorry,' he said to Bennelong. 'I know a warrior is never frightened. But the white ghosts do not know how to behave sometimes.'

For the first time Bennelong looked at him. 'You are a little white ghost now.'

Nanberry put up his chin. 'I am Nanberry White, son of a great man among these people.'

'You're nothing. An ant, a beetle.'

Nanberry trembled. He didn't know if it was anger, shame or pain. 'What I ask?' he said to Father White.

'Ask him how he got those scars,' said Mr Tench.

Nanberry translated.

This time Bennelong laughed. He pointed proudly to the scars on his chest and upper arms.

'Those are from when he was made a man,' said Nanberry.

'And the deep ones on his arm and leg?' Father White sounded interested. 'They look like spear marks.'

'Yes,' said Nanberry.

'Violent lot,' said Mr Tench. 'What about the scar on his hand?'

Once more Nanberry translated.

Bennelong laughed again. He seemed happy to talk now, though he faced the men, not Nanberry, as though the boy was a far-off bird, singing to itself.

'He got that scar carrying off a woman from another clan.'

'She didn't want to go?' Mr Tench sounded amused.

Bennelong responded with a long explanation. Nanberry tried to find the words to translate. 'She was angry. She yelled and yelled. She bit his hand. There was lots of blood.'

'What did he do then?' Mr Tench was enjoying the story.

'He knocked her down. He beat her till she ... I do not know ... asleep?'

'Unconscious,' said Father White grimly.

'Unconscious. She had all blood, lots of blood.'

'Quite the lover,' said Mr Tench, grinning.

Nanberry didn't understand.

～✺⊙

Every day, after that, Nanberry was taken to Bennelong to translate and teach him English words.

He hated it. Sometimes Father White came with him and it was not so bad. Other times Father White had to be at the hospital, and Mr Tench took him instead.

Bennelong spoke to him now. But it wasn't *to* him; it was to the men. He used Nanberry like a ... a boat carrying the sentences to and fro, a way to understand the speech of the white men without learning more than a few words himself. Nor did the white men try to understand much of the natives' languages.

Even when Bennelong said that two other Cadigal had survived the smallpox — Colbee, Caruey — he didn't look at Nanberry to see if the news hurt him. Even when the Governor took Bennelong and Nanberry to a hut on the great headland called Woolara, to look for sails in case the big ships came back, it was as though only Nanberry's mouth was there. I am parrot mouth, he thought.

He stood on the headland overlooking the sea with the man who lived at the lookout post and the Governor. Bennelong threw a great spear, it landed exactly on the rock he threw it at despite the wind that whipped about them.

He shivered. He didn't like Woolara. It was a place of battle and many dead. He sat on the rocks and stared out to sea, ignoring Bennelong's and the Governor's laughter behind him.

Suddenly he realised that all was quiet. He climbed up the hill. Down on the harbour the boat with the Governor and Bennelong vanished behind the ridge.

'Stop!' he yelled. He began to scramble down the beach.

The lookout keeper ran after him. He grabbed his shoulder.

'You're to stay here a few days, lad. Talk to the natives if they come this way.'

Nanberry shook his head. 'No! There are ghosts here. I want Father White. I want to go home!'

The Surgeon's hut was home, he realised. The Surgeon was the one who protected him now.

How could they have left him here? Did Father White know?

'You'll go home in a few days, lad,' said the man. He led the way into the hut.

Nanberry followed him. The shadows were swallowing the day. Soon the ghosts would be out, whispering around the hut, under the howl of the wind.

─✦◎

It was hard at the lookout hut. But no natives came. There was only a blanket on the floor for him; he had grown used to the comfort of a bed. There were no good stews or roasted duck, just salt meat boiled with dried peas, stinking and sour. There was no Maria to tell him to wash his face. Worst of all, there was no Father White to smile at him and tell him he was a good lad.

Nightmares left him quiet and shaken: dreams where every person screamed at him, white blisters on their skin; and other dreams where he walked alone, always alone, along a beach that had no end. There was a hut but he could never find it. Never, never, never. Always he walked alone ...

The lookout man, Mr Southwell, was kind enough. He wanted to know what he called *native ways*. Nanberry showed him how to dig a grave and pour on earth, and how to rub sticks to make a fire.

But his hands weren't strong enough and the hot north wind ate every spark he made before it had time to burrow into the dry leaves he'd gathered. At last he gave up and sat on the rocks. Mr Southwell sat with him, the man staring out at the sea for the ship that didn't come; the boy staring into the harbour, waiting for the man who called himself his father.

No supply ship came. But at last a fishing boat skimmed across the water, with six convict rowers.

And at the prow sat Father White.

Nanberry ran down to the cove below the headland. Even before the boat was pulled up onto the sand he splashed into the water and swam out, grasping the edges of the boat and hoisting himself up. 'Father White!' he cried. 'Father White.'

'Missed me, have you?' asked Father White. He reached over the rail and ruffled Nanberry's hair. Maria kept it short so it curled around his head.

Nanberry held onto the boat till the rowers hauled it up onto the sand. Father White stepped out. He looked at Nanberry for a second, then held out his arms.

'I'm sorry they left you here, boy,' he said as he held Nanberry close. 'I thought you would have liked to be out in the wild again for a few days. Be away from the township and the smells.'

'No,' said Nanberry. 'Stay with you. Always stay with you.'

Father White held him close again.

Chapter 24

NANBERRY

Nanberry sat at the table, his elbows pressed politely close to his body, his freshly ironed shirt crisp and warm against his skin. There were scrambled eggs and toast and honey for breakfast.

He had helped make the toast, holding the slices of bread up to the fire on a metal three-pronged toasting fork. He had found the honey too, climbing up a tree and filling a bucket with the dripping comb. Father White had patted his head, and said he was a *fine lad*, then smiled and suggested that perhaps next time he climbed a tree he shouldn't take all his clothes off, especially when there might be ladies about.

But how could your knees grip a tree trunk properly in trousers?

There was a lot to learn, even when you had been English through nearly a whole circle of the stars.

For a while he had wondered if his skin would turn white too, now that he wore clothes and lived in a ghost house. But his skin was as dark as before.

He did not let himself think about the Cadigal. They were dead these days: dead to him, even if two others still lived. You did not think about the dead, in case their ghosts came to haunt you. And that was true, for whenever he thought about his family and his friends, he felt like the convicts must have when they were lashed for not working or for being rude to important people. But his pain was inside him, not on his back.

It would be easier to bear pain on my back, he thought.

He did not talk to Bennelong, or Bennelong to him any more. Bennelong had enough English words now to talk directly to the Governor, who he called beanga, or father. Sometimes Nanberry saw the two of them walk around the town, the Governor in his fine coat and Bennelong in one almost as fine, the iron ring still around his leg, his convict keeper trailing them with the other end of the rope in his hand.

'Well, are we all ready?' Father White smiled. Nanberry forced himself out of his dream. It was good to see Father White smile. He was still worried about the big ships that didn't come, about the convicts and marines who grew thin and tired because they would eat only what came from the stores.

There was little food left there now. But there was lots of food in the Surgeon's garden, and plenty of fish in the sea.

Nanberry had grown almost as tall as a spear. Maria had put longer legs on his trousers and made a coat of Father White's fit him. She had pulled apart ragged stockings to knit him new ones. Maria could knit cloth that was as warm as o'possum skin.

Nanberry watched Father White dab his lips with his napkin and stand up from the breakfast table.

'I'm ready, sir.' Maria stood at the table with her hat on, and her coat, even though the day was warm. Nanberry tried not to bounce with excitement.

Today was a great day. A ... What was the word? ... a *grand* day. Today Father White and he and Maria were to move into a new house, a big house made of bricks, with a slate roof, not this hut where water dribbled in when it rained.

Something squeaked from the window ledge. Nanberry grinned. Father White and his people and his bungu — no, his *o'possum* — were to move.

It was still strange living with an o'possum. Almost as strange as sleeping on a bed off the floor and having times for meals instead of eating when there was food or when you were hungry. There was food in the morning and during the day, and just before the sun set too. If you ate at the right time you could eat as much as you wanted, except for *wheat bread* and *salt meat*.

Nanberry didn't mind. Salt meat stank. It wasn't proper food. Bread was good, especially with honey, but cornbread made good toast, and corncobs were even better.

Father White put his head out the door and made some sort of signal. Men came — men in bare feet and dirty rags, not like Nanberry's clean pressed shirt and trousers. Nanberry looked at his clothes proudly. Father White had even shown him how to make his boots shine.

The ragged men began to lift all that could be moved. Already the sacks and boxes from the storeroom had been taken. Now beds, tables and Maria's big pot were grabbed and hauled away.

Father White put on his hat and coat. He led the way up the track between the huts, Maria walking behind holding a bundle of her own things. Nanberry and Father White carried nothing, like true warriors. The summer sun beat down on them, making him sweat in his clothes.

Something screamed behind them. Nanberry turned. It was the o'possum, shrieking at the convict who carried his basket. The angry animal jumped out of the basket and clambered up a tree. It chittered angrily down at them again.

Nanberry laughed. So did Father White. Even Maria gave a smile. 'Maybe the o'possum will stay here,' she said hopefully.

Father White smiled. 'The new house is only just up the hill. I suspect he'll find us.'

'Just as long as he doesn't find the sack of apples again,' muttered Maria as they reached the house.

It was so big! Nanberry ran from room to room as the men put beds and tables down. Maria was bustling about and telling them what to do. A Cadigal man would have bashed her on the head with his axe for speaking to him like that, but here Maria was important because Father White was important, just as Nanberry was important too.

The house had a big kitchen and a storeroom — and a *study* too. *Upstairs* — stairs were stacks of wood you could run up and down — were rooms for him and Maria and Father White. There were *shutters* at the windows to keep out the wind and a smooth wooden floor that bounced a little when he jumped up and down on it.

His room was as big as the old hut's kitchen! It had a window that looked down to the harbour, so he could see if a big ship sailed in.

'Put the bed there,' he said to the convicts as they lugged it into the room. He knelt on the pallet and looked out the window again. He could see the harbour from his bed, and someone with dark skin splashing in the waves. It was Booroong.

'Father White, may I go and swim, please?'

'Drat the boy ... can't you do something useful?' Maria bustled in with an armful of sheets.

'Let him have a day of play,' came Father White's voice from the hall.

Something small and dark ran up the stairs, then dashed under the bed. A small furry face — an angry face — peered out. The o'possum gave a short sharp scream.

'Your friend has found us already,' Father White said to Maria.

Maria snorted.

Nanberry laughed again and ran downstairs.

Booroong was only a girl. But it would be good, just for a while, to speak to someone without having to work out the words. Besides, he knew lots more English words than her and could show them off.

Nanberry ran down to the waves, yelling as he leapt over the rocks and into the water, diving down into the blueness, then swimming up towards the sunlight, his wet clothes dragging at his body. Booroong laughed as he poked his head out of the water and waved at her.

It is almost like it was before, a small voice whispered, when you swam while your people feasted and life was good.

Nanberry shut the voice away. He lived in a grand house. He had Father White, who was proud of him. He was not like Bennelong, with a chain around his leg.

It was good — yes, it was good — to be English.

Chapter 25

SURGEON WHITE

The fishing boat bobbed and the waves splashed its sides. Nanberry peered down at the nets, excited by the splash of fish. The Surgeon smiled. The lad's laughter was one of the great comforts of his life.

All at once the boy looked up, his gaze entranced. 'Father White! The big ship is sailing!'

The Surgeon looked over towards the rocky headland, his heart leaping with hope that it might be a ship from England. But it was only the tiny *Supply*. The *Supply* was the only ship the colony had left, now that the *Sirius* had been wrecked on Norfolk Island. It had been taking another load of convicts and supplies to the small outpost there — and the troublesome Major Ross, to try to stop him urging his marines to open rebellion.

The *Supply* was heading for Batavia, in a desperate attempt to buy food to keep the colony alive through winter. There had been little from this year's wheat harvest, although the corn crop had been good. The weekly ration was only two pounds of flour now, two pounds of salt meat or ten pounds of fresh fish, and a cup of rice-and-weevils or dried-peas-and-weevils. It was enough to keep a man alive. But only just.

The colony had huddled on this barren shore for nearly two and a half years now and still not a sail had been seen from England. Why hadn't a ship come?

Sometimes it seemed as though home must have vanished off the earth. At other times he wondered if this land had wandered further south in the great ocean, so no one would ever find them again.

Foolish thoughts, for a scientist. But no one could help the dreams that came at night.

The Surgeon stared at the hovels that lined Sydney Cove, the small farming plots, the vast green wilderness of trees behind them. There were still hardly a dozen brick houses in the colony and even those would probably crumble in ten years. The rest were mud and wattle, roofed with bark. Could they even last a third winter?

He shook his head. There was no clothing to be had in the stores now. No medicines, except the remedies, so new to him, that Arabanoo had told him about, like the oil from the eucalyptus leaves that helped the itch and congestion of the lungs. No more dried peas, no wine.

His fishing brought in enough to feed his household, no more. Even the fish had mostly vanished from the harbour. Only Bennelong still ate all the bread that he wanted in the colony now. The Governor was afraid that if the native knew how little food and gunpowder the colony had he might tell his old friends were he to escape.

If the Indians attacked now they couldn't defend themselves. Starvation or murder, thought the Surgeon, which will happen first?

He looked at his adopted son again, peering down to see whether a fish swam near their nets. He had been right. The lad was a comfort to him. At least he could see that the boy — and Maria — didn't starve.

'I'll take you out shooting tonight,' he said suddenly.

The lad grinned up at him like he had offered the crown jewels. 'I can fire a big musket?'

'Yes, lad.'

'We will shoot a kangaroo,' said Nanberry joyfully. 'I will show you where they graze. We will be warriors!'

'Yes, lad.' The more meat the better, thought the Surgeon.

The Surgeon watched the *Supply* change course, avoiding the rocks. Poor leaky little ship, with the treacherous reefs and storms between here and Batavia. If only they could all sail away on her, but she could carry fifty men at best. Could she even get to Batavia? Could she make it back here? Even if she did, she would be away for at least five months. How many would survive till then?

The tiny ship was nearly past the headland now. And then it was gone …

An empty harbour. Empty stores and empty hopes.

It was time to haul in the nets, to do a final round at the hospital, checking on the convicts who had unnecessary scurvy, the fools injured in fights because they hadn't learnt that so far from civilisation every life was precious.

We are a small speck in a vast land, across an even vaster ocean, he thought. Oh Lord, who sees a sparrow fall, watch over us and protect us. Send us a ship, some food, some stores. Don't let us die here forgotten.

Chapter 26

SURGEON WHITE

Winter arrived — their third winter here, with even less food in the stores and the marines trudging barefoot in the mud, their fine black boots worn out.

The Surgeon shivered at his desk in the hospital, trying to break up the lumps in his inkwell so he could sketch a new bird — a fascinating pigeon he'd seen in his garden yesterday, fat and grey with a white stripe around its neck, strutting around under the trees as though it didn't want to fly. Nanberry called it a wungawunga and that was almost the sound the bird made.

Outside the hospital the wind blew shivers of ice against the leaky walls. Was there snow beyond the mountains? It felt like it. But there could be anything out there. Lakes, deserts ...

There was no way to tell. Nanberry was too young to know. Bennelong might — but the man had finally escaped, once he had gained the Governor's trust and had the shackle removed from his leg. Even now he might be urging the natives to wipe out the colony ...

A woman screamed outside, and then another. The Surgeon leapt to his feet and grabbed his bag. For a second he wondered if the natives had really attacked.

The cries came again. But they weren't screams of terror, he realised. They were excitement.

He dropped the bag and ran to the door. Two women rushed past, clutching their babies in their shawls against the wind. One of them grinned at him, showing the gaps between her yellow teeth. 'The flag's up! The flag on the headland is up!'

A flag meant that a ship's sails had been seen, far out at sea. A ship! Surgeon White shut his eyes, and gave a quick prayer of gratitude. A ship bringing the food, the clothing, the medicines they so desperately needed. A ship bringing news. A ship that said: 'We have not forgotten you, tiny colony at the end of the world. You are not to perish here.'

More women ran past the hospital with children in their arms, kissing them and each other. One hag with filthy hair would have kissed the Surgeon but he drew back.

He threw on his hat and coat and seized an eye-glass, then ran outside and up the hill to see for himself. And there it really was — the signal flag, flapping in the wind.

There was no sign of the ship itself yet — it might be hours before it sailed into the harbour. But already he could see the Governor leaving his neat stone house. The Surgeon ran down to the cove, heedless of his dignity, to join the party.

The rowers pushed the Governor's boat out into the harbour with their trousers rolled, then hopped in and began to pull at the oars. Behind them officers tumbled into fishing boats, ordering men to row, and row fast, desperate to reach the ship. That ship might carry letters with news of the families they had been forced to leave behind in England, as well as stores.

Surgeon White scanned the great blank blue canvas of sea and sky between the harbour's headlands. For the first time he felt a whisper of fear.

What if the ship wasn't English? What if it were French, or even Russian or American? The French knew that they were here. What if war had been declared while they were away? The colony was hardly surviving as it was. If a French ship attacked they would be helpless …

And suddenly there it was: a large ship, graceful on the waves. And on her mast … He swallowed, and shut his eyes briefly in gratitude again. The English flag.

'She's sailing too close to shore,' muttered one of the men next to him. 'She'll be on the rocks if she takes that course.' The man stood and began to wave frantically.

White grasped his eye-glass. Disaster indeed if the ship had come so far only to be wrecked, her cargo lost at the last minute. But the sailors aboard must have seen the signal. The ship altered course slightly.

The man next to him sat down. Surgeon White could see the name of the ship now: the *Lady Juliana*, and the word 'London'.

Beside him the Governor drew a breath of relief. 'Saved,' he said quietly.

Surgeon White nodded. Even with Major Ross on Norfolk Island, the marines were at the point of rebellion, demanding the alcohol that was supposed to be part of their wages. The only thing that had stopped them was the knowledge that there was no more wine, or rum, or even rations, for the Governor to give them.

'No point my meeting the ship myself now,' muttered Phillip. 'I need to get the work parties together, get the stores unloaded as soon as we can.'

The Governor signalled to one of the fishing boats that were following his boat.

The dinghy drew close so the Governor could step aboard. The Surgeon admired his sense of duty once again. This ship might have news of Phillip's loved ones, the first news in so many years.

A sudden scatter of clouds above them began to weep, a winter squall with ice-cold fingers. The rain stopped as they drew closer still to the big ship.

The Surgeon felt his heart hammer in his chest. Perhaps one of the letters aboard was his recall to England. He had served nearly five years in this job now, if he counted time in England, preparing for the voyage. He had done his duty here for nearly two and a half long years, his duty enough on the voyage. Surely it was time for another posting ...

'Pull away, lads!' yelled the rowers. 'Hurrah for a bellyful, and news from our friends!'

The *Juliana*'s rope ladder bounced as it was flung down so they could scramble up. White was one of the first aboard. He looked around for the Captain. 'Letters!' he cried, forgetting all politeness. 'What is the news from England?'

The Captain stared at him, his face broken in a sour grin among his wrinkles. 'You want news? Where do you want me to start? The King went mad, did you know that?'

The Surgeon stared. 'You're joking, man!'

'I am not. But he's well enough now or so they say. And the Frenchies have put their king into prison — and their queen too. It's rule by mob there now — and we're at war with 'em.'

Surgeon White shook his head. It was too much to take in. Impossible ... a king didn't go mad, nor did mobs tear a king and queen from their thrones. Was the man joking? But the Captain looked sincere; nor were any of the sailors nudging each other as though the colonists were taken in.

'We knew none of this,' he said slowly. 'We've heard nothing of the rest of the world — nothing at all.'

'Aye, well, you wouldn't. You wouldn't know about the *Guardian* either.'

'The *Guardian*?'

'The store ship sent after you, before we set out. Should have reached you months ago. But she was wrecked on an iceberg near the Cape.'

White stared at him. So they hadn't been forgotten. But that was poor comfort now, with all the stores lost as well as the poor sailors on board.

'But *you* have stores?' he asked urgently.

'Little enough. Only loaded supplies to get us here.' The man looked at him speculatively. 'Might have some extra to sell though, if you can meet the price.' He grinned. 'Got something else you might fancy below too.'

'What?'

'Two hundred and twenty-five convict women. Women! How does that sound to you? Enough to tickle any man's fancy, eh? And them being convicts you can do what you want with 'em.'

'More convicts? But we need food, man. Medicines, clothes, candles, blankets. We can hardly feed the wretches we have here.'

The Captain wasn't listening. What did it matter to him if the colony starved? He'd soon sail away again. He rubbed his hands and nudged the Surgeon. 'Had the wenches all to ourselves all the way here. The rest o' the fleet is following, with the men.'

White edged away from the man, disgusted, suddenly aware of the stench around him. Not just the natural smells of any ship that had been long at sea — bad meat and salt; the stink of sailors with teeth lost to scurvy — but a dreadful reek.

He became aware of a muted moaning from below. He had been too excited to hear it before. 'What's that sound?'

'Just them women. Now, about the stores you asked about. There's flour, and dried fruit, and port too ...'

But Surgeon White had already run to the hatchway. 'Open it,' he ordered.

One of the sailors slowly lifted it up.

White faces, starved and hollow-eyed, blinked at the sudden light. The stench of death and rats, of vomit and muck, struck him so strongly he stepped back. A voice called with desperate cheer, 'Anythin' you want for a biscuit, dearie. Anythin' at all. Just you ask for Maggie!'

White looked back at the Captain. 'God help us, man. Are the convicts on the other ships as desperate as these poor wretches?'

But the Captain was already trying to sell his stores to someone else.

Chapter 27

SURGEON WHITE

It was a scene from Hell.

The sides of the new hospital tent flapped like a ship's sails as Surgeon White strode among the bodies of the dead and dying, giving orders. There had been no time to make beds for so many, nor even pallets of straw. The men and women in this tent had only a blanket between them and the cold ground. But it was the best that he could do.

Most of his new patients were naked, their rags so filthy and crusted they had to be cut off their bodies and burnt. There were men as well as women now, for the other ships of the Second Fleet had unloaded their human cargo, as starved and weak as the convicts on the *Lady Juliana*. Shadowed eyes looked enormous in skeletal white faces. Some screamed at the light after so many months in darkness. Others muttered, their teeth fallen out, their legs swollen, lost in the madness of scurvy. Rat bites had turned foul, lice crawled from matted hair.

It was a nightmare. How long had he prayed for ships to come? And now they had, bringing not the stores they needed, nor certainly a letter of recall, but the ill and starving.

The stench of the smoke from the burning clothes and blankets filled the colony. It was impossible to be clear of it. Impossible not to hear the moans and cries. Not far away the pile of bodies grew: those who had died as volunteers brought them to shore from the ship, those who had died since. Most of the new convicts had been so weak they didn't even know that they had reached the land they'd sailed for.

There was no time to bury the dead now; there was hardly time to tend the living.

One thousand and thirty-eight men and women had sailed from England. Two hundred and seventy-three had died on the eleven-month voyage. Four hundred and eighty-six — he clung desperately to the figures, as though by accurate accounting he could somehow help them — had been rowed from the ship too weak to stand. Many had died on that last trip to shore, never feeling the soil of the land they had been sent to. Others lay wide-eyed and gaunt-faced on the grass, dying before a hand could comfort them.

One hundred and twenty-four had died here already.

Even the most hardened convicts of Sydney Cove had run to help these victims as the rowing-boat crews had unloaded them like sacks of wheat. The poor and hungry of the colony had brought their tattered blankets to warm the newcomers, their ragged blouses to cover their nakedness. Men he had regarded as black-hearted rogues cried as they lifted white faces to help them sip fresh water. Women he had damned as whores spooned flour-and-water soup into cracked and fevered lips.

The convicts below decks had even hidden the bodies of their dead friends during the voyage, desperate for their rations, adding to the stench and rot in the hold. Most of the convicts —

alive or dead — had been so muck-covered as they were carried out that you couldn't see the skin below the crust of filth.

He wanted to yell accusations, to have the captains put in irons. But they were elsewhere, cheerfully selling the food that they had stolen while their human cargo starved. One had even had the gall to open a shop. Their best customers were the officers, like that upstart Balmain.

There was nothing the Governor could do, for the captains had at least brought the government stores as ordered. All they had taken was the convicts' food — and there was no law that said that convicts must be fed or even given water or daylight. The captains had broken no law of England, only the laws of humanity and God.

The Surgeon would not buy their stores, though he too hungered for familiar food — wheat flour, rice, peas. He would not profit from men like these, nor add to their profit.

At least the captains hadn't dared to break into the official stores sent to the colony. The colonists would eat, for a while, even with so many more to feed. Now his job was to try to separate those who were weak from starvation and scurvy from those with fever: typhus mostly, although maybe dysentery too.

At least today the portable hospital tent had finally been put up. The sailors on the *Justinian* swore it had been put up in a few hours back in England, but it had taken days to work out how to do it here. The fever cases were quarantined there, hopefully stopping typhus or dysentery killing the rest of the colony. He'd ordered the worst of the scurvy cases — their arms and legs bloated, their teeth fallen out, their gums bleeding — to be taken up to the colony hospital and the huts around it, with directions to feed them teas brewed from wild greens and fruits, and gruel made with flour and water and wild spinach.

Which left tents like the one he was in now, ragged and

leaking, for those who were dying of simple starvation or putrid skin ulcers from the filth they had been forced to live in.

Surgeon White gazed at the bodies on the ground.

Some of these poor wretches might recover, with food and time and nursing. He tried to imagine them healthy again, strolling in the good sunlight of New South Wales.

Maybe some of them might know how to farm — or even how to work.

Now the colony's farms were left while every able-bodied man or woman helped nurse the newcomers. Except the marines, of course. They still did what they did best — nothing, or making preparations to sail back to England when the ships left. And good riddance. A specially formed Corps, the New South Wales Corps, had been sent to replace them. The Surgeon prayed that these were better men: men who'd help the colony, not just play at parades and regimental dinners while others worked.

The Surgeon stood back as a convict helper carried yet another dead body out of the tent.

And another thousand convicts were due in a month. Please, Lord, the Surgeon prayed, let them not be as badly treated as these poor wretches. Let there be stores enough to feed them. Let the ships bring men who know how to farm, women with courage and good sense.

We can only do our best, thought the Surgeon. His body needed rest; his mind longed for the green comfort of England; his stomach was long past nagging at him for food.

He turned towards the huts that housed the fever patients, to check that the quarantine was still in place, to bleed the worst cases. To do his best, as long as he was able.

Chapter 28

RACHEL

Rachel Turner sat on the grass down the hill from the hospital tents. Except it isn't real grass, she thought, but stumpy tufts. And the trees here were too blue and the sky too high and clear.

It had been nearly a year since she'd been out in daylight — and over two and a half years since she'd sat under a blue sky — but she was sure she remembered what trees should look like.

Not like these.

This was a land of forest to the horizon, far too much of it, and only huddles of mud huts and ragged tents for a town. Even the few stone and brick buildings were surrounded by mud. Soldiers went barefoot, dressed in rags; convicts patrolled the streets and assisted in the hospital. Around her a few others who had survived the voyage managed to stumble out of the tents and stare around.

This was a strange world indeed.

But Rachel had been in worse. Prison, with rats and slimy

straw and buckets of filth unemptied for days. The horror of the ship's hold. She wondered if the whole fleet had been as bad as the *Lady Juliana*. A few buckets of stew let down for the lot of them to grab at, three mouthfuls a day if you were lucky. You only got proper food, ship's biscuit and salt beef, if you gave the sailors and marines what they wanted.

She'd said yes to a man once and look where it had got her. She wasn't doing it again. She'd rather starve.

And so she had.

She closed her eyes against the too-bright light. At least she was here, and not bearing a sailor's bastard either, like so many others, some poor scrap that the father wouldn't claim, off with his ship again before the babe was even born.

At least she was alive. Even if the trees *were* strange, she decided to like them. She'd had enough of city streets, the stench of other people.

Twice before she was sure she'd soon be dead — once when the judge condemned her to death for stealing the silk scarf, the petticoat, the apron. That young barrister, Mr Garrow, had got witnesses who swore the Master had given them to her as a present, that they'd seen her and him in the taverns, with him talking all sweet and kind and buying her gin and mutton pies. And all the time his wife lying in her bed, giving birth to his baby …

The Master had lied. Five times, he'd lied: once saying he loved her, that he'd give her nice things. Once, to his wife, saying how Rachel had stolen the clothes. The third time he'd lied had been to tell Rachel that if she confessed she'd stolen the clothes to his angry wife then he'd see she went free and got another job.

The next time he'd lied had been to the Bow Street runner his wife had called, when Rachel had obediently said she'd taken the clothes, sending her to gaol. The last time he'd lied to the judge, calling her a thief.

She was no thief. Mr Garrow believed her. No barrister had ever argued in a court before, bringing witnesses to say someone was innocent. But Mr Garrow had, because he believed her and believed in her.

But the judge hadn't liked Mr Garrow arguing for her. Prisoners were guilty — why else would they be there? The judge had put on his black hat. He said that Rachel must die, hanged by her neck for the crowd to jeer at.

She'd sat on the filthy straw of Newgate, waiting for the gaolers to come to take her to the gallows. Instead she'd heard cheering in the streets outside.

She crowded up to the bars with the other prisoners, till one of the gaolers came in, slurping from a pint of porter. 'The King is cured!' he yelled. 'Long live the King!'

'A pox on the King!' That was Big Maggie. 'He's mad, ain't he? And he's alive and we is goin' to be dead. Why should we cheer for him?'

The gaoler leered at the ragged women in the cell. 'Because, fine ladies, King George ain't mad no more. An' to celebrate they says you lot ain't going to be hanged.'

Every woman in Newgate got seven years' transportation to New South Wales instead of death, in honour of the King's cure. Rachel wondered grimly if they'd haul her back across the sea to hang her if the King went mad again.

She took a deep breath. The stink of the *Juliana* was still with her, in her hair; the stench of the clothes burning in piles around the cove hung heavy on the town.

But there was clean air here too. It tasted of winter, despite the sunlight. She shut her eyes again briefly against the glare. She still wasn't used to the light, not after the months of dark in the ship, the shadows of prison. Even when she'd been free in London the sky was always grey with smoke, or yellow fog. She'd hated the smoke and fogs most when she'd first come to London to work as a servant. She'd been only twelve, an innocent from a tiny village, dreaming of a grand life as a servant in London Town, a housekeeper one day maybe, or even a blacksmith's wife, with a servant of her own.

And this is where her dreams had led her. Ragged and starving in Sydney Town, a prison at the far end of the world.

A shadow bent over her. She opened her eyes again. A man picked up her wrist, and felt her pulse. 'Symptoms?' he asked briefly.

'Wh-what?'

He peered down at her over his waistcoat and gold watch chain. A man of importance, she thought, despite his mended coat. 'What's wrong with you? Fever? Bowels running?'

'I just shut my eyes, that's all. The light is so bright.'

He let her wrist go. 'You don't need anything?'

She gave a half-smile. 'I'd like my life back. Failing that, a bowl of stew.'

For a second she thought she saw sympathy in his eyes, but he spoke almost harshly. 'We have little enough food,' he said. 'But what we have, we share.'

And then he was gone, back to the hospital tents to help some other poor wretch, she thought.

How did the King expect them to live, when he sent them to starve in New South Wales?

Chapter 29

SURGEON WHITE

The winter wind still wailed up from the harbour. Surgeon White placed another note against the names on his list. He'd written 'Died' against too many names, but plenty of others now had 'Work Detail' next to them. The men who had recovered enough were put to work clearing land at Rose Hill for more maize and potatoes. The women were assigned as 'housekeepers' to members of the new New South Wales Corps, or crammed into huts together to mind their young, or the babies they were soon to bear.

He looked down at the next convict in line. It was a young woman. She had found some way to wash, for her hair as well as her face looked clean. He'd talked to her before, he realised. She had even made some attempt to put her hair up under a stained but clean cap. Once, perhaps, she might even have been pretty.

'Name?'

'Rachel Turner, sir.' He found her name on the list.

'Are you with child?' he asked abruptly.

She gazed up at him, her voice steady. 'No, sir.'

'Are you well enough to work?'

'Yes, sir.'

'Then report to the Work Master down at the stores. We'll find another place for you.'

'In some man's bed?'

He froze. Had fear made the woman reckless? Why else would a well-spoken servant girl say such a thing to a gentleman? 'What do you mean?'

'I see the way the men look at us. You've got a colony of men here. Soon as I get out of hospital I'll be fair game.'

'We have women.'

'But not enough, sir. And no one to protect us.'

'Few of the wretches here seem to want protecting.'

'Have you asked us?' she said bitterly.

He stared at her. 'Can you cook, Miss Turner?' The words left his mouth before he realised.

'Would you believe me if I said yes?'

'Just answer. Can you cook? And clean and sew?'

'Yes, sir. And do them well,' she added, 'though it's been over two and a half years since I had a chance.'

'I need a servant. My present girl is getting married.'

She raised an eyebrow. 'Is she now?'

He looked down at her sternly. 'Married by the Reverend Johnson. She goes from my protection to her husband's. The banns have been read. There is no immorality in my house, Miss Turner.'

She said cautiously, 'You have a real house! How many would I be working for?'

'There is just me, when Maria goes, and my adopted son, Nanberry. He is a native.'

'A native!'

'They're not all naked savages. He wears clothes like any English boy, and he speaks better English than most of the men here. You will treat him with respect, as befits my son.'

'I can do that. So just the two of you?'

A smile lifted his mouth. He looked different when he smiled. 'And one other.'

'Who is that?'

'An o'possum.'

Chapter 30

RACHEL

She found her way to the house by asking. Everyone, it seemed, knew Surgeon White.

It was a good-enough house; nowhere near as big as the Master's back home, but solid. The enormous garden behind it held fruit trees and rows of vegetables, and a paved area with a trough out the back for washing vegetables or mucky hands or feet, or plucking feathers.

She had nothing to bring; no change of clothes even. She knocked on the door. A small girl opened it. Rachel looked again and saw it was a young woman, but tiny, her head hardly up to Rachel's shoulders. She wore a respectable servant's apron, but it had a frill around it, and there were frills on her sleeves too. The frills were the first sign of fripperies Rachel had seen since they landed.

'You're Maria? I'm Rachel Turner.'

The girl looked her up and down — though mostly up — suspiciously. 'The Master told me to expect you. Come in.'

Rachel followed her down the hallway to the kitchen. The room was warm, wonderfully warm, with a strange woody smell from the fire and an even better smell from the stew bubbling in a giant pot on the hearth. No salt beef or pork in that, she thought. It smelt like fish and potatoes, the best thing she'd smelt in too many years.

She looked back at Maria. It had been years too since she'd seen a girl so healthy, her hair so shining and clean. 'Do you mind if I sit down? I'm only out of hospital this morning.'

'The Master told me.'

'That smells good.' She nodded to the pot.

Maria picked up a bowl from the dresser and wordlessly served Rachel a large portion. It was delicious, and not just because the food was fresh.

'There's thyme and parsley in this?'

Maria gazed at her. 'You *can* cook then.'

'Yes.'

'The Master said you could.' Maria shrugged. 'You might have been lying.'

'I don't lie.'

'Then how did you land up in New South Wales? We're all of us crooks and liars here.'

'I was innocent.'

Maria's smile had no humour in it. 'There isn't a convict in the land who doesn't say that.'

'In my case it's true.' Rachel shook her head. She was too unsteady still to argue with the girl. And there was no point making enemies in a new place. She tried to sound friendly. 'The Surgeon said you're getting married. Congratulations.'

For a moment Maria's face softened. 'Jack is a good man. Not like most. The Master saved his life! And his leg too. He's farming up-river at Rose Hill now, wheat and corn and potatoes. He's got hens and two pigs and everything.' Her face glowed at the idea of the hens and pigs. 'He says I'll eat like a queen. One day he'll buy me a silk dress too.'

'A silk dress?'

Maria looked at her levelly. 'One day we'll have dressmakers here, and silk dresses too. We'll have a proper town at Sydney Cove.'

Rachel stared at her. How could this girl think that this collection of huts and convicts on the edge of the wilderness could ever be a proper town? That it might ever have a shop that sold silk dresses?

Let her have her dream, she thought. And then, what if she's right? All cities had to start somewhere. She'd heard that American cities had been huts once. Who knows what might happen here?

This girl had sense. Both of them were stuck here. Even when they'd served their sentences she doubted that either would have the money to pay for her passage back to England. And what was there for them back there? Best to dream what might be, rather than dread what might never happen.

'When do you get married?'

'Tomorrow.' Maria still stared at her. Rachel grew uncomfortable. What was wrong with the girl? She'd done nothing to annoy her, had she?

'He'll never lay a hand on you, you know,' Maria said suddenly.

Rachel blinked. 'Who?'

'The Master. He's a gentleman. Not like most here. He'll treat you proper, but he won't take you to his bed. So you make sure you work hard and do right and don't waste your time making sheep's eyes at him.'

Rachel almost smiled. So the girl was protecting the Master who had looked after her. It said a lot for her — and him.

'I'll work,' she said.

'I'll show you your room. You'll have to share the bed with me tonight. After that ...' She smiled, as though she couldn't help it.

'You'll be with your Jack.'

Maria nodded, leading the way up a narrow set of stairs. 'That's Nanberry's room. He's a good lad, even if he's a native.'

'Does he have a spear?' asked Rachel nervously.

'No! The very idea. You'll get no trouble from him. Mad for ships, he is. Just remember that he sits at the table with the Master like a gentleman, and don't expect him to do no servants' work. That is the Master's room. He doesn't like it if you go in when he's in there, nor in his study downstairs neither. He keeps his specimens in there.'

'Specimens?'

'Birds in bottles of spirit, leaves and dried flowers and such. Some of them don't half stink. But they make him happy, and it's our job — your job now — to *keep* him happy. He does a lot for people, Surgeon White. Now this is my room, your room from tomorrow.'

She opened a rough plank door into a small room. An open window looked out down to the harbour, its shutter folded back to let in fresh air. But the bed was a proper one, with bedstead and feather mattress and quilt, all smelling clean and fresh. Rachel sniffed in delight: yes, even a scent of lavender. There must be a bush outside.

'There's water in the basin if you want a wash.' And Maria left, shutting the door behind her.

The water was cold, but welcome — there had been little fresh water for washing down at the hospital. There was no looking glass, but she tidied her hair as best she could. She was just lifting her skirts to go downstairs when something growled at her.

She stopped, and listened. The sound came again, an almost

hoarse laugh, and then another rumbling growl. It was under the bed. Something was under the bed. Not a dog. She knew what a dog's growl sounded like.

She stepped back towards the door and bent down. She could just see a pair of eyes, glaring at her from under the drooping edge of the quilt: big black eyes. The monster growled again.

She screamed as the beast rushed out at her. Its claws dug into her legs and clambered up her dress; it perched on her shoulder, its claws digging into her skin again. Slowly she turned her head to look at it.

No monster, despite the size of its eyes and growl. It was no bigger than a large cat, with claws like a cat's too. It stared at her, and made a chattering sound. It still sounded angry.

She moved slowly to open the door with her other hand, then carefully walked down the stairs, trying not to jolt the creature.

'Maria ...'

The girl looked up from the shirt she'd been ironing. She laughed. 'You've met the Master's o'possum.'

'Will it bite?'

'Yes, and scratch you too, but not as long as you don't startle him. Here.' She handed her a cob of corn. 'Give him this.'

Rachel held the corn up. The animal took it and jumped down onto the table, glaring at her as though it was her fault it had taken so long to get its treat. It held the corn in its tiny paws, and began to gnaw.

She had never seen anything like it. She stared at it, entranced, as it absent-mindedly scratched an ear then went on munching. 'It's beautiful.'

'Aye, well, it can be a nuisance too.' But Maria was smiling. 'You'll see all sorts of strange beasts here. Animals with long tails that jump instead of run. All manner of birds too. The Master's written a book about them,' she added, as proud as if she had written it herself.

Rachel stroked the creature's head with a finger. The fur was the softest she had ever felt. The creature accepted it for a moment, then threw the corncob down and jumped with surprisingly strong legs onto the floor and out the window.

'His basket is on the table by the window. You have to keep the shutter open so he can get in and out. And he likes to sleep under the bed sometimes too.' Maria picked up the iron again and spat on it to see how hot it was.

'Can I do that?'

'You can iron?'

'Yes.' Rachel smiled. 'I'd offer to scrub the floor, but I can't see that it needs it.'

Maria handed her the iron and watched as she pushed it over the cloth then exchanged it for another heating by the fire. For the first time she looked approving. 'Come upstairs when you've finished the ironing,' she said at last. 'You'll need another dress, and another petticoat and apron and some cuffs and collars. The Master likes you to look fresh. I've some cloth laid by — old sail cloth, not dress material, but it'll do. If we both get to it, it can all be done by tomorrow.'

Rachel said nothing for a moment, trying not to cry. How long had it been since anyone had done anything for her, without asking for something in return?

'Thank you,' she said at last.

Maria nodded, satisfied.

Chapter 31

NANBERRY

SYDNEY COVE, 16 JULY 1790

Nanberry bowed, just as Father White had shown him to when you met a lady. 'How do you do, madam?'

The strange woman stared at him. She backed away towards the fire. 'He speaks just like a proper person!'

'Shush!' Maria gave Nanberry a quick look. 'He can understand every word you say.'

'But he's a native!'

Why was the woman so scared? Nanberry wondered. She was thin too. 'Would you like some stew, madam?'

'She's just had two bowlfuls. And you don't need to "madam" her neither. She's a servant, like me. Her name's Rachel.'

Nanberry grinned. He was glad they had another servant. He was going to miss Maria's stews and cornbread. 'Can you make cornbread?'

The woman looked at him cautiously. 'Yes.'

'And apple dumplings?'

'Listen to the boy.' Maria patted his arm affectionately. 'I'll make you apple dumplings for tonight, and I'll show Rachel how to make them too.'

'Good.' Nanberry reached into his coat pocket and held out a small package. He had wrapped it in paperbark and tied it with dried grass. 'Father White said we should give you presents because you are getting married. He is going to give you the silver saltcellar, and salt to put in it. But this is from me.'

Maria took the package and untied the grass. She stared at the bunch of colourful feathers inside. 'What is it?'

'It's for your hair. Father White said that ladies in England put pretty feathers in their hair,' he added anxiously. 'These are the prettiest I could find. That is from the guma bird, and that is the one called parrot ... Why are you crying?'

'No one has ever given me feathers for my hair before.'

'They will make you pretty,' said Nanberry. He thought Maria was much too skinny to be pretty, but it made her smile. He turned to the new woman. She still looked at him as though he was a shark who might bite her. 'Would you like feathers too?'

'I ... I don't know.'

Nanberry stared at her, trying to work out why she looked so scared, then turned back to Maria. 'I will find you honey for the dumplings.'

Honey wins smiles from everyone, he thought.

Chapter 32

NANBERRY

Nanberry swam in the cove below the hospital, feeling the cold currents merge with the sun-warmed surface water on his skin. Father White waved to him from the rocks. He swam back to the shore and brushed the water from his chest, his wet trousers clinging to his skin. They were too short again, he thought happily. He was growing even taller.

'Put your shirt on, lad. The Governor needs you. Let's hope your trousers dry before he sees you.'

Nanberry grinned. It was good to be important. The Governor called for him often now, to speak to natives. Natives were those who didn't wear clothes or live in houses, like he did.

'Bennelong has been seen,' Father White added. 'He's with a great party of natives feasting on a beached whale. The Governor hopes to persuade him to come back to the colony.'

Nanberry's smile vanished.

He sat next to Father White and Mr Tench as the rowers pulled at the oars. It took a long time to cross the harbour, but it was good to watch the coves and headlands pass, to see the cooking fires of his people — his old people, he corrected himself — rising again among the trees.

At last he could smell the whale, faintly at first, and then a huge stench that covered even the brine of the sea. The whale must have been dead on the beach for many days already. He remembered jumping on swollen whale guts when he and his friends were small. The guts had burst, spraying them with stuff that dripped and stank. The boys had run into the sea laughing, and …

He thrust the thought away. Ghosts now, every one of them. Memories hurt too much. It was true: it was not good to think of the dead.

Soon the boat was near the beach. The whale had been half eaten: a giant shape all blood and torn flesh. Perhaps 200 people from several clans lay around it, sleepy from feasting. Suddenly someone saw the English boat and gave a cry. Women ran into the trees, taking the children with them.

'Tell them we are friendly,' Father White said to Nanberry.

Nanberry stood up in the rocking boat. 'We are friends,' he cried in the Cadigal tongue.

None of the men on the shore bothered to answer. Nanberry glanced back at Father White. No matter how many times warriors ignored him, he still grew hot with humiliation whenever it happened. He wasn't a Cadigal boy to be ignored now! He was English, the colony's translator!

'Try again, lad,' said Father White.

Only a handful of warriors stood by the whale now. The rowers leapt out and tugged the boat onto the beach as the warriors watched.

'Ask for Bennelong,' said Father White.

'They won't answer me,' said Nanberry reluctantly. Father White nodded. It was only too obvious that the warriors would keep ignoring the boy.

'Bennelong?' called Father White.

A warrior stepped forward, all bones and thin, straggly beard. The man had a great spear wound on his upper arm, still swollen and black with blood, and an almost healed wound on his head.

Nanberry stared. This couldn't be Bennelong! He'd been fat when he lived at Sydney Cove. How could he have grown so thin in a few months?

'Do you have hatchets?' the thin man asked Father White, using the Wangan words that were close enough to Cadigal for Nanberry to understand.

It was Bennelong. There was no mistaking the voice.

'He wants a hatchet,' Nanberry said to Father White.

'How did he cut the whale without a hatchet?' asked Father White. 'Ask him where is his own hatchet?'

Nanberry translated.

Bennelong held up his woomera, with its sharp oyster shell at one end. 'Hatchets,' he demanded again.

'Tell him we have no hatchets with us, but we have other presents.'

The new skinny Bennelong gazed at the officers as they laid down shirts and knives for him on the beach. He seemed happy about the presents, but wary of being caught again. As soon as the officers stepped back he leapt over to the whale carcass, and sawed off three large chunks of meat. He thrust them at one of the rowers, who took them reluctantly. Bennelong spoke again. Once more Nanberry translated.

'He says the whale meat is a present for the Governor. Bennelong wants to see the Governor, his beanga. He wants hatchets in return for the meat.'

Father White shook his head at the stinking meat, then turned to the rowers. 'Tell the Governor that Bennelong wishes to see him. Tell him Bennelong looks thin and ill. I think the Governor can persuade him to come back with us.'

The rowers pushed the boat out again, leaving the officers, Nanberry and Father White on the shore. Slowly the women and children emerged from the trees.

'Ask him why so many natives are here,' said one of the officers.

It seemed obvious to Nanberry — they were feasting on the whale — but he put the question anyway.

For the first time Bennelong looked straight at him, disgust in his eyes. 'Don't you know what we are doing?' he asked in the Cadigal speech.

'Yes,' said Nanberry, confused.

Bennelong casually reached out and struck Nanberry across the cheek, just as he had the year before. The blow stung, so hard it almost knocked him to the ground. His ears rang. Father White held him protectively. Bennelong shouted something, once again not even glancing at Nanberry.

'He wants scissors to cut his hair,' whispered Nanberry, ashamed and humiliated.

Father White reached into his medical bag. He put scissors down on the sand, then stepped back again to Nanberry. Bennelong picked up the scissors and started to cut his hair. The dark locks fell onto the sand. Bennelong began to trim his beard.

'Ask him where Barangaroo is,' said Mr Tench. Barangaroo was Bennelong's wife.

It seemed Bennelong understood this, for he didn't wait for Nanberry to translate, he laughed. 'She is gone. She is the wife of Colbee now.' Bennelong nodded at the man next to him.

Nanberry blinked. He and Colbee hadn't even recognised each other. Colbee too looked different, thinner in the face and with a longer beard.

How could I not know my own uncle? he thought. And then: How is it that my own uncle doesn't know me?

I am becoming English, thought Nanberry. I do not feast on whale blubber on the beach. I wear clothes. I eat my meals at tables.

'I have two fat women,' boasted Bennelong. He used a mix of Wangan and Cadigal words. 'They are much better than Barangaroo.'

Colbee laughed.

More and more people crowded back onto the beach now: children peering around their mother's legs; and the old women standing to the front, naked except for the bungu-fur string around their waists, their skins shiny with whale oil and fish guts to keep off mosquitoes. Nanberry edged closer to Father White. There were so many of them, and so few officers. Some of the warriors had long thin fishing spears, their barbs sharp in the sunlight.

At last the boat appeared again, carrying the Governor, Mr Collins and Captain Waterhouse, who was the chief of the small ship *Supply*. Convicts rowed the boats and soldiers stood guard with muskets.

Bennelong muttered something, too low for Nanberry to hear.

Too many soldiers, thought Nanberry. He thinks they want to capture him again. He's right.

Bennelong walked swiftly back down the beach, and stood, half hidden in the trees, as the rowers beached the boat. Governor Phillip jumped out and strode up the sand.

'Where is Bennelong?' he called out.

'I am Bennelong!' Bennelong beckoned to Governor Phillip to walk along the beach towards him.

Phillip hesitated. 'I don't want to scare him away, or make him think we are going to take him prisoner again.' He smiled briefly at Nanberry. 'Friendship works better than chains, I think.'

The Governor signalled to one of the sailors, who collected bread and salt beef and handkerchiefs and a bottle of wine from the boat, and gave them to Mr Collins. Governor Phillip held up his hands to show he was unarmed. He and Mr Collins carried the gifts towards Bennelong, who stood where he was. The Governor put the presents onto the sand. Bennelong grabbed the wine, pushed the cork into the bottle and took a swig. 'To the King!' he shouted.

'He remembers that much English,' muttered Father White.

'Captain Waterhouse!' called Bennelong, waving the bottle of wine. The big sailor began to walk towards Bennelong and the Governor.

All at once a mob of warriors surrounded the Governor, Mr Collins and Captain Waterhouse. It was impossible to see the Englishmen among the crowd. Nanberry recognised one of them. It was Willemeeerin, a giant Guringai warrior. He held a long barbed hunting spear, not a lighter fishing spear like most of the others. He glanced at Father White. Should they order the soldiers with muskets to go and rescue them?

Father White frowned, trying to work out what was happening. They still couldn't see the Governor, though there were no shouts or yells, just a mutter of conversation, and Bennelong's laughter as he drank the wine. Perhaps Bennelong has remembered more English, thought Nanberry. Perhaps he will come back to Sydney Cove. Nanberry rubbed his cheek where Bennelong had struck him. It was swelling now.

He hoped Bennelong stayed away. He hoped Bennelong vanished forever.

Suddenly he realised that all the women and children had vanished again. Only warriors stayed on the beach now. The Englishmen shifted uncomfortably. 'What's happening?' muttered Father White.

Suddenly someone shouted, and a man gave a scream of agony. The warriors broke ranks and ran back into the trees. The end of the beach where Bennelong had stood was immediately deserted except for the three white men, two standing, the third lying on the sand. It was the Governor. Willemeeerin's giant spear had pierced his shoulder. Blood spurted from the wound, black on the white sand.

He's dead, thought Nanberry. The Governor is dead.

A fishing spear flew from the trees, and then another. Mr Collins and Captain Waterhouse glanced down at the motionless body of the Governor, then began to run to the boat. The spears fell like rain now.

Father White pulled Nanberry back to the boat and shoved him below the seats. 'Keep your head down,' he ordered.

Spear points cracked against the side of the boat. Nanberry felt the rowers push it out into the shallows, beyond the reach of the spears, then hold the boat steady to wait for Mr Collins and Captain Waterhouse, still running on the sand, to reach them. Nanberry peered out again, over the edge of the boat.

Suddenly the Governor moved, his hands clawing at the sand among the fallen spears. 'Help me!' he cried. 'For Heaven's sake help me!'

He was alive.

Nanberry glanced around the boat at the officers from the New South Wales Corps. Why didn't they run with their muskets to help the Governor? Weren't they warriors? But the officers crouched behind the side of the boat, away from the spears.

Mr Collins hesitated, then kept running to the boat. Captain Waterhouse ran back, ducking his head as though that might protect him from the flying spears. More spears fell around the two men as Captain Waterhouse grabbed the one protruding from Phillip's shoulder, then paused. 'It's barbed, sir,' he yelled. 'It will kill you to pull it out.' He tried to snap the massive spear in half instead.

Phillip screamed in torment. Another spear flew across the beach from the trees, hitting Captain Waterhouse's hand. He pulled his arm back, his blood mixing with the Governor's, then despite the danger bent over the Governor again.

'We need to get the Governor to the boat,' said Father White. He stood up. Mr Collins held him back, just as the spear snapped in Captain Waterhouse's hands.

'He's got him,' said Mr Collins.

Several feet of wood still protruded from the Governor's shoulder. Captain Waterhouse began to help him along the beach, the weight of the half spear left in his shoulder slowing them down.

Another flurry of spears filled the air. Nanberry could hear the *whoosh*, then the thuds as they hit the sand. He poked his head up above the edge of the boat.

Phillip was grim and white-faced, only just managing to stumble with Captain Waterhouse's help. He reached down with his good hand and took his pistol from his belt. He fired it at the hidden warriors in the trees. The man who had steered the fishing boat finally lifted his musket to his shoulder and fired too. The stink of black powder and sulphur almost overpowered the stench of whale. At last the two officers raised their muskets too, while the sailor reloaded, but when the officers pressed the triggers nothing happened.

'Powder's damp,' muttered Father White. 'Not even the muskets fire in this damned place.'

Why did they wait so long to fire? thought Nanberry. Why didn't they attack the warriors?

He gazed at Captain Waterhouse, still half carrying the Governor, blood welling from his hand. That man is a warrior, he thought. He sails ships. He faces danger.

More spears fell, and more, but none hit the boat. Warriors like Colbee and Bennelong could hit a small rock accurately from the other end of the beach.

They have speared the Governor, the white men's leader,

thought Nanberry. Just him, and no one else. They chose to spear him in the shoulder, not kill him.

This is revenge for the settlement, for the disease, for the stolen women and canoes, for the humiliations.

Captain Waterhouse and the Governor were nearly at the boat now. Father White waded out onto the beach again. He helped Mr Collins lift the half-conscious Governor onto a seat. The rowers began to heave at the oars.

'Keep him as steady as possible,' ordered Father White. His hands pressed around the Governor's wound to try to stop the bleeding. 'I will need help to cut it out.'

The Governor was pale and panting. Blood soaked his shirt. His jacket had vanished. Nanberry knew that Bennelong had taken it. He wondered whether the Governor would die.

He wondered what would happen to the colony then.

Chapter 33

RACHEL

Rachel had just had a bath — a long one in the tin bath by the fire in the kitchen. It was her first proper wash in weeks, with no worry about Nanberry or the Master coming back unexpectedly and seeing her.

Now her hair was nearly dry again. Her skin was so fresh she felt like singing.

She hummed an old song from home as she peered into the big pot, its outside blackened now from years of cooking over a fire. The stew was done — a haunch of kangaroo simmered all day to make it tender, flavoured with savory and sage, with carrots and potatoes from their own garden. A plum pudding hung from its cloth in the food safe, boiled early this morning before she'd put on the stew.

She had made cornbread the way Big Maggie said an American sailor had showed her, soaking last summer's ground corn in boiling water till it was soft, then adding butter and an egg, and then baking it on the hearth. It was good to have eggs again, now the hens had started laying after winter. She fed them every morning, early, for if she fed them late in the afternoon the o'possum might steal their corn and cabbage stalks.

She sighed. The Surgeon was proud of his pet o'possum, but she was the one who had to clean up its droppings and its puddles under her bed. You couldn't house-train an o'possum, it seemed, as you would a dog. It left its smell all over the house, a peculiar o'possum scent that you could catch a whiff of as soon as you came in the front door.

She supposed the Surgeon was used to strange smells from the hospital. But she'd had enough of stinks in her life. It annoyed her that her good clean house should smell like a stable. An o'possum under her bed and a black savage at her table. But it wasn't her place to complain.

She glanced out the door. It was almost dark — far past the supper hour — but there was still no sign of the Surgeon. What could have happened? The colony had few candles and lanterns. No one went out after dark if they could help it, except thieves by moonlight. She pulled the pot off the fire and left it warming at the edge of the hearth, then sat turning the Surgeon's cuffs again.

Rrrrraaaaaarrrk! The o'possum had scrambled up onto the windowsill. It stared at her impatiently, as though she should know that it always woke up at dusk and needed its breakfast.

Rachel put the shirt down and fetched its tin plate then filled it with cold potatoes. The o'possum foraged outside each night now, but still demanded food from its humans. Half the colony hungry, she thought, and potatoes so precious they hang a man for stealing them, and I'm feeding them to an o'possum.

Where was the Surgeon? And Nanberry, for that matter?

At least *he* didn't act like a savage. In fact it was a wonder how well he spoke English. He did what he was told too, and his manners were fit for a king's table.

Where *were* they?

It was growing darker. She put hot bricks in the Surgeon's bed, hesitated, then put one in Nanberry's bed too. Savage he might be, but he was still only a boy. Wherever they'd been, they'd be cold by the time they got back.

She'd twice put more wood on the fire by the time they arrived. She gasped when she saw the Surgeon's face: grey with worry and tiredness. There was blood on his jacket. For a horrible moment she thought it was his.

Panic bit her. What would she do if anything happened to the Surgeon? Then she saw that he moved easily, with no sign of a wound. Wordlessly, she helped him out of his jacket and gave him a clean one off the peg.

'Sit,' she ordered, pushing a chair with a cushion nearer the fire and bringing a stool for his feet. Nanberry was clearly almost as exhausted. The boy looked like he had been crying. She pushed him into a chair too, then fetched their food and a small table to put it on.

She sat on a hard, twisted kitchen chair herself. She waited till they had eaten their stew, then refilled their bowls before she asked: 'What happened?'

'The Governor was speared this afternoon.' The Surgeon's words were short and clipped.

'By a native?' Many of the convicts had spears now, mostly stolen from native camps.

'Yes.'

Rachel felt the world shake around her. The Governor was the rock on which the colony stood. 'Is he ...?'

'Not dead. The wound is to his shoulder. Balmain and I removed it as soon as we got him back here. He will recover, I think, but he's in great pain.'

The Surgeon shut his eyes for a moment. 'If only we had some safe way to ease pain like that. I offered him laudanum, but he wouldn't take it, said that he needs to be alert if there is more trouble.'

'What sort of trouble? Will the savages attack?'

The Surgeon glanced at Nanberry. 'Well, lad? What do you think will happen now?'

The boy's face grew strangely blank, as though he was trying not to show what he felt. 'I … I do not think they will attack.'

'Did you see who threw the spear? Was it Bennelong?'

'A man called Willemeeerin.'

'Maybe the native was frightened,' said the Surgeon.

Nanberry shook his head. 'A warrior like Willemeeerin wouldn't be frightened.' The boy's voice was soft now. 'I think it was a punishment for the things the English have done.'

Rachel snorted. 'What have we done then?'

The boy's voice was even softer. 'You've taken the land, taken the fish and game. Made the water dirty.'

'It's called a town, that's what it is. Even if you heathen don't know any better.'

'I am not a heathen.' The boy looked as though he might cry again. 'I listen to Reverend Johnson. I dress in trousers. I'm not like Bennelong. I'm not!'

'No one said you were.' She looked at the boy's face, then patted his hand. It was hard to remember, sometimes, just how young he was. 'Don't you mind. You're a grand lad and don't you forget it. Now you run up and wash and get into bed.'

She waited till she heard the boy's footsteps overhead, and the crash as the o'possum leapt to another branch outside, before she said, 'How bad is it really?'

'As I said.' His voice was infinitely weary. 'The Governor's in great pain. But with good care he will live.'

'He'll have the best care in the world,' she said gently. 'Do *you* think there will be more attacks from the natives?'

He stared into the flames. 'The Governor has ordered that no native be killed in retaliation.' He shrugged. 'We couldn't survive an outright war with them. There are too many of them, despite the smallpox, and too few of us. Only one of the muskets even fired today. The natives could kill us all in an hour, if they only knew it.'

He bent his head, looking unutterably weary. 'I must go back and see how the Governor is faring, then to the hospital. I have been gone from it all day.'

'You need rest,' she said.

'How can I rest, Miss Turner? There is work to do.'

'A few hours' sleep. You'll work better later if you stop now.'

He smiled at her, briefly. 'Perhaps you are right. Just a few hours' rest.'

'Why do you do it?' she asked suddenly. 'Spend so much time, all your strength, caring for others? The other surgeons spend most of their time on their farms. But if you're not at the hospital you're on some expedition for the Governor.'

'He needs men he can trust,' said the Surgeon. 'There are few enough of them.'

'And he can trust you. We all trust you. But why? Why not take time — just a little time — for yourself?'

'I sketch my birds —'

'By firelight, for men of science to see. That's not for yourself.'

He was silent. At last he said, 'It is my duty, I suppose. It gives me pleasure to do my duty. To help my fellow man, to do the best I can. Does that seem so very idiotic?'

'No,' she said quietly. 'To me it seems the most admirable of all things. Now you go up to bed too. No writing in your book tonight.'

'I am not a child,' he said mildly.

'I know. But sometimes you need care nevertheless.'

He smiled at her, then trudged wearily up the stairs.

Chapter 34

NANBERRY

Rachel had sent him to take dinner to the Surgeon at the hospital — a good meat pudding. Now Nanberry dawdled on the way home.

He was bored. It was too cold to swim. He could weed the vegetables with Big Lon, but that was boring too ...

The days stretched long sometimes. It was good when Father White had time to fish or look for birds or take him hunting. It was good when someone needed him to translate, or explain native customs. But sometimes the space between meals and sleep seemed to go on forever.

What would he have been doing if the English had never come?

He smiled. Hunting bungu and bandicoots with the other boys, probably; making grass traps, skinning the small creatures and roasting them on their own cook fires before going back to the main camp; pestering the warriors to show them how to spear fish — not with a big spear, forbidden till you were initiated, but with a small practice spear. He would love to have a friend ...

He blinked. A young man stood by the rocks; a young man with dark skin, but wearing trousers, ragged but still proper clothes. He was older than Nanberry — almost an adult. His face was stretched out of shape with pain. One hand was pressed against his arm, trying to stop it bleeding. An axe — an English axe, not a stone one — lay at his feet.

It wasn't a total surprise. There had been more native people about the colony in the past few weeks. For Governor Phillip hadn't died. Father White had made him well — or almost well, for Father White said the wound still hurt. And the Governor now wanted to encourage the native people to get to know the colonists — as friends, not vanquished subjects.

The young man saw Nanberry. At once his face lost its pain. He is trying to be a warrior, thought Nanberry, even though he has no initiation scars, nor a bone through his nose or gap in his teeth.

'Good afternoon,' said Nanberry. He spoke English automatically.

The young man looked at him with eyes so like his own. 'Good afternoon.'

'You speak English!'

The young man blinked. He didn't understand. Nanberry switched to Cadigal. 'Who are you?'

'Balloonderry,' said the young man around a mouthful of pain.

Nanberry looked at the wound. 'That is bad. But my father can make it better.'

'Your father?'

'My father is Surgeon White. I'm Nanberry White. Come on.'

He turned back towards the hospital. The young man — Balloonderry — didn't move. 'Why don't you come?'

Balloonderry nodded towards the hospital huts. 'There are bad people there. They'll steal my axe. They tried to tie me up before, when I went to comfort my sister.'

'My father won't let them do that now.'

'You're sure?'

'He is my father,' said Nanberry simply. 'How did you get the axe?' he asked curiously. English axes were prized around the harbour.

'My sister gave it to me. Booroong.'

So this was Booroong's brother. That explained the trousers and the *good afternoon*. He would be of the Bunamattogul people then, like her, from Parramatta. Booroong still lived with Mrs Johnson but Nanberry thought she wasn't happy there.

'You are under my protection,' said Nanberry grandly. Then he added cautiously, 'Brother.' He waited to see how Balloonderry would react. It was a big thing to offer brotherhood. And Balloonderry was older than him too. But he had been without friends so long ...

Balloonderry considered, the blood still dripping from his hand onto the tussocks. At last he said, 'I am Nanberry Balloonderry.'

Nanberry grinned. 'I am Balloonderry Nanberry. Balloonderry Nanberry White,' he corrected. 'Come on. I'll look after your axe.'

This time Balloonderry followed him.

⁓⚭

'So,' said the Surgeon. 'You've found a friend.' He sounded approving. Nanberry hadn't been sure how his father would react to a native friend. Because Balloonderry *was* native, despite the trousers.

'Let's have a look at that.' The Surgeon stretched out the wounded hand. 'Axe slipped? I've seen a lot of wounds like this.

You sharpen a bit more than you're used to, then *wham*. Lucky it's a clean cut.' He picked up his needle and thread. Nanberry translated and then murmured reassurance as Balloonderry looked wide-eyed at the needle.

But he bore the stitching without flinching or crying out. Nanberry was proud of his friend. Balloonderry would make a fine warrior ... He shut his mind to that.

'There,' said the Surgeon. He poured alcohol over the wound, then washed the blood off his hands in the bowl. 'Keep it clean and dry, young man. Come back here if it gets red or puffs up or you start shivering.'

Nanberry translated again.

'I will do that.' Balloonderry's voice was firm, the colour coming back to his cheeks now the ordeal was over. He stared with interest at the hospital hut, the surgical implements in Father White's brown bag, the bottles of alcohol, lavender oil, rose oil, eucalyptus oil and laudanum, the pliers for pulling out teeth, the tweezers, the irons, the amputation case with its bone saw and short and long knives; he pointed at the jar of leeches.

'Why? You can't eat leeches.'

Nanberry translated.

Father White beamed. 'That's my leech kit. There's the salt to make them vomit the blood once they have sucked it out. You need your leeches hungry.'

Once more Nanberry translated. Balloonderry laughed. 'You roll leeches off. You don't put them on.'

'You put them on bruises, or to bring fever down,' said Nanberry. He had learnt that much from Father White. 'And that is the cup and knife set for taking blood. That is good when there is a fever too. The English know many such things.'

'If they know so much why do so many of them die? You need to learn the proper ways to treat fevers. Our ways.'

But your ways couldn't cure the smallpox, thought Nanberry.

The Surgeon still looked at them indulgently. 'Off with you now. I have a rotten tooth to extract. Trust me, you don't want to be here for that. And be careful with the axe,' he added.

'Father White, may I take Balloonderry back to the house to eat corn?' Nanberry wasn't sure what the Surgeon would say. When he was with his first family all visitors were welcomed and fed, as long as they hadn't come to steal women or cause trouble. Yet he had never seen a visitor fed at the Surgeon's house. Perhaps only the Governor allowed people who weren't his family to eat at his house.

But the Surgeon smiled. 'That's a fine idea. You can teach your friend some more English. The Governor wants more of the natives to be friends of the colony.'

So they don't spear him again, or other English, thought Nanberry. But Balloonderry wouldn't be the colony's friend. He would be mine. 'Thank you, Father!'

'Funny lad,' said the Surgeon, ruffling Nanberry's hair and embarrassing him, though Nanberry tried not to show it. 'Of course you may have friends to tea. Now you'd better let the porter bring the next patient in.'

It was good to be away from the hospital again. Nanberry could see that Balloonderry was glad to leave too. 'Come on. Our house has ...' He paused. There was no word in Cadigal for *sacks*. '... lots and lots of corn. Rachel will boil it and put butter and salt on it. Rachel is ...' There was no word for *servant* either. Or *prisoner* or *pet*, he thought. 'Rachel cooks.'

Balloonderry hesitated. 'If I go with you will they tie me up?'

'Of course not.' Nanberry thrust away the memory of Bennelong and Colbee in chains. 'They don't do that now. My father was your friend just now.'

Still Balloonderry hung back. 'Tomorrow maybe.'

Nanberry grinned. 'Tomorrow then. I will teach you English,' he added eagerly. 'I will show you the English manners. You can wear one of my shirts and —'

Balloonderry laughed. 'Why would I want to learn English?'

'Because ... because the English are important.'

'The English are gunin bada.' Balloonderry used a rude expression.

'But Father White stitched up your hand! You use an English axe!'

'The axe is a good axe. But the English are still gunin bada.' For the first time Balloonderry looked at Nanberry sternly. 'The English are weak. A storm could blow them away! You should be learning how to be a warrior. Can you use a spear? A fire stick? How can you know what needs to be done if you're not with your people?'

'These are my people,' said Nanberry quietly.

'Then how can you be a warrior?'

'I don't need to be a warrior.'

Balloonderry stared at him. Nanberry thought he saw pity on his new friend's face. At last he said, 'I won't come to eat corn.' He used the English word. He considered a moment then added, 'But you are still my brother.' Balloonderry began to walk off, holding the axe in his good hand. As he rounded the rocks he turned. 'Good afternoon,' he said. Then he was gone.

Chapter 35

NANBERRY

Nanberry looked at his image in Father White's mirror, and grinned. He was *going to dine* at the Governor's house, with important people. Rachel had mended his jacket, and let down the hem of his trousers again. Now he looked important too.

His hair was held back in a queue, tied with a black ribbon, just like his adoptive father's. He wore one of Father White's hats, with strips of blanket sewn inside to make it fit.

The Surgeon placed his own hat on his head. The hat was stained and the rim was tattered, but no gentleman would go out — especially not to dinner with the Governor — without his hat. 'You're ready to go, lad?'

Nanberry nodded.

Rachel handed them their bread rolls, each neatly wrapped in a napkin. Governor Phillip's shooter made sure his master had meat for himself and his guests, and there'd be fruit and vegetables from his garden. But Phillip had handed his own supply of wheat to the common stores. The ration was down to a pound of flour a week now — only enough for a small bread roll per person every day. Guests had to bring their own bread to dinner.

The sun was setting behind the mountains in a red haze of distant bushfire smoke. Dingoes howled up above the Tank Stream.

Nanberry shivered. The dingoes had been feasting for months on the dead from the convict ships, scattering the bones. One woman swore she had swung up a skull still wearing shreds of hair with her bucket of well water.

How many ghosts whispered around the colony now?

Most of the English were thin and weak, just as Balloonderry had said. Their huts stank, and so did they.

But the Governor's house is all that is good, all that is truly English, thought Nanberry, with its solid roof and white stucco front, freshly painted with limewash every few weeks. In a colony of mud, it gleamed.

He trod up the shell-lined path with Father White, trying not to think what Sydney Cove had looked like when it had still been Warrane: a place of ferns and cabbage trees and clear water, and mussels in the mud flats where the stream ran into the sea.

A manservant opened the door. He took their hats and hung them on hooks on the wall, then ushered them into a big white-painted room, with curtains drawn against real glass windows, that strange stuff that was hard but you could see through. Nanberry would have liked to touch the glass. But instead he stood next to Father White, who talked to Mrs Macarthur about a new bird he had discovered the day before, a kingfisher with a bright blue tuft of feathers.

Mrs Macarthur did not seem interested in birds, or in talking to Nanberry either. But he could have stared at her for hours. He had never seen a woman with skin so pink and white, or a dress that shone like that and made crinkling noises when its folds moved. Her hair shone, piled up on her head, and her hands were the smoothest he had ever seen.

'Dinner is served.' It was the manservant again. The Governor offered Mrs Macarthur his arm, the good one that hadn't been hurt.

Nanberry walked next to Father White, then took his place in the middle of the table, the Governor at one end, Mrs Macarthur at the other. Each guest put his or her bread roll on their side plate — except for Mrs Macarthur, whose plate had a roll already. She smiled her thanks to the Governor.

Candles flickered in their silver candlesticks. The Governor still had candles. The servants began to bring in the dishes.

Nanberry stared. One of the servants was a native. The Governor's policy of giving gifts to the local people, instead of chaining them up, was working. More were living in the town now, though he hadn't seen Balloonderry again. Now it seemed one was living with the Governor.

But as a servant, thought Nanberry. I am Surgeon White's son. The servant's face was swollen where a tooth had been knocked out at his recent yulang yirabadjang, his initiation.

Suddenly Nanberry recognised him, despite the swollen face. It was Yemmerrawane, a Cadigal, like him. Yemmerrawane and the older boys had shown him how to trap small birds with dried fig sap, how to tell the difference between a snake track and the trail of a wallaby tail, how to blow air into badagarang guts to make a ball.

Nanberry hadn't even known that Yemmerrawane had survived the smallpox. Bennelong had said that only two other Cadigal still lived. But a few others, too, it seemed had survived when their families died from the plague.

How many more of the boys I played with are alive? wondered Nanberry.

Now Yemmerrawane wore the dark clothes of an English servant, and was laying the dish of asparagus among the plates of boiled potatoes and carrots. He didn't seem to notice Nanberry but stood back against the wall with the white servants, while the guests were helped to meat — a giant saddle of mutton carved by the Governor; and slices of chicken from Father White, his hands working with all the dexterity he might use to take off a wounded man's leg.

Nanberry spread butter on part of his roll, as Father White had shown him, and ate as the talk flowed around him. The chicken was good, but not as good as Rachel's roast young rooster with thyme stuffing. Mrs Johnson was on one side of him; another officer he didn't know was on the other. Neither spoke to him.

Mrs Macarthur put her knife and fork together on her plate to show that she had finished eating. Nanberry signalled to Yemmerrawane. The young warrior bent close to him.

'Take Mrs Macarthur's plate away,' Nanberry whispered to him helpfully, assuming that Yemmerrawane would not know English manners. 'The knife and fork together is a sign the English use to tell their servants when to take the plate.'

Yemmerrawane said nothing. He moved to take Mrs Macarthur's plate, then one by one he took the plates of all the other guests.

Except Nanberry's. Nanberry sat there, embarrassed, the last of his chicken gravy staining his plate. The white servants had gone out to fetch the next course of food. At last he signalled Yemmerrawane again. Yemmerrawane refused to meet his gaze.

'Please take my plate.'

Yemmerrawane smiled, showing the fresh gap in his teeth. He stayed where he was, next to the wall, carefully not looking at Nanberry.

'I said take my plate!'

'Nanberry.' Father White's voice was quiet. 'That is enough.'

'But Father …'

Governor Phillip at last noticed what was happening. He rang the bell on the sideboard behind his seat. A white servant appeared. Governor Phillip murmured to him. Nanberry sat there, humiliation hot as a blanket on his face as the white servant took his plate away.

Why had Yemmerrawane insulted him? Was it because Yemmerrawane was a warrior, had been initiated, and Nanberry had not? Or because Nanberry was an Englishman with black skin?

It was as though Bennelong had slapped him again.

Nanberry was no servant, like Yemmerrawane. He was the adopted son of Surgeon White. He should be treated with respect, not just by Yemmerrawane, but by the other English at the table. But none of the settlers had even spoken to him, except the Governor when he had greeted him earlier. As though I am a pet, he thought, like the o'possum, to be fed and stared at.

Time stretched out. Wine was poured, a bowl of fruit brought in — early peaches from the Governor's orchards, the first of the melons, strawberries, raspberries. Once more a white servant served Nanberry, not Yemmerrawane. Nanberry ate. The peach flesh was white and juicy. He had never seen a fruit so large and soft. But it could have tasted like wood ash for all he cared.

Nuts were served: English nuts from the Governor's trees, or brought in the big ships from far beyond the horizon, almonds and walnuts, not kurrajong or bunya.

At last the meal was over. He and Father White followed one of the servants — again not Yemmerrawane — who held a lantern of precious whale oil to light their way home.

It was dark inside the house, but Rachel had left a slush lamp, a wick floating in a dish of emu oil, burning by the stairs. The Surgeon lifted it and began to climb up to his bedroom.

'Father …'

The Surgeon turned. 'Yes, lad?'

'I … I am sorry if I embarrassed you tonight.'

It was too dark to see the expression on his adoptive father's face. 'You weren't at fault.'

No, thought Nanberry. It would be easier if he had been. He could learn to behave properly, just as he had learnt how to dress, how to speak like an Englishman. It was the English who wouldn't learn. And the Cadigal too. Neither really knew the other — or wanted to learn — even though they had lived on the same harbour for nearly three years.

He knew the Governor liked him. He used him to translate when he needed to speak to the clans around the harbour and even as far away as Parramatta. He had been a guest at the Governor's table, while Yemmerrawane was, after all, just a servant, waiting on them all. Father White and even Rachel were good to him too.

But …

'I don't belong. I have no friends.' The words were almost too quiet for the Surgeon to hear.

'What was that, lad?'

'I have no friends. I work for the Governor, I do my jobs here. But I don't belong. Father, I want to leave.'

'Go back to your own people?'

'You are my people now!' The anguish in his cry echoed up the staircase. Outside the o'possum gave a startled grunt, and leapt to another tree.

'I'm sorry, lad. I know … I do understand.' The Surgeon's voice had a thread of bitterness. 'I know too well what it's like to be lonely among a mob of fools. But I don't know how I can help.'

'Send me to sea. Let me be a sailor.'

'What?' Father White stared at him in the flickering light of the slush lamp. 'You've no idea what you're asking. It can be Hell on earth on those ships, lad. Poor food, the lash if you do the slightest thing wrong. I'm a naval surgeon, boy. Do you know how many sailors never make it home from their first voyage? Half are dead by forty, old men, teeth lost to scurvy, a leg crushed or an arm. How many sailors with whole bodies have you seen?'

'I have seen sailors with dark skins,' said Nanberry softly. 'Sailors from Africa. Sailors who are natives from America. Here, to the English, I will always be a savage. To the Cadigal I am nothing. But on a ship ... in other lands, perhaps ...'

He wished he could see the Surgeon's face. At last the voice on the stairs above him said, 'Very well. I'll speak to the Governor. I'm sure he'll agree to send you as Captain Waterhouse's cabin boy for the next trip to Norfolk Island and back. Will that do you?'

Nanberry felt his face become a grin. He had thought he would never laugh again. Now he felt like dancing. He would go on a ship! With Captain Waterhouse, the bravest man in the colony!

'Thank you, Father!'

'Don't thank me till you find out what it's like. You may find you hate it. You probably will.'

'I won't,' said Nanberry confidently. He had known what he wanted without realising it since he had seen the first big ship. To sail into that thin line between the sea and sky ...

'Go on, up to bed with you.' Father White held the slush lamp high so Nanberry could see his way. 'I'll sit down here for a while.'

'To write your book?'

'Perhaps. Good night, boy.' The Surgeon's voice was gentle as he returned to the kitchen.

Nanberry climbed the stairs. The memory of tonight's humiliation vanished. Soon he would be on a giant ship. He would be a sailor. Let Yemmerrawane laugh at that.

Chapter 36

RACHEL

The noise downstairs woke her. At first she thought it was just the o'possum, trying to get into the food safe and the corn. But then it came again. She reached for her shawl, unlatched the shutter to let in moonlight and trod quietly down the stairs, her hair in its bed plaits down her back.

The Surgeon sat in the kitchen, barely visible by the red glow of the coals in the fireplace.

'Sir?'

He looked up. The tears glinted on his cheeks.

She had seen him with his arms still drenched red after surgery; had seen him walk among rows of corpses, calmly giving orders for them to be buried. She had seen him with the Governor's blood on his shirt. She had never seen him cry before.

She hurried towards him. 'Sir, what's the matter?'

He shook his head. 'Nothing. No matter. Go back to bed.'

'Not until you tell me what is wrong.'

'Wrong?' The despair in his voice made her shiver. 'What is right? We have come to a clean land and made it a stinking swamp. We came with brave ideas of a new city and have only a huddle of huts. Our colonists are drunkards who would rather steal than work. Our soldiers sulk and see every labour as below them. There is nothing good about what we have done to this land.'

'There is you. You are a good man. The best I have ever known.'

'Me?' He made a sound almost like a laugh. 'I have been worst of all. How many hundreds of natives died and I couldn't save them? And now this boy ... the one I thought I *had* helped ... I have failed him too.'

She stood still and quiet in her white nightdress. 'How have you failed him?'

'I have let him think he might be an Englishman, but he is not. Back home he would be a curiosity. A servant, if he is lucky. He ... he asked me if he could go to sea tonight. To be a sailor.'

'You agreed?'

'I have said I'll get him a job as a cabin boy. Captain Waterhouse is a good man. His ship is better than most.'

'Is a sailor's life so very bad?'

The Surgeon stared at the stars glimmering through the window left open for the o'possum. 'It's hard company. So many sailors are press-ganged, forced onto the ships when they are drunk, or ordered to sea instead of facing the hangman's noose.'

'But others choose to go. For adventure. To see the world.' She hesitated. 'And some who are press-ganged choose to stay with their ships, even when they reach another port.'

'It's that or starve.'

'Not for all.'

'No. Not for all. Maybe ...' He shook his head again. 'Rachel ... I am just so lonely. It has been three and a half years now, with no one to talk to. No softness in my life ...'

He had never called her Rachel before. She took another step towards him; put her hand on his shoulder. He reached up and stroked her hair.

She had sworn never to do this, but her master was a good man. A man who did good. A man who needed her. She said, 'I am here.'

Chapter 37

NANBERRY

Waves with white froth, swelling high above the ship, trying to smash the little vessel to tinder. A hammock warm from the body of the man who had gone to take his place up on deck as the next lot of crew had their few hours of sleep. Mutton so salty it left blisters on his mouth and ship's biscuit that crawled with weevils. No place to relieve himself except on the perch at the rear of the ship, the sea slapping below him. Sunlight cleaning the sky and spearing off the sea.

A world of sea and sky, and the far-off thin scrape of the horizon.

He had been sick the first two days; had had to run to do Captain Waterhouse's bidding in between vomits over the rail. By the end of the second day he crawled to his bunk, on his knees with weariness.

On the third day he woke up with his stomach where it should be. Even emptying Captain Waterhouse's chamberpot didn't make it heave. There was fish and potato stew for breakfast. He ate ravenously, perched on a great coil of rope, the sails flapping, ropes creaking, the lookout high above on the mast. One day *he* would be up there, high over the ocean. An albatross sailed lazily past it. He felt like waving to it. 'Hello, friend! I am master of this world too.'

And then the smudge of green that was Norfolk Island. Impossible to find a green speck in an endless ocean, but somehow Captain Waterhouse had done it, not just once but many times.

This was how Governor Phillip had found New South Wales, after a journey almost as long as the seasons all put together. He had followed the stars like the moon found its way across the darkness. For the first time he felt true awe of the English. Houses, muskets, metal axes, fields of corn were nothing compared with the glory of surging with knowledge across a trackless ocean.

It was hard. He was the youngest on board. Even if his work was mostly cleaning for Captain Waterhouse, fetching and carrying, it still pushed his body to its limits. But he loved it. This was what a warrior did: accepted pain and hardship, whatever it took to do all that a man was capable of doing.

He would be a sailor, a man who conquered not just another few warriors, but the sea.

The southerly filled their sails as the ship bounced into the smoother waters of the harbour. The wind smelt of ice, of the mysterious land the other sailors had told him about, where the water turned solid and could burn your fingers and rot your toes away, where rain fell in white flakes from the sky.

One day I'll go there, he vowed. One day I'll go everywhere.

But it was good to see the harbour again — to smell the trees, the soil, the cook fires. It was even good to smell the privies of the colony, as the ship anchored and the ship's boat brought the sailors back to shore.

He had half hoped Father White had heard the *Supply*'s sail had been seen out at sea and would be waiting for him in the crowd on the quay. But the message mustn't have reached him, or perhaps he had work he couldn't leave.

Nanberry waved goodbye to Johnnie One-Leg, the cook, and Fat Jack, who was so thin you could feel his back when you poked his belly, and shouldered his duffel bag for the walk up the hill, ignoring the yells around him.

There was always a crowd when a ship came in: women after the sailors' money, grog sellers, shanty owners offering a place to sleep. But mostly the convicts and brats and soldiers were just there because a ship arriving was something new to see, like a hanging or a flogging, something to break the boredom of their days.

Once, you had known everyone in the colony by sight, even if you didn't know who they were. But more and more convict ships came now, more sick and starving to be tended at the hospital till they could work on the farms or roads. The colony was full of strangers now. There wasn't a face in the crowd that he knew.

He stared. The people at the other end of the cove weren't looking at him and the other sailors from the *Supply*, but at a canoe pulled up on the muddy sand. It wasn't a woman's bark canoe; it was the biggest he had ever seen, chopped from a whole tree trunk. A net inside was filled with the silver gleam of fish.

He wriggled his way through the crowd, careful to keep tight hold of his duffel bag in case some rogue grabbed it. Who could have built a canoe like this? A young man with dark skin, in a red shirt and tattered trousers, passed over a giant fish in exchange for a loaf of bread. As Nanberry watched, the youth lugged out a sack of fish. He grinned and grabbed a hatchet from a balding convict in return.

It was Balloonderry.

'Balloonderry!' he called.

Balloonderry laughed. 'The sailor is back,' he said in their own language. 'It's good to see you, Nanberry Balloonderry, my brother.'

'It's good to see you, Balloonderry Nanberry. The canoe?' he added eagerly. 'Did you build it?'

Balloonderry grinned. 'It took me a whole season to make one that floated. I used my white-ghost axe. The white ghosts down at Parramatta are hungry for fish. Just like the white ghosts here. They don't know where the schools hide when the winds come, or when the mullet feed. I am the best fisherman in the colony.'

'You like the English now?'

Balloonderry hesitated. 'They are interesting. Some of their things are good.' He met Nanberry's eyes. 'But I am still Eora.' The word meant *of the people* — the whole people. There were so few Cadigal, Guringai, Dharug now. The old clan barriers were fading.

'You haven't been initiated,' said Nanberry carefully.

Balloonderry looked at him sternly. 'I have been showing the Governor the land of Parramatta. I have been doing many things. But I will be initiated soon.'

'You know the Governor now?' How could so much have happened since he last met his friend?

Balloonderry laughed again. He said carefully in English, 'I stay at Governor Phillip's house at Parramatta. Today there are many, many fish. I bring fish here.'

His English was good. Not as good as Nanberry's, but better than Bennelong's or Booroong's, better than any other black person Nanberry knew. Once again he felt pride that this young man was his brother. 'You speak like an Englishman,' he said.

'It's useful,' Balloonderry admitted in their own language. 'The white ghosts are too stupid to learn our tongue.' His eyes strayed to the *Supply*, swaying at anchor on the tiny waves of the harbour. 'And you sailed in that?' There was no mistaking the admiration and envy in his voice.

'Yes.'

'It is so good to see you, brother.'

'And you.'

Balloonderry gazed at him. 'Come and stay down at Parramatta. We'll fish together. You can tell me about sailing in the big ship.'

It would be a while before the *Supply* sailed again. Nanberry needed to see Father White, to eat Rachel's cooking, to sleep on a mattress and not think the ground below his feet was going up and down.

He grinned. 'Yes,' he said. 'In a few days I will be there.'

Chapter 38

NANBERRY

It was good to be home, to tell Father White about the towering waves and hear his stories of ships he had sailed in too. Why had he never known how many ships Father White had sailed on when he was younger?

Rachel fussed and made him wash his hair before he came inside, to get rid of the ship's lice. She boiled his clothes too, holding them on a stick and shoving them into the big pot while he changed into his spare trousers.

He loved it all.

Rachel and Father White shared a room now. He didn't give the matter much thought. That was what men and women did.

Even after a week at home, it was good to sleep as late as he wanted to, his body recovering from the effort of the voyage. It was even good to feed the o'possum young gum leaves, to watch the silly creature hold them in its paws and nibble them, staring back with its big black eyes.

Best of all was to sit at supper as the early night wrapped its coldness around the colony, the fire flaring in the hearth, Father White on one side of him and Rachel on the other, the table piled with weevil-less fresh bread, butter that didn't stink, roast lamb with potatoes and greens, a giant pudding filled with apples from the storeroom and dried grapes.

'More lamb, sir?' Rachel filled the Surgeon's plate again. Nanberry held out his plate too.

The Surgeon took a bite of lamb. 'I forgot to tell you — you know that young native fisherman who's been supplying the garrison down at Parramatta?'

Rachel nodded. 'I traded some hearth cakes for his fish when he came to the quay last week.'

'Well, you may not get the chance to buy any again. Some rogues wrecked the lad's canoe a few nights ago down at Parramatta. The boy was quite cut up about it. Appeared at the Governor's house at Parramatta covered in red mud, danced about and yelled.'

'What did the Governor do?'

The Surgeon shrugged. 'They found the men who did it. Convicts, jealous of the boy's trade. They got a good flogging. Phillip gave the lad a few trinkets and told him one had been hanged. A lie of course, but it seemed to calm the boy down.' He took another bite of lamb.

Nanberry sat still. His friend's canoe — that wonderful canoe, like no other ever made, the canoe that had taken a whole season to perfect, destroyed. His friend, lied to. Given 'a few trinkets' to replace a canoe.

Rage filled him; he didn't let it show. He was good at not showing what he felt now. Sailor or warrior, you 'took it on the chin' as Captain Waterhouse would say. You never let it show that the blows hurt you.

There would be no journey down to Parramatta now. He doubted Balloonderry would even stay there, betrayed and bitter as he must feel.

The meat tasted like dirt now. Nanberry pushed away his second helping.

Chapter 39

NANBERRY

'Two head wounds, eight scurvy cases, a case of the stone, a madman who thinks the flies are talking to him and a baby with a fistula. What a day,' said the Surgeon as Rachel hung up his coat and knelt to take his boots off. She put them outside for Big Lon to polish.

'Any other news?' Rachel gestured for Nanberry to sit at the table. She had fried the kangaroo collops in the giant skillet, and added a dust of flour and water to make their gravy. The cornbread was already on the table, along with the butter, and a jug of Rachel's fresh ale.

'More officers' quarrels. I stay out of it. Oh, and that native fisherman. He's in trouble again, it seems. The skull fracture patient they brought up from Parramatta a few days ago was able to talk this morning. Told me that the native speared a convict. I asked the Governor about it this afternoon, when I called in to check his shoulder.'

'It's still hurting him?' asked Rachel.

The Surgeon nodded. 'It's more than inflammation, I think. Perhaps an infection in the bone.'

'But the native?' asked Nanberry quietly.

'What? Oh yes. Balloonderry. Phillip said the lad had the hide to paddle another canoe right up into the harbour after his crime. Wanted to ask him for a pardon, I suppose. Phillip ordered the guards to arrest him.' The Surgeon shook his head. 'That Bennelong is staying with the Governor again. He shouted a warning and the young man vanished.'

'When did this happen?' asked Nanberry. He tried to keep expression from his voice. Father White knew Balloonderry's name. He didn't think he would connect it with the friend his foster son had made the year before, though.

The Surgeon shrugged. 'A week ago? I didn't ask. Pity — Phillip told me that the lad had promise. He was even thinking of taking him to England to show the Royal Society what a native is like. But he's for the gallows now — if they don't shoot him first.'

Nanberry sat frozen. His friend in trouble. More than his friend — his brother. The exchanging of names had been an impulse, but the bond still held.

Suddenly Big Lon pounded on the door. The Surgeon sighed. 'Will the man ever learn to knock politely?'

'No,' said Rachel. She stood and opened the back door. Big Lon was panting. He must have run up the hill.

'Sir, the Governor sent for you. Word is there's a band of natives assembled across the cove. That there Balloonderry is the ringleader. Governor's gettin' a party to fight them and bring the blighter back. He wants you down at the barracks — likely to be injuries with them big spears, sir.'

The Surgeon nodded wearily. 'Merciful Heavens. Is there no end to this?' He stood up. Nanberry waited till he had left with his brown medical bag, then slipped out of the door too.

How long would it take the soldiers to get ready? A long time, he thought — they'd get into their uniforms, check their powder and muskets. They'd march, in their heavy boots, their muskets over their shoulders.

He could follow where they went. He could warn his friend. If he was seen he'd be punished — even hanged, perhaps. That's what they did to anyone who helped someone who had speared a white man. Even Father White mightn't be able to save his son from hanging.

Nanberry grew still. He was Nanberry, the Surgeon's son, in his good clothes, his hair tied back. But if he took off his clothes, untied his hair ...

It was strange to stand naked in the night air. I am not Nanberry White, he thought. I am ... who am I?

Nanberry Buckenau Balloonderry. My brother's brother. He began to run through the night, keeping to the bush behind the straggle of huts. An owl hooted above him.

It was hard to run at night, despite the moonlight, bright enough for shadows. He stumbled, skinned his knees. He kept on going.

Slowly it became easier to see by moon- and starlight. It was as though his feet knew where to go. He looked down, hearing the whisper of long-gone Aunties: 'Look at the ground, not the bright sky, if you want to see in the dark.'

The night wind felt sweet on his skin.

Then faintly he heard it, down by the harbour: the thud of soldiers' feet. *One two, one two* ...

They were marching to attack.

Where were Balloonderry and his companions? No time to find them now. 'Jiriyai!' he screamed. He had forgotten the war cry, but it came to his lips now. Soldiers! 'Jiriyai!'

'Jiriyai!' The call echoed back between the trees. He ran down to the water, moving more slowly now among the rocks.

The moon sent a breeze of silver across the sea. All at once rock shapes turned into warriors with white paint on their bodies. Young men — not yet initiates — stood with them. Even the young men had spears.

Balloonderry stood tall in the moonlight, his spear even taller by his side.

'The soldiers,' Nanberry panted. 'They're coming.'

Balloonderry grinned. 'Nanberry, my brother, we know. We are waiting for them.'

'But they have muskets ...'

'We know that too.'

They could have been pictures on the rocks, they were so still. Nanberry shook his head. He had expected them to run away as soon as he warned them.

They were going to fight.

The sound of marching drew closer. The soldiers appeared around the curve of the beach, their muskets over their shoulders, their bayonets fixed. They still hadn't seen the warriors, waiting by the rocks.

He should run before they saw him, before they recognised him. He should run before they attacked. The last time there had been a clash of warriors and soldiers he had been on the side of the English, a boy cowering in a boat.

He was on the wrong side. Or was he?

Balloonderry didn't look at him now. Instead his gaze was on the soldiers.

Suddenly one of them gave a cry. They had seen the warriors. 'Halt!' The soldiers stopped. The ones in front knelt in the sand, and aimed their muskets. The others stood behind them, aiming too.

No one moved.

'Balloonderry, I arrest you in the name of the King. Step forward and no one will be hurt.'

The silence grew. Then Balloonderry laughed.

He stepped forward, his smile friendly. His spear had vanished. He held out his empty hands in a gesture of peace. The warriors behind him grinned too, their teeth white in their beards, although they still held their spears.

Slowly, step by step, Balloonderry crossed the sand to the waiting soldiers, his hands still out, the smile still on his face. The other warriors followed him. Only Nanberry lingered in the shadow of the rocks.

What was going on? Surely Balloonderry wasn't giving himself up! He'd be hanged on the gibbet on the hill, his legs dancing as he died ...

It felt wrong, the slow step of the warriors, the smiles ...

Suddenly Balloonderry snatched at a musket. All at once Nanberry understood. The soldiers were no warriors. Take away their muskets and they were helpless against spears and war axes.

Black shadows scuffled with red uniforms in the moonlight. It was impossible to see exactly what was going on.

I should help, thought Nanberry. But he might make things worse. This had been planned, but he had no idea what the rest of the plan might be.

A spear gleamed as it flew in the moonlight. A musket cracked. A man screamed — a native man, but not Balloonderry.

Then the warriors were gone, black shadows lost in a black night. The soldiers stood, confused, alone on the moonlit sand.

Nanberry moved back silently till he was hidden by the boulders. Where had the others gone? Why hadn't they taken him with them?

But he was Nanberry White. He needed to put on his clothes again, and run to his father's house. The Surgeon would be waiting at the barracks, to tend any wounded.

The soldiers muttered. They began to straggle back along the beach, no longer marching in formation. Nanberry started to walk back up the hill. He half hoped that Balloonderry might call him quietly from among the trees. But only the owl hooted.

I risked myself for nothing, thought Nanberry. Nothing changed because I ran to warn them … No, he stopped. I am what's changed tonight. Yesterday I was an English boy. Tonight I ran to warn my brother.

Black brother. White father. He looked at his hands in the moonlight, his naked body. His black body. His knees hurt. He rubbed them, then began to limp back home.

Chapter 40

NANBERRY

He hung around Government House and the soldiers' parade ground now. He used his trip to Norfolk Island as an excuse to chat to the soldiers on guard. He slept at Father White's house. He ate at his father's table. No one knew that now he listened. Now he watched.

That was how he heard that Governor Phillip knew that Balloonderry's warriors were camped a mile beyond the brickworks and had sent orders to find them — and shoot them if they attacked with spears.

This time he stripped off his clothes in daylight as soon as he was away from the parade ground. Nanberry the native, not Nanberry White. He ran, the bushes pricking at his skin, grateful for the muscles won as a sailor.

There was no campfire smoke spiralling into the sky to tell him where they were, but he could smell where smoke had been.

He turned and scrambled up the gully. The lilly-pillies were blooming, white flowers that smelt of honey, and the grass orchids with their sweet tubers underground ...

He thought he had forgotten. He hadn't. His bare feet were so silent on the ground that the warriors looked up, startled, as he burst into the campsite.

They looked to be the same men and youths who had gathered before. They lay against trees or sat by the ashes of the fire, picking the last meat from a roasted badagarang. They didn't wear white paint today, but their spears were long, barbed war spears, not fishing ones. At first he couldn't see Balloonderry, then noticed him among the others.

'The soldiers are coming! They plan to shoot as soon as they see you this time!'

Balloonderry stood up without haste. 'Then we will make sure they don't see us. Thank you, my brother.'

The other warriors picked up their spears and ngalangala, their war clubs, and began to stride into the trees.

'Where will you go? Back down to Parramatta?'

Balloonderry hesitated, then nodded his acceptance of Nanberry's loyalty. 'Across the harbour. The English won't bother walking there, and we can see their boats if they try to hunt us.' He paused. 'Do you think the Governor will stay angry?'

'You want to come back to the colony?'

'I don't want to be hunted like a badagarang. I want to fish the harbour again.' He met Nanberry's eyes. 'The Governor said I might go to England. I want to see new lands, to ride in the giant boats, like you. Do you think he will forget?'

'No,' said Nanberry honestly. 'The English think it is serious to kill a man. A white man,' he added.

'There is no punishment he will accept, except my death?'

Nanberry had lived as an English for over two years now, but there was so much he didn't know. He shook his head — an

English gesture. 'I will ask my father. Perhaps he might know.' Someone yelled an order in the distance. 'You should go!'

'Yes. If the Governor says I can come back, will you send me a sign?'

'What?'

'An oar,' said Balloonderry. 'Thank you, brother.'

'Balloonderry Nanberry,' said Nanberry.

'Nanberry Balloonderry,' said Balloonderry. 'You will be a warrior,' he added quietly. 'One day you will.' He turned his back and vanished after the others into the bush.

Nanberry was almost back at the settlement when he saw the soldiers. He hid in a bush as they tramped by with their muskets, followed by the Governor and some officers with swords and pistols, their red coats stained now, no longer as bright as when they had arrived.

He laughed. Those brave red coats, those big black boots. How could any warriors fight when their red coats made them such easy targets? When black boots made so much noise? How could the English be so clever sometimes, but so stupid too?

'You! What are you laughing at?' It was a convict, one of the officers' servants. Nanberry came out of his bush. He wondered if the man recognised him, naked, his hair down. He didn't care either way.

'The warriors have gone,' he said. 'The soldiers won't find them now.'

'How do you know?' The man was suspicious.

Nanberry laughed again. Let the convict report him — the man hadn't seen him do any wrong. He began to run — not to escape, but for the sheer joy of it, feeling the earth under his bare feet, the air on his skin. No trousers to chafe him, no shirt to make him sweat.

'Hey, you! Come back!'

But there was no way the servant, small and ragged, could catch him. Had the man ever even run along a beach?

He was free! He was Nanberry! He was Nanberry ... White.

He stopped running, found the bush where he had stripped off and reached for his clothes, then returned to his father's house.

Chapter 41

NANBERRY

The *Supply* sailed again. Nanberry didn't sail with it. He told Captain Waterhouse that he would like to sail on the next voyage though, if Captain Waterhouse would let him. Captain Waterhouse agreed, probably because of his friendship with Father White.

Summer descended on the colony. Smoke from the bushfires in the mountains mingled with the smoke of cooking fires outside the huts, or from the colony's few proper chimneys. Flies feasted in the horse and cattle dung. The smell of human excrement filled the air. The Tank Stream grew thick with green weed that turned to brown. It stank as well.

Days passed. He slept, he ate, he wandered around the town. He ate dinner again at Government House with Father White. This time there was no black servant to sneer.

He listened as Mr Collins urged the Governor to pardon 'the native lad with so much promise'. He found an oar, and kept it hidden, so he could send a message to his brother if the Governor said he'd give a pardon. But Balloonderry had disappeared.

～❦❦◎

The knocking came at breakfast. The Surgeon sighed. More people in the colony meant more illness, more urgent summonses to the hospital. But this knocking didn't sound like Big Lon or the hospital porters. Rachel opened the door and stared. 'Sir ...' she called to the Surgeon.

It was Bennelong. He wore his shirt and trousers, but no boots or hat. He looked unsure of himself. Bennelong had never looked like that before.

'Come,' he said to Father White. It sounded like a plea.

'What is it, man?' demanded the Surgeon.

'Balloonderry ill. Most ill.'

Nanberry froze. Would his father tend a person who might be hanged if the Governor caught him? Would his father call for soldiers to capture him? But the Surgeon simply stood up and took his coat and hat from the peg. He nodded at Nanberry. 'Ask him where the lad is.'

～❦❦◎

It wasn't far. His brother lay on the ground by the blackened remnants of a campfire. His skin was hot. Sweat beaded his face. He stared at the sky with eyes that didn't see.

The Surgeon halted, then turned to Nanberry. 'I've seen this lad before,' he said slowly. 'You brought him to have his hand stitched.'

'Yes,' said Nanberry.

'You know him?'

'Yes,' said Nanberry. He hesitated. 'He is the fisherman who speared the convict.' He knelt beside Balloonderry. 'Babana? Brother?

Balloonderry didn't reply.

Nanberry searched his brother's skin, but there were no white blisters. Just the heat, the mindlessness of fever.

'Father? What's wrong with him?'

The Surgeon felt Balloonderry's pulse, then laid a hand on his forehead, and checked the whites of his eyes. He shrugged. 'A fever. Not the smallpox, I think. Measles, perhaps — there's been an outbreak of that among the children. Influenza, or even just a cold. It could be one of a dozen things. The natives get so sick with many of our illnesses.'

'Can you make him well?'

'We can look after him and hope his fever breaks. Go and tell the porters to bring a stretcher. We need to carry him to the hospital.'

'You won't let the Governor hang him?'

The Surgeon sat back. 'Lad, I don't know what the Governor will do. But while he is at my hospital I promise he will be safe.'

Balloonderry was put in the same hut that Nanberry had once lain in. Nanberry sat with him as Father White checked his pulse and temperature again. Balloonderry muttered something, then grew still again, panting slightly like a dog.

'Is he worse?'

'Yes. His pulse is more rapid.'

'But isn't that good?'

'No. It means his body is struggling with the fever. But his breathing is clear, at least.'

'What can I do?'

'Wipe his face and chest with a wet rag, to try to cool the fever. I'll send some lavender oil over: add a few drops to the water. It might soothe him, help to cool him too. I'll send meadowsweet tea. Try holding a little to his lips with a spoon, but don't tip it down his throat unless he tries to swallow, or he might choke.'

'Are you going to tell the Governor?'

'He already knows,' said the Surgeon gently. 'I sent one of the porters to tell him. Is this young man a friend of yours? A relative?'

'He is my brother.' He knew the Surgeon might think they were blood brothers, not name brothers. But the English didn't seem to understand *name brothers*.

He felt the Surgeon's hand, reassuring on his shoulder. 'We'll do our best for him. I'll be in my office. Call a porter to get me if he becomes restless. I can give him laudanum, but I don't want to if I don't have to — it can make the breathing weaker. I'll send a message to Rachel to organise some food.'

The hut door creaked open on its rope hinges. Bennelong came back in. He carried a wattle branch and a coolamon of water. As Father White and Nanberry watched he dipped the branch into the water and stroked it over Balloonderry's body, over and over, to cool it down.

Better than a wet rag, thought Nanberry. 'Father, the lavender oil —'

'I'll send it down.' The Surgeon hesitated. 'Lad, in truth, it won't make much difference. With a fever like this there is nothing we can do.'

For two days Balloonderry lay and sweated, staring at the bark roof. Once he began to scream, a nightmare in his fever. But as soon as Bennelong touched him the screaming stopped.

Bennelong didn't leave his side, except for brief moments outside. Nor did Nanberry.

The Governor called in several times, standing still and simply watching. He seemed sad. Nanberry thought there was more to his grief than the illness of one young man. There was no talk of chains or hanging Balloonderry now.

On the third day Willemeeerin arrived. Bennelong ushered him into the hut. 'He knows how to drive out the spirits that make men sick.' The man who'd speared the Governor put his mouth to Balloonderry's body. He closed his eyes and let the illness take him. He shuddered and moaned, feeling Balloonderry's pain.

At last Willemeeerin lay, exhausted, on the dirt floor of the hut. Balloonderry's face was blank, his eyes were staring, unchanged. His breath was so slight it might vanish any second like a puff of smoke.

Bennelong looked at Nanberry. He spoke in their own language. There was none of the arrogance of the warrior to a boy now. 'We need to take him away. Across the water, where his ghost won't hurt us.'

'No! He may still get better.'

'No,' said Bennelong. His voice was kind. He touched Nanberry gently, a leaf touch on the arm. 'He is dying. Do this for your brother. Help me carry him down to the cove.'

Bennelong carried Balloonderry's head; Nanberry his legs. But as soon as they left the hut others joined them, the warriors and young men who had been part of the war party, here to escort Balloonderry's body. They must have been waiting, thought Nanberry, watching for us to come outside.

This time he didn't follow them. His brother had what he needed, in these last hours of his life. He had the harbour, the blue sky. He had the people he loved, the ones who had stood by him when he was hunted down. Their hands would carry him now.

Nanberry watched them go, down to a canoe that waited on the shore. He watched as the canoe was paddled out into the water. And soon he heard the women's cries and knew that his brother had died.

The warriors and young men brought the body back. They placed it in a hut, down by the water, given by the Governor for the purpose. 'A fine lad,' said the Governor to Father White. He sighed. 'A tragedy, that it should end like this.'

Father White glanced at Nanberry, then back to the Governor. 'Yes, sir,' was all he said.

Women and girls wailed outside the death house while convicts dug a grave at Government House. Bennelong brought Balloonderry's canoe, a new one, freshly made, not the one wrecked by the convict men.

The warriors laid the body in the canoe, with a spear, a throwing stick and Balloonderry's fishing spear and lines. Young men waved bunches of grass.

Nanberry followed, with Father White, the officers, the Governor. Nanberry wore English clothes now. He had no place in the official part of Balloonderry's burial. That was for his brother's true native companions.

Drummers lined the road leading to Government House. Bennelong had ordered them, and the Governor had agreed. They beat the drums slowly, *thud, thud, thud,* their drumsticks muffled.

The warriors bearing the canoe reached the grave, and began to lower their burden in.

Someone gave a startled laugh. The grave was far too short. The warriors trimmed off the ends of the canoe, then rolled Balloonderry's body into the hole, with his head positioned so that his ghost might see the sun as it passed overhead.

White and black began to fill the grave. At last the earth was mounded up. One of the young warriors placed branches around the dirt, and then a log, which he covered with grass. He sat there, staring at the sky.

You do not mention the names of the dead.

Once Nanberry White had had another name. He couldn't use that name now. He followed the Surgeon and Rachel back to the house without speaking.

I am Nanberry Bo-rahng, he thought. Nanberry and the shadow of the man who was once my brother.

What might we have done together, if he had lived? Would we have gone fishing? Would he have convinced me to become a warrior, to go through the ceremonies with him? Perhaps we would have sailed on ships together.

Don't think of the dead, for ghosts can hurt. How could the loss of what you had never known hurt more than the loss of what you'd had? He felt more desolate now than he had nearly three years ago, when his whole family had died.

He took off his hat, his English hat, and put it on the peg next to his father's. Tomorrow he would go down to the harbour and see when Captain Waterhouse was expected back.

He was Nanberry Bo-rahng White. Nanberry No-name White. Now it was time to go to sea again, to accept the life that he had chosen.

Chapter 42

RACHEL

'Pretty lady! Pretty lady!' The ragged urchins grabbed at her skirts as she lifted them out of the dirt of the street. This road past the Governor's house was the only proper road in New South Wales.

The Governor's house was empty now. Governor Phillip had returned to England, ill and exhausted, taking Bennelong and another native with him to show to everyone back home. But the road was still kept up perfectly, a mile long and perfectly straight, unlike the muddy lanes that wandered between the colony's hovels. It had a foundation of logs with dirt tamped hard to make a firm surface.

She handed the urchins the hearth cakes she'd brought for them (with the Surgeon's permission): hard baked biscuits made of cornflour. There were more and more children running wild around the colony now, with dribbling noses and thin starved cheeks.

All too much of the wheat and corn crops were turned into alcohol these days. The children's mothers were either drunk or simply didn't care that their children went hungry. And their fathers: well, probably no one had any idea who their fathers were.

She walked on, lifting her skirts again out of the mud and horse droppings, up to the headland. The small crowd had gathered under the trees for the Reverend Johnson's Sunday church service. The Surgeon was already there, sitting on an upholstered chair up the front with the other officers. She found herself a seat on a long bench, towards the back.

Even if they had walked to the service together they would have sat apart, like master and servant, not together like husband and wife.

It hurt, but she said nothing. Other men took convict wives, though none of them were proper gentlemen like the Surgeon, with good jobs back home to go to. Perhaps, one day — when she had served her sentence maybe, in just over two years' time, when she had the right to go back to England, seven years after they had put her in gaol to wait for the hangman's noose — the Surgeon would say …

No, that was a dream. She made herself focus on the sermon. But the Reverend Johnson spoke as lengthily as ever, and as boringly too. It was good to stand for a hymn, hearing their voices join together, the song of praise carried on the wind across the harbour. She smiled. She had a lot to be thankful for, despite the lack of a wedding band on her finger. A comfortable home, and a man who treated her with kindness and respect. A life, instead of the noose, back in England …

There had been a time on the *Lady Juliana* when she had almost wished she had been hanged. Not now.

'Amen!' The man beside her bellowed out the word. She glanced at him. Tall, so broad-shouldered he was almost like a bull, black-eyed, the look of a sailor about him, not a convict.

What was he doing here? Few sailors bothered to come to the Reverend Johnson's services.

He caught her look, and smiled. She looked away as the Reverend opened his Bible for the readings.

Others lingered to gossip after the service, but she had the Surgeon's dinner to see to. She had made her way through the crowd when she realised the sailor was walking next to her. He lifted his hat — a good one — showing neat black hair pulled back into a queue. 'Good morning, miss.'

She nodded politely, but kept walking.

'Thomas Moore, ship's carpenter, at your service.'

She hesitated. She should ignore him — no lady, or respectable servant, spoke to a man without an introduction, especially in the colony, where rogues needed no encouragement to think a woman willing. But somehow she found herself saying, 'I am Rachel Turner.'

'It's an honour to meet you, Miss Turner. It is *Miss*, isn't it?'

She smiled. 'It is. But you must excuse me. I have my master's dinner to attend to.'

'Then may I walk with you?'

She paused again. But he had been at church and she liked his face. 'For a way,' she said.

'I saw you before, giving food to the children.'

She stared at him. 'Is that why you came to the church service? You followed me?'

'No. I go to church whenever I'm onshore.' There was truth in his voice. 'It's a pity the colony don't have a proper church. But I'm sure it will, one day.' He smiled again. 'A cathedral, maybe, where we can give God thanks for our deliverance across the seas.'

'The colony needs granaries to store the grain more than churches.' She was echoing the Surgeon's words. 'I can't see a colony of mud-and-wattle huts ever boasting a cathedral.'

'Can't you? I can.'

She stared at him. 'This place is a prison, no more.'

'If you'll pardon me, it's a lot more, Miss Turner. There's enough whales in these waters for a thousand whaling ships — ships that will need food to feed their sailors. There's land for sheep and markets for their wool too. Once the American colonies were mud-and-bark huts. Look at 'em now.'

'Have you been to America?'

'I have.' The smile came again. 'Do you have your Sunday afternoons free, Miss Turner? I could tell you about my travels. A walk along the cliffs would be grand.'

'No. I'm sorry.' To her surprise she found she was.

'I will see you at the service next Sunday then?'

Suddenly she knew she had to be honest with him. This was a pleasant enough man, but he could want only one thing from her. 'Mr Moore, I'm not looking to be a "sea-wife" to a sailor who's got a girl in every port, a man who may never sail this way again. I'm sorry.'

He met her eyes. 'And I'm not looking for a sea-wife either. Very well, Miss Turner. If one day you find me knocking on your door you'll know it's a proper wedding ring I'll be offering you, with a house and a job onshore.'

She flushed. But there was no way he could mean it. No man offered that after a single meeting. No sane man came to live in this colony willingly, not one who could have a good life anywhere else. 'I might marry another by then.' She tried to make it sound like a joke.

'Then you'll have my good wishes.' He gave her that smile once more. 'Until we meet again, Miss Turner.'

He had been sincere, she realised. But even if he did return — and there was no guarantee he'd find a ship coming this way, even if he wanted to come — he'd lose interest when he found out she was another man's mistress.

But she could feel him watching her as she walked along the street, shaking her head at the children to show she had no more biscuits to give them today. Another good man, she thought. At least there were two good men in the world.

But neither, she thought with a stab in her heart, likely to be a husband for me.

Chapter 43

RACHEL

Summer had burnt the tussocks brown. The plums were ripe in the orchard, the bees buzzing and the hens pecking around the fallen fruit, damaged in a hailstorm the night before. Rachel wiped the sweat from her face — the cooking fire made the kitchen hot — and slowly dried the plates from dinner.

Nanberry was back from yet another voyage to Norfolk Island, filled with stories of storms and broken masts, of the green island set in the blue sea. She made him scrub off the lice and muck out in the washhouse before he came inside, then fed him roast mutton and potatoes, freshly picked corn and hot buttered bread, with plum pudding to follow.

He ate like he hadn't seen food as good for months — which she was sure he hadn't — and the Surgeon looked on, his face for once happy and peaceful.

He and Nanberry sat together in the study now, talking about the birds on Norfolk Island, while she cleaned up and put the bread on to rise for tomorrow's baking. There was more wheat flour in the colony this year, grown out at Rose Hill, now called Parramatta, enough to make it worthwhile keeping a yeast plant going and making proper bread, not soda bread that went stale an hour after it was baked.

At last she heard Nanberry's footsteps going up the stairs to bed. Surgeon White appeared at the door. 'That was a fine meal. Thank you.'

'Sir …' It said a lot, she thought, that he had never told her to call him by his first name, although she sat at the table and ate with him now, instead of standing by like a servant. 'There is something I need to tell you.'

He sat on one of the kitchen chairs. 'What is it?'

'I'm with child.'

She'd wondered if he'd look happy, or shocked, or angry. Instead he simply nodded. 'I thought you might be.'

Had he heard her being sick in the morning? He was a surgeon, she thought. Of course he would have guessed. She waited for him to speak again. What happened next was his decision. Not hers.

'Rachel.' He spoke quietly and carefully. 'I can't marry you. Any day now I might be recalled to England. You can't come back with me.'

She had promised herself she wouldn't plead with him. But she couldn't help it. 'I can go back to England at the end of next year. I'll have served my full sentence then. Or you could stay here …'

He shook his head. 'My life here … these are days I want to forget, Rachel, not remember. The filth and horror, the thousands dead. Back in England I will have a proper house, servants, friends of my own kind.'

'And not a convict wife.'

'No.' The sorrow in his eyes was real. 'Not a convict wife.

If I married you there would be no good job for me back home. No respectable neighbours to dine with. Not for us or our children.'

'The neighbours need never know!' Her voice was fierce.

'They'd find out,' he said gently. 'They always do. So would my employers. A man can hide his past here, perhaps. Not back home.'

She was silent. He was right. He had never promised her marriage. They both knew it. Even here, he was a gentleman and she was not of his class. Even without her convict past, the tongues would wag if he married the likes of her. Gentlemen did not marry servants.

He looked at her steadily, this good man, locked into the rules of 'gentleman'. 'Rachel, I promise that you and your child will never want for anything. When I leave here, I'll make sure you are an independent woman, with a house and money of your own. I will care for you, I promise, all your life, and the child too.'

'I know,' she said.

She turned her head away so he wouldn't see her tears.

Chapter 44

RACHEL

Her pains began in the early afternoon. She wished she had another woman to tend her. But her few friends, mostly from the *Lady Juliana*, had either died, or were too far away, like Maria. She had made no new friends. The women nearby were either drunks, or officers' wives like Mrs Macarthur, not interested in friendship with the Surgeon's 'housekeeper'.

She sent Big Lon to tell the Surgeon he was needed at home — no need to tell the crease-faced convict why. She sat in the kitchen, waiting for the next pain, trying not to remember Pockface Judy, back in Newgate, lying on the straw screaming as they took her baby from her arms straight to the workhouse, where it would most likely die in days, poor mite. You didn't get to keep your child in prison, not unless you had the money to bribe the gaoler. And few of the babies born in the swaying filth in the depths of the ship had lived, unless their fathers claimed them and took them and their mothers up out of the hold.

She was scared. She was right to be scared. She knew of too many women who'd died in childbirth, especially the older ones. Back in the village when she was a child Old Meg came with her bag of napkins and herbs when it was time for a baby to come. Most of Old Meg's mothers lived. But in London a servant was as likely to get an old crone with filthy nails to attend her, just to die of childbirth fever, red-faced and sweating, within a week.

At least she would have a surgeon. At least her baby hadn't been starved because his mother was desperate for food or half poisoned with gin. At least …

The Surgeon's dark shadow blocked the door. She tried to smile at him. 'Your child is coming.'

Chapter 45

SURGEON WHITE

The baby was beetroot, waving red fists as it yelled, its face scrunched up like a tiny monkey's. It exactly resembled the hundreds of other newborns he had held — and looked completely different too.

His son. His tiny, perfect, incredible son.

He glanced at Rachel, sleeping now, pale and still in the bed. He had sent a message on the ferry to Maria, out at Rose Hill, to come and help for a few weeks. She had come on the return ferry, glad of the chance to make a few coins, for the harvest had been poor.

Maria was downstairs, now chopping the last of the winter parsnips for a chicken broth and giving the peelings to the o'possum, as though she had never been away. Nanberry was on another voyage to Norfolk Island. The Surgeon held his son, wrapped in a swaddling cloth made from a carefully hemmed part of an old sheet, worn so thin that another kick from the baby might rip a hole in it.

He had dreamt of this day. His wife would be in her silk-hung bed, there would be carpet on the floor, and brocade curtains; they would hold a christening with silver cups and teething rings, and a fine dinner for all the guests afterwards, to toast the baby's health. Instead he was in a house of crumbling convict bricks; his son's mother was a convicted felon, still serving a sentence for theft.

He was not a well-regarded London specialist with honourable colleagues and friends; his brother officers were thieves and rogues, more intent on making as much money as possible, now that Governor Phillip had left, than on governing the colony.

But today none of it mattered. This small child meant more than anything he had ever known.

Rachel stirred in the bed. 'What shall we call him?'

'Andrew Douglass Keble White.'

She frowned. 'But that's what you called Nanberry.'

'Nanberry didn't want the name. Andrew Douglass was the Captain who recommended me for this post.' He smiled at her, this lovely woman, the mother of his son, his companion and his friend. 'Without him I would not be here.'

And the baby would never have been born. This miraculous child. His son. He touched the child's hair with one finger. It was dark already, like his, and he had the blue eyes of the very young. The baby let out a yell again.

'He's hungry.' She held out her arms.

He let the baby go reluctantly. He sat on the bed, watching them both. 'He will be my true son,' he said softly. 'Everything my eldest child should have will be his.'

Rachel smiled vaguely, too worn out to wonder at the meaning of his words. But the Surgeon knew. His son would not be brought up a convict brat. His son would be a gentleman, like his father.

His son must go to England.

Chapter 46

NANBERRY

Nanberry sat in the kitchen, teasing the o'possum, holding a crust of bread by the creature's nose, waiting till it ran up his legs to get it, then holding it high out of reach.

Graaah! the o'possum muttered. It climbed onto Nanberry's head and stood on its hind paws. But the bread was still out of reach.

Rachel looked up from rolling out her pastry. 'Leave off teasing it, do.'

Nanberry laughed. He bent and put the bread on the floor. The o'possum jumped down and picked up the food in its paws. It ate it reproachfully, growled again, then jumped up and out of the window.

The baby gave a chortle and then a cry from its cradle by the fire. The cradle had been made by a ship's carpenter, and the smooth wood was well joined together, unlike most of the makeshift furniture in the colony.

'Pick him up, there's a lamb, while I finish this.'

Nanberry peered doubtfully at the baby, who was waving his tiny fists. 'Babies smell. At both ends too.'

'Then he needs changing again. And it's a good smell, you silly boy. A baby and milk smell. Here, I'll take him.' She lifted the baby, then laid him on the table and took a clean napkin from the pile on one of the chairs.

Baby, baby, baby, thought Nanberry. It was all his father and Rachel could talk about now. The whole house revolved around the baby. Except the o'possum. He grinned. The o'possum had more sense.

Tomorrow he'd sail to the Cape, not as a cabin boy, but as a proper sailor, through the most dangerous waters in the world. Giant waves that crashed ships into splinters, sea monsters with gaping jaws, islands of ice that lured ships to their doom. A new land with different trees and people from this place and tiny Norfolk Island, with carriages pulled by horses, and giant buildings larger than anything he'd seen here, and giant animals called *elephant* and *lion*, with teeth the size of carving knives.

He could hardly wait.

Chapter 47

SURGEON WHITE

The first of the thunderstorms had come, bringing hail that flattened the corn and stripped the baby peaches from the trees. But he would not be here to see either the peach or corn crop.

Surgeon White stood in his office at the hospital and stared at the pages in his hand, just delivered from the newly arrived *Daedalus*, along with its cargo of pale-faced wretches, sick or dying of scurvy and fever. But after so many years they were no longer his concern. Not now.

The paper was yellowed from damp and the voyage, the ink already fading even though the orders had only been written a year ago. His hand trembled as he read the words.

He had longed for this moment for years! At last he could sail from this accursed land! He had been ordered back to England, to civilised company. Back to the world.

Almost as good — and astonishing — was the news that his

Journal of a Voyage to New South Wales had not only been published, but been a massive success, translated into German and about to be translated into French. He was a respected writer and had never known it. There was money waiting for him in England, far more than just his wages while he had been here. Enough money for a proper house, his own carriage and horses ...

At last, finally, he was going home.

Let others deal with the ships of living corpses who screamed when they saw the sun, their bodies like walking sticks leaking dysentery, or typhus that spread like butter in the heat. He would be back in green England.

The Surgeon put the letter down and stared out the window. Now — somehow — he had to tell Rachel.

She was sitting in the chair by the kitchen fireplace, the boy on her lap, spooning mashed carrot and potato into his mouth. The child was just beginning to toddle now, holding onto chairs to steady himself. Soon he'd be running ... Pain gripped the Surgeon's heart. And he'd not be here to see.

Rachel smiled as he came through the door. 'He'll be finished in a moment. I made us a steak and kidney pudding and treacle dumplings ...' She stopped, and looked at his face. 'What is it?'

'My orders have come through. I'm recalled back to England. I sail on the *Daedalus*.'

She stared at him. 'But ... I've a month of my sentence to serve yet. Can't you wait till my papers come?'

'Rachel,' he said gently. 'You're not coming with me. You know that.'

She stared now at the child, all expression vanished from her face, then nodded. 'It's true. You never promised me that. Only that you would take care of me.'

'I will. I've arranged for you to keep this house as long as you want it. There'll be rent from the farm here, meat, milk, whatever they cost. I'll have money sent to you regularly, enough to keep you in comfort.'

'And Andrew.' She still gazed at the baby's face, not at him.

He shut his eyes. He knew what this would do to her. 'Rachel ... the child must come to England as soon as he is old enough to travel.'

'What?' It was obvious that she had never even thought of this. 'No! You can't do that!'

'He is my son,' he said softly. 'A father has every right to say what happens to his child. What is better for him? To stay here, as a convict brat, or come to England as a gentleman? I will send Andrew to school, Rachel — a proper boarding school. Buy him a commission in the army, perhaps.'

She stared at him, her face like the stone cliffs above the cove. 'And if you marry? What then?'

'I will never marry a woman who does not respect my son and give him a loving home. Andrew will always be my eldest son.' He crossed over to her and held out his hand. 'I have never lied to you. Never promised more than I could.'

'No,' she whispered. She took his hand in hers.

'Then trust me on this too.'

She shut her eyes, perhaps to stop the tears. 'A baby wouldn't survive the voyage. Not without his mother.'

'I know. There is no hurry. When he's five, perhaps, or six.'

A silence. At last she said, 'When do you leave?'

'As soon as the ship can be restocked.'

'So soon!'

'There may not be another ship for months. Rachel, I'm sorry,' he said. 'I wish it didn't have to be this way. But we both have known that this was coming.'

She wiped Andrew's face, then stood, the little boy held over her shoulder. 'I'll go and start your packing.'

He watched them leave. The boy had still to say his first word. I will miss that, he thought. Hearing him say *Papa*, watching him learn to walk, losing his baby teeth.

And Rachel too ...

She would never know how close he had been to saying: *Come to England, as soon as you are free.* Despite what it would mean he had almost said the words.

She had been more than a mistress, more than a housekeeper, more even than the mother of his son. She had been a friend, someone he trusted utterly, a good woman. He would leave part of his heart here with her and the boy.

But he couldn't stay here. Couldn't stay and let the place destroy him, as it had Phillip. A man could only take so much. And if he went home he could make a future for his son.

This was for the best. It had to be for the best.

He wanted to go upstairs to Rachel, to spend as many of these last hours with her and the boy as he could. But she needed time to accept the news. She wouldn't cry in front of him, he knew. She wouldn't plead. Not Rachel.

Instead he stepped into his study, looking over at his specimen jars and leaf press, deciding which of them to take, for luggage on the ship would be limited and some would be spoilt by the damp air. He would bring some of the eucalyptus oil he had distilled: it was useful for afflictions of the lungs and skin. The dried eucalypt sap that had proved so effective against dysentery, just like the fern root had been: if he could create a demand for that it might bring him even more than his book. His preserved frogs and snakes, the bats, the paintings of the birds, each one exquisite, though none as beautiful as Rachel as she gazed down at his son ...

All at once he remembered the French ships, long ago when they first landed at Botany Bay. The French were taking live animals back with them, for men of science to study back home. A live kangaroo would certainly make an impression …

And just as certainly die on the ship. He shook his head. There was no point even trying.

Grahhha! Something rattled the shutters in the next room. It was the o'possum, demanding to be fed again. Rachel must have shut them to keep out the draught.

'Come along now, here you are,' Rachel's voice sounded like she had been crying as she let the animal in. He crossed over to the door and watched her; the o'possum perched on the kitchen table, taking a cob of corn from her fingers.

Corn, bread, hard tack … that animal ate anything. And it was small enough to keep in a cage in his cabin.

True, an o'possum wasn't a particularly interesting beast — so like an American o'possum it was hardly worth describing in his book. But on the other hand it was tame, would eat from his fingers. No one had ever managed to tame an American o'possum. He imagined it sitting in its cage while the members of the Royal Society listened to the talk he would give. The ladies would coo and the men feed it biscuits.

'Big Lon!'

The convict ran up from the woodshed. 'Sir?'

'Find me a cage. One big enough for the o'possum.'

Big Lon stared. 'Why, sir? The animal is tame enough.'

'Because I am going home at last. And the o'possum is coming with me.'

Chapter 48

RACHEL

Rachel stared at the o'possum in its cage. She'd expected it to snarl or try to bite. It had shrieked and yelled at first. But now it crouched in its cage, bewildered. It looked smaller, somehow: all big black eyes and fur. She shook her head and walked upstairs, carefully lifting her skirt, and peered at Andrew, curled up in his crib for his afternoon nap. The child had no idea that his father was going to leave them, even before Christmas came.

She wondered what to do next. Something, anything, to keep her occupied, to stop her thinking. The Surgeon's trunks were packed. His clothes were thin, not much better than rags despite all her mending. But he'd need them on the voyage, at least till he could buy better — at the Cape on the way home, perhaps. He'd need one good suit to wear when he landed in England, till he could find a tailor to make him more.

Big Lon would continue to work the garden, to grow vegetables for them and bring the wood and water. The Surgeon had arranged for extra food to be sent from the land he owned each week too, and goat's milk, or even medicines from the hospital, whatever they had that she needed. She and her son would want for nothing that this colony could give them.

Except for him. A lover. A father. The centre of a happy home, where her son could grow up in peace, their happiness and charity spreading to others. It was all that she had ever wanted.

Stop thinking, she told herself. Do something. He was at the hospital now, overseeing the distilling of more eucalyptus oil to take to England. Precious hours when he could have been with her, and with their son …

Portable soup, she could make him that. Bones and vegetables boiled down till they turned into a hard jelly that would keep for months — the hard months aboard ship with no fresh food. There wasn't dried fruit in the colony for him to take.

She filled the stew pot with vegetables, herbs, chicken bones and beef bones, and called to Big Lon for a bucket of water and more wood. Soon the stock was simmering, the house filling with the scent.

Still no sound from Andrew upstairs. Still no Surgeon's footsteps. She wandered into the study to gaze again at his trunks, his specimen jars, the crates of dried plants. The o'possum glanced up at her from its cage, then seemed to shrink back into itself again.

Perhaps, like her, it had simply given up.

For the first time rage filled her. He was taking an o'possum, but not her! You could boast of a pet o'possum, but not of a convict wife. He was leaving her, imprisoned even though she had no ball and chain around her leg, held in a prison colony across the world. There was no escape, not even when she'd served her sentence. No escape for her, just like the o'possum.

She picked up some leaves to feed it. The animal watched her, its dark eyes wide. She had moved before she knew it. She picked up the cage, opened the door. The animal sat there as if it didn't know what was happening. Maybe it was simply half asleep.

'Run, you stupid creature! Wake up! Run!'

She tipped the cage on its side, tumbling the o'possum to the floor.

It moved then, sitting up, staring at her. She shook her head in despair. 'Run!' she cried again.

And suddenly it did, scampering to the window, jumping out. She peered out of the window, but it had already gone.

She looked at the cage, the gnawed corncobs on the floor. She put them back in the cage and placed it where she'd found it — but with the door open — then swept the floor. When the Surgeon finally came home, dark circles under his eyes, she was stirring the soup. She turned to him. 'All well at the hospital?'

'As well as I can leave it.'

She heard boots in the hallway. Porters, come to take his trunks.

'Handle those jars carefully!'

She watched as he went into his study; she waited, breathless, till she heard his footsteps coming back.

'The o'possum has gone!'

'Gone? How can it be gone?'

'It must have opened the cage door,' he said slowly.

'Who'd have thought an o'possum would know how to do that?' She turned back to the soup.

'Mama!' The sound came from upstairs.

The Surgeon stared at her. 'He's talking!'

She nodded. 'Just that word so far. I'd best get him before he tries to come down the stairs.'

'I'll come with you.'

She said nothing, feeling his eyes on her as she climbed up to the bedrooms, picked up Andrew, and began to change his wet napkin. The Surgeon leant against the doorjamb, still watching them both.

'I'm sorry about your o'possum,' she said at last. 'He would have been a fine thing to show off in England. Maybe he'll come back tonight.'

'No.' His voice was gentle. 'I don't think he will come back. Not once he's been held prisoner in a cage. You don't willingly return to prison.'

He was talking about more than the o'possum, she knew. He was saying that even if he was offered a posting back here, he'd refuse it.

He held out his arms for Andrew, and gathered the child to him. Tears ran down his cheeks, but he said nothing, just breathed in the scent of the baby's hair.

'Will you do one thing for me?' she asked abruptly. 'One thing only. It's all I ask.'

'What is it?'

'Tell the fine lady that you marry that the convict woman loved you. Can you tell her that?'

'I'll tell her. I'll tell her that I loved the convict woman too. I'll tell her that Andrew is the son of my heart, my eldest son, no matter how many children I have in wedlock. He will never be less than that. I will have no woman marry me who cannot accept those words.'

It had to be enough. All that she would get. She let herself cry now, feeling his arms around her and Andrew too. The last time, she thought, for he wouldn't embrace her in public, not down at the harbour. Not even once.

This was goodbye.

Chapter 49

NANBERRY

Nanberry swung his kit bag over his shoulder, and sauntered up the track to home. Hens clucked, pecking at the weeds in between the huts. A goat baaed up the hill, pulling at its tether. Somehow in the past few years the dead-looking twigs in the gardens had become big fruit trees. He sniffed. Peaches were ripening somewhere near.

Peach pie, he thought. Rachel's apricot dumplings …

He had so much to tell them. It had been a grand voyage, all the way to the Cape and back. The things he'd seen! Waves that towered so high the ship seemed to be sailing uphill, till finally it teetered on the white crests and went plunging down. Whales that frolicked about them, as if they knew they weren't whalers but, like themselves, travellers in this great ocean.

And Cape Town … His face clouded at that. It hadn't been quite what he had expected. No trips into the country to look for elephants or lions. His shipmates had advised him to stay near the docks — in this land of black skins, only whites, the Dutch or English, were welcomed in the shops and hotels. It was different in England, according to Cookie, the one-legged sailor who cooked their stew in the tiny reeking closet of a galley. Black men could get all sorts of work in London, and women, he dug Nanberry in the ribs, some white women were right taken with a black skin.

But even the docks had been fascinating. He'd seen a monkey and a team of all-white horses. Traders had rowed their little boats out to the ship, selling silks and fruit and carved animals. He'd bought Rachel green silk ribbons, and a carved carriage for Andrew, with wheels that went round and round, and a new pipe for Father White.

He flung open the front door and yelled, 'Hello!' then hung his hat on the peg by the door.

Baby Andrew chuckled in the kitchen. Rachel appeared, wiping her hands on her apron. 'Nanberry! Come in, sit down. Oh, I wish I'd known, I'd have got some meat in. There's bread and cheese ...'

'No meat?' He had never known this house not to have meat.

'Well, there's just me and Andrew these days, and there is no one to hunt for us now ...' She stared at him. 'You don't know.'

'Know what?'

'He said he would leave you a letter. It would be delivered to your ship, so the Captain could read it to you before you came home.'

'I left the ship on the first boat ashore,' he said impatiently. 'If there's a letter someone will bring it to me here and Father White can read it out.' Father White could read as well as write, but not him or Rachel. Why did a sailor or a woman need to read? 'Rachel, what's wrong?'

Her face was carefully expressionless. 'Your foster father has been recalled to England. He sailed last November.'

Nanberry felt his world lurch. 'Without telling me?'

'There was no time. His orders came. He had to go when the ship sailed.'

It was as though the deck had suddenly vanished from under him, leaving him stranded in the ocean. A moment ago he had been Nanberry, sailor, foster son of the great Surgeon White. And now ... nothing. No man of his clan to claim as family ...

'We are to keep this house. There will always be a home for you here.'

He shook his head, hardly hearing. What use was a house? He needed a clan, people to belong to.

'Sit down,' she said gently. 'I'll get you the bread and cheese. Big Lon can go up to the hospital and get some meat.'

He followed her to the table, hardly seeing. As soon as he was sitting, the small boy toddled up to him and tried to climb onto his knee.

'He's grown,' he said, automatically lifting the boy up.

'Yes.' She smiled as she watched the boy try to pull Nanberry's beard. It had grown longer since he'd been at sea, though he was afraid it still looked as straggly as a goat's beard.

He ate the bread and cheese to fill his belly, not really thinking of what he was eating. What was it like for Rachel with the Surgeon gone? She was a free woman now, it seemed, not assigned to be another man's servant. She was living here on her own, with just her son for company.

How could a woman live alone? No Cadigal woman would, with just her child. He didn't know any woman in the colony who did either. He shook his head. He'd thought he'd understood the English world. But once again he had been made to realise that he could see only the edges.

He stood up. 'I'm going out.' He needed friends — the men he sailed with. At least he knew where he was with them.

'I'll cook you a proper welcome-home supper. Roast mutton maybe? And a plum pudding too.'

He nodded, again not really listening to her words. She was just a woman. What did she know of men's business? What if another man took her? Would this still be his home then?

The wind blew hot and hard out in the road. It was a bushfire wind, carrying a hint of far-off smoke, not just that from the cooking fires of the colony. He made his way down to the docks, to the hotel where he thought his friends might be. Yes, there was Cookie in the corner, huddled around a tankard. He started towards him.

'Hey! No natives allowed.'

He stared at the barman in his once-white apron. 'I have money.'

'I'll believe that when I see it.' The man stared at him. 'You speak good for a native. I remember when Bennelong were here. Bennelong'd dance for any cove who'd give him a rum. You speak better'n Bennelong.'

Nanberry took out a threepence — Cape Town money, but good here. The man looked down at it. 'Well, mayhap you do have money. But I'll bring your drink outside. I'm still not having natives in my tavern.'

Nanberry looked over at Cookie, but the man was lost in his drink — drunk already perhaps, and there was no sign of anyone else he knew.

'Keep your ale. And the money.' Nanberry flung the threepence onto the dirt floor, sticky and stinking with spilt rum and ale, and made his way down to the shore.

The waves calmed him. They always did. People came and went, but the waves went on.

Who was Nanberry, really? Not English — you needed a white skin, it seemed, to be English, no matter how well you spoke the language or knew good manners at a table. He was a sailor, but a sailor couldn't always be at sea.

To the people of the colony he would forever be a native. But to the people he had been born among he was still no one: a boy who had never been made a man, not even allowed to throw a spear or know a woman.

He heard ghost whispers in the breeze.

The Cadigal and other clans that he had grown up with had been lost to the disease. But new clans had formed. He remembered enough about the bush to find them.

The whispers tickled his ears again. No voices, but he still knew what they said.

It was good that his foster father had left. Now he had to face just who he was. White men would never accept him in their world onshore. No white woman would take him as her husband.

He stood up, stripped off his clothes, rolled them into a ball and slung them over his shoulder.

It was time that he became a man.

Chapter 50

NANBERRY

He wore a crown of plaited reeds and a bracelet of reeds on his arm. His face was painted white; on his chest was a broad black stripe. The darkness was soft around him, the firelight very bright. He stood as still as possible, digging his toes into the ground so that he didn't cry out as the old man shoved the oyster shell up into his gum, back and forth, loosening his front tooth. The world was swaying when at last the man put down the shell.

Another man approached, his skin oiled and gleaming in the firelight. Behind them warriors chanted. Nanberry tried to make out the words. He still remembered everyday language, but these were ritual words, banished from his mind for many years.

The second man had a long bone in one hand, a stone in the other. He laid the point of the bone against Nanberry's tooth and tapped it with the stone, once, twice, three times, then suddenly a heavy blow.

Blood gushed into his mouth. He could feel the tooth lying on his tongue, the blood flowing down his throat. He fought to stay upright, not to show pain, not to vomit from the blood.

The old man reached into his mouth, then held up the tooth. It looked so long, far longer than any tooth did in a mouth. The old man sang as he raised the tooth aloft. Once more Nanberry tried to make out the words.

Then it was done. The song around him changed. A spear was put into his hand, a bark container of water held up to his mouth so he could wash away the blood.

He was a man.

Why, he thought, his knees trembling, almost beyond pain now, do I still feel empty?

He had lost this world when the Surgeon had rescued him, all those years ago. He was neither Cadigal nor English now, but only a small part of both. I am a ghost too, he thought. I walk upon the world but I have no meaning. Maybe I died when the sickness came, and only know it now. Even the pain in his mouth couldn't make him feel real.

Hands led him to a tree. He sat, his back to it. Someone handed him a cooked fish. He pressed it into the hole in his gum to stem the bleeding, feeling the blood slow to a seep in his mouth.

The dance continued around the firelight. Caruey, the only other Cadigal of his age Nanberry knew to have survived, and another young man stood as their teeth were loosened, then struck out.

Time flowed past him, dark as the blood from his mouth. It was another dance now, another song. Above them the moon rose, large and white. Like the waves, thought Nanberry. Nothing stops the waves or dulls the moon. We suffer here, but the waves still flow and the moon still shines, beautiful and unchanging.

A bat flickered past the fire. Somewhere wallabies would be drinking, o'possums nibbling at their leaves. What happened to the Surgeon's o'possum? he wondered. Rachel might know.

His sense of being an outsider began to ease. The men here accepted him. No matter what, he was a Cadigal warrior now. Perhaps next week he would hunt badagarang with them, learning how to use spears again, this time as a man. No more muskets for him now, but the power of the giant spear of a warrior. They would light the fires to bring the grass, to clear the undergrowth. They would watch the women sweep the droppings from the waterholes and do their duty to the land.

Being a warrior meant accepting your duty: to perform the rituals; to stand by your friends. If there were battles with the English, or against other clans, he knew which side he must be on.

But there would still always be a captain eager to have a sailor who knew the ropes and sails, who had faced the waves of the Cape and the terrifying calms of the doldrums. There was still an English house, with Rachel and her son.

He knew now that his room would still be there, his bed, the clothes he wore on land, no matter how far he travelled, on the sea or back into the bush. Nor would the Surgeon forget him, even if he was far away. One letter waited for him. There would be more.

Yes, he knew who he was now.

Slowly he began to relax into pain and weariness. There was beauty and belonging in this world. He had the bush. He had the sea. He had a home with Rachel, at least while no man claimed her.

That would have to be enough.

The chant changed once again. And now he understood every word, the child's language he had almost forgotten coming back to him.

He was Cadigal still. And he was English.

He smiled, despite the pain, his swelling mouth. He was Cadigal and English! He could see more in this land than any Englishman ever could, the way he had found birds for Father White. He could travel on giant ships and see the world, as no other Cadigal could do.

He was warrior and sailor.

It was tradition to take a new name after the yulang yirabadjang. But he would refuse, just as he had refused to take the name Andrew so long ago.

'I am Nanberry Buckenau White!' He would wear his name with pride.

Chapter 51

RACHEL

Nanberry had sailed away again, climbing up the ship's rigging as though he had done it all his life, with a new gap between his teeth and a tattoo of a ship on his arm.

She waved him off, down at the harbour, carrying Andrew in her arms. The baby held up his chubby hand to wave farewell to his foster brother as the ship's boat pulled out from the shore. Now she walked slowly back up the hill.

The house would feel empty. It had been so good to have someone to cook for, to look after while his mouth and face healed. Silly boy, to go and do a native trick like that. And that tattoo, something else men did just to show they could bear the pain. Let them bear a child and they'd know all about pain, with no need for knocking out teeth or needles and dye.

She smiled down at her son, peering over her shoulder at the harbour's bustle, then quickly wiped the smile away, looking down at the ground in case any man thought the smile was encouragement. There was no protection for a woman in New South Wales, not from convicts or soldiers of the Rum Corps. The officers of the Rum Corps (not that anyone called them that when they could hear it) had come out at the same time as she had, to serve in the colony. But the only ones they had served were themselves. They did what they wanted, took what they wanted. They hanged anyone who tried to stop them. It was hard, living by herself, putting the bolts up on the doors and shutters at night in case some drunken soldiers tried to get in; making sure no light showed to let them think a woman might be inside.

Big Lon still worked the garden each day, growing the fresh vegetables and fruit the Surgeon believed to be so important to a child's health. He chopped their wood and brought them water, but he went back to the barracks each night. She couldn't see Big Lon protecting her and her son from anyone either.

But at least she had money — the rent from a land grant the Acting Governor had given the Surgeon. The tenant sent meat and milk once a week as well. Already sea chests had arrived for her. Each chest contained coins in a purse hidden in bolts of cloth for clothes and sheets — good sensible linen and flannel. There had been a toy horse for Andrew and a letter in each chest that took her a day to read, for she wouldn't ask anyone else to read her out something so private.

The chests and letters had come from the Cape. In a few months he'd reach England, and in another year perhaps they'd hear from him again, that he had reached port safely. He said that he was safe and well; he said to kiss the child from him; and he said he was hers, always affectionately. No word of love. But he was keeping his promise, caring for them. She was sure he always would.

But a woman needed more than linen and flannel, or even silk if it had ever occurred to him to send it. She'd had a silk scarf once, the one that the Master had given her back in England, the one he had claimed she'd stolen. The one that had sent her here …

Yes, a woman needed more than silk. More than love, even. The Surgeon had been the first man to talk to her about why the birds flew north in winter, or how men got scurvy. Her world had been so small, survival and nothing else. He had opened a window to a wider life, but now it was shut again.

Yells floated across from the marketplace just up from the harbour. A crowd had grown, jeering men and toothless grinning women. She shuddered, and turned Andrew's face away, in case he caught sight of whatever they were watching. A flogging, perhaps, or a public hanging. The crowds loved sights like that.

She had just started down the track to the house when the breeze caught the words. 'And what am I offered for this fine wench then? Six more years she got to serve. A bit o' feeding and she'll be good as new …'

Her skin grew cold. They were auctioning the women off the latest ship, the one that had brought her sea chest and letter. The Rum Corps officers had first pick, of course, inspecting the women as they lined up on deck, taking the youngest and plumpest and prettiest. The officers' friends could choose next, also paying nothing for the privilege. The other women were auctioned to whoever would pay the highest price.

'No more'n that?' The auctioneer's voice was scornful. 'Sold then, for a pint o' rum to the cove with the withered hand. And I bet she'll warm it up for you, eh? Now the next wench is a right good piece. Don't laugh now, me dearies. She may be tiny but she's a good worker, and freshly widowed, so she knows what to do, eh?' The crowd snickered.

'The natives killed her husband just ten days ago and …' The woman let out a cry of anguish.

'Maria!' Rachel whirled around and began to run, holding Andrew against her. Her arms ached but she didn't dare put him down.

How could Maria end up at the auction? A widow, the man had said. Maria was still a convict. If her husband had died the officers must have decided she was worth selling. Legal or not, there was no way to stop them …

Rachel struggled to get closer; the crowd was too thick. But she could see the auctioneer standing on the back of the cart and Maria next to him. She looked so small. She had always been tiny, but now her face was thin and pinched, with shadows under her eyes like they'd been smudged with charcoal. Yet even here she looked neat, her dress worn but well mended.

'Just look at her! She can sew and clean, can't you, lovey? And she's a right good cook. She can sow yer barley and shuck yer corn, as well as keep you warm at nights.'

'She ain't big enough to keep a man warm!' The man next to Rachel gave a gap-toothed grin, as though it was the wittiest thing he'd ever said. Which she supposed it might have been.

Maria stared blankly at the crowd. Her eyes were empty.

'Ah, the little ones have more fire in them. You take it from one who knows.' The auctioneer gave a wink. 'Whatever you pays for her you'll make back again. She could cook for a whole tavern. You could hire her out by day and have her back each night. Or hire her out all night too! Now, who'll start the bidding? You, sir?'

'Threepence!'

The auctioneer snorted. Maria made no sign that she had even heard.

'One pint o' rum!'

'One pint! Do I have two?'

'Two pints!' It was a young man with beefy arms and a rough tattoo of a mermaid on his forearm.

'I'm offered two. Who'll make it three? Oh, for a taste of this young lady's pie. She'll scrub for you, cook for you, never mind the rest of it —'

'Ten shillings!' Rachel had to yell over the noise. It was all she had. But she couldn't let Maria be sold like this. If only the Surgeon was here, she thought. He would never let this happen. But there was no one to help her now.

'Ten shillings! Now that's more like it.' The auctioneer nodded to her. Rachel flushed, lowering her head, clutching Andrew to her. It was dangerous to be noticed, but impossible not to help.

She glanced up again. Maria peered around, showing the first signs of life. Rachel held up her hand briefly so she could see it. Maria bit her lip, hope washing across her face.

'Ten shillings and sixpence!'

It was from a soldier, his red coat stained with sweat under the arms. He must have decided Maria could be sold for more, if someone was bidding that much for her.

Rachel tried to calculate. She could sell her spare dresses. 'Twelve shillings.'

'Twelve and sixpence.'

The soldier leered at her. All at once Rachel realised what he was doing.

He was determined to beat her bid. He had no intention of paying any money. He could bid any sum he wanted to. No one could force a member of the Rum Corps to pay their debts.

And there was no way she could bid more.

Maria knew it. Rachel saw her shoulders droop, and the same blank look descend on her face. Maria had another six years to serve. She was so small, so thin. If a man worked her hard could she last that long? There was no surety he would even let her go when her time was served. Many women were kept bound as long as the man they served wanted them. The courts were run by the Rum Corps too. Impossible to expect justice there, especially for a woman.

'A guinea!' It was a new voice, vaguely familiar. Rachel peered across the crowd. She knew that face! It was the ship's carpenter she had met years before, after church. What was his name again? Mr Moore. She flushed. He had seemed such a good man. Now he was bidding for a woman, like all the others.

'Ten guineas!' the soldier bid again, his grin even wider. He lifted a stone jug from the ground and took a swig. The crowd roared with laughter, aware of the joke now. Ten guineas was an enormous sum, months of wages. Ten guineas for a woman like this — impossible, incredible. He may as well have bid a hundred pounds.

Rachel looked across at Mr Moore again. He frowned, staring at Maria on the cart.

'Well, sir? Another bid?'

Mr Moore shook his head.

'Sold then, to the officer over there.'

The crowd cheered. The auctioneer shoved Maria over to the edge of the cart. The soldier elbowed his way forward and lifted Maria down like a sack of potatoes. 'There's nothing to her! I want me money back!'

The crowd shouted with laughter again. There would be no money paid, no money given back. It was a joke, a joke for all of them.

Except for Maria, thought Rachel. She tried to think what to do. One of the surgeons at the hospital might help her. They might even be able to get Maria assigned to someone else. Mrs Macarthur, maybe. If she told Mrs Macarthur how good Maria was with her needle she might want her as a maid. She'd be safe there, at least …

There was no sign of Maria now, nor of the soldier or Mr Moore. The crowd was too thick. Nor was there any point pleading with the soldier, not drunk as he was.

Andrew began to whimper, afraid of all the noise. She soothed him automatically, patting his back as she held him against her shoulder. She began to walk away, back towards the house, planning her next move …

'Mistress Turner!'

She looked back. Mr Moore strode down the road, carrying a ragged bundle under one arm. The other hand held Maria's. He let the hand go as Rachel ran to her, hugged her. 'I was so afraid for you! I'm sorry, so sorry, I had no idea. I offered all I could …'

Maria said nothing, but clung to her, Andrew squashed between them. He struggled to get down. Rachel lowered him, his hand held tight in hers, then looked at Mr Moore. She had forgotten how big he was, his shoulders straining at his jacket. 'Sir …' She didn't know what else to say. How did he come to have Maria here, when the soldier outbid him?

His lips narrowed. 'The ruffian back there was glad enough to take a guinea once he'd had his fun.'

'So you bought her?'

'A man does not buy another life, Mistress Turner. All men are equal in the sight of God. But it seems your friend has been assigned to me now, yes.' He bowed, first to Rachel and then to Maria. 'I think it best if she stays with you.'

She had to thank him, but still she could find no words. Maria was shaking as though she would collapse at any moment. Andrew fidgeted, pulling at her hand, eager for his dinner. And any moment the crowd might find them here and gather for further fun.

She curtseyed quickly, then put her arm around Maria. She bent to pick up Andrew, but Mr Moore had already picked him up. She waited for the boy to put out his arms to her, but instead he laughed as Mr Moore hoisted him onto his broad shoulders. 'I will see you to your door.'

She curtseyed again, as best she could while still holding

Maria. The way to their house had never seemed so long. She took the key from the pocket of her apron, and unlocked the door — the Surgeon had paid for a lock the year before — and ushered Maria inside.

Should she ask him in? She flushed. Would he require ... payment ... for his favour? But he had already lifted Andrew down.

'Thank you —' she began.

He bowed. 'I am glad I could be of service.'

She hurried in to Maria as he strode back up the street.

Chapter 52

RACHEL

Maria sat huddled on one of the chairs in the kitchen, still in her hat and coat, staring down at her hands. Rachel bent, and kissed her cheek.

'Mama? Who that?' Andrew stared at Maria, wide-eyed.

'I'm your mother's new servant.' Maria's voice was only a whisper.

'She is Mama's friend. She will live with us now.' She took Maria's hat, then gently helped her out of her jacket. There was meat pudding, ready to heat again for their dinner, and the pot was near to boiling on the hob. She added wood to the fire, and pushed the pot above the flames.

Maria stirred. 'I should do that.'

'You should rest.'

Rachel plopped the pudding in its cloth into the boiling water, then added potatoes. There are stewed apples in the pantry too, she thought, sweetened with the honey Nanberry had brought her. If only he was here, she thought, though Nanberry had no influence in the colony these days, now that Governor Phillip had left; no one bothered translating the native tongues any more. But his presence was a comfort. He could at least fight off a drunk who tried to force his way past the door or steal their potatoes.

She put Andrew on his chair, pushed him up to the table, and put the plates in front of them all. But even when Andrew began to spoon up his pudding Maria still sat, unseeing.

Rachel reached for the spoon and lifted it to Maria's mouth as she had fed Andrew till not so long ago. Maria's mouth opened and she swallowed. Andrew watched as Maria ate her meat pudding, the colour coming slowly back into her face. Rachel cleared the plates, then brought in the stewed apples. She was spooning it into bowls when Maria said, 'They killed Jack. The natives. I found him in the cornfield with a spear sticking out of his chest.'

Rachel glanced at Andrew. But he was more interested in the apple, smearing it over his face as he gulped it down.

At last the tears were running down Maria's face. 'I wouldn't go out with Jack that day. I was tired, so tired. I said he could pick the corn himself; I was staying home. And when he didn't come for his dinner I went to look for him ...'

'It wasn't your fault,' said Rachel helplessly. She hadn't even heard of an attack at Rose Hill. She heard no news at all, now the Surgeon had gone. The French might be invading and who would think to tell the woman who had once been housekeeper to the Surgeon?

'The natives had stripped the crop, every cob of it. And there he was ...'

'Shh. It's all right now. You're here, you're safe.' She hesitated. 'Perhaps you can sell the farm.'

'Captain Patterson has given it to someone else.'

'But he can't do that! You should have been able to sell the land and house at least —'

'He can do whatever he likes,' said Maria wearily. 'A woman can't own land, not without the Governor's special permit. And we have no Governor.' She stroked Andrew's cheek. 'He has grown so much. Such a handsome boy.' She looked up at Rachel. 'I will work hard.'

Rachel shook her head. 'We will share what we have, and the work too. You can do sewing again. And when I am rich,' she tried to make Maria smile, 'you shall make all my silk dresses.'

'I can at least make Andrew's first pair of trousers. It … it is good to be back,' she said softly. 'I was scared out there, even before the attacks. So much space, too many trees. Jack was a good man. But milking cows, stripping the cobs of corn … I'm too small to be a proper farmer's wife. I even missed the o'possum.'

'He's not been seen since the Surgeon left.' No more o'possum droppings to sweep up each morning, no wet patches on the floor … 'We'll do well,' she told Maria softly. 'We will do very well.'

Chapter 53

RACHEL

February was the hardest month in the colony. A blanket of humid air sat about the town, sending the sweat dripping down her petticoats, sealing in the stench of sewage, cooking smoke and filthy clothes and bodies. But here was magic to sweep away a few of the smells ...

Soap! Rachel stood in the tiny shop and cradled the precious stuff. At last there was enough fat to spare in the colony to make soap! No more straining the wood ashes for the lye that burnt her hands and wore the clothes to shreds too soon. Real soap!

She had left Andrew playing with Maria — he was at the age when he was into everything and, besides, there had been a fresh outbreak of typhus when the convicts from the *Marquis Cornwallis* arrived. It wasn't safe for a small child to come near crowds now. Thank goodness she had someone she trusted to leave him with, someone to talk to as they sat sewing in the shade of the orchard, hoping for a breeze up from the harbour, watching Andrew chase the rooster, trying to get a tail feather.

Free rations were still given out in the storehouse up the hill, though now there were also government stores at Rose Hill — no, she corrected herself: Parramatta. Only convicts and government servants received rations these days. Convicts who had served their terms — like her — and become farmers or tradesmen or labourers either grew, made or hunted what they needed, or bought it at stores like this.

But the prices were far higher than most could afford. The Rum Corps had ruled that everything in the colony had to be sold either by the Corps or with their permit, under pain of the lash or serving in chains on the road gangs. Every farmer, soap-maker and sea captain had to sell his goods to the Corps at whatever small price the officers set. The Corps then resold the goods at ten or even fifty times the price.

The colony's new Governor, Mr Hunter, was powerless against so many officers. His authority came from halfway across the world, with no one to enforce it. So the officers of the Rum Corps grew richer still and it was more dangerous than ever to live in the colony.

Rachel was careful, only ever going out in the mornings when most soldiers would still be sleeping off the rum from the night before. Maria never went into the streets at all, though she was happier now. Yesterday Rachel had even heard her singing a song to Andrew.

And it had been a good morning — a meeting with Mrs Johnson about a home for the orphaned children. Somehow in the past year Rachel had become part of what passed for reputable society in the colony — a regular churchgoer with good manners and careful ways, respectable enough to drink Indian tea with the Reverend's wife and admire the new glass in the church windows.

And now soap! It had been expensive, but worth it. And there was little else to spend money on. Surgeon White still found ways to send sea chests to them on almost every ship, filled with cloth and sugar and even once a small box of tea. She headed towards the door, the soap in her reticule, brushing past a man in a top hat. He lifted it politely as he stepped out of her way.

It was Mr Moore.

Rachel gave a startled curtsey. Mr Moore lifted his hat again and bowed. He was dressed more formally than he had been before, in new-looking dark trousers and a dark coat, as well as the top hat. She was just about to speak when a young woman in a bonnet that certainly hadn't been made in the colony raised her gloved hand to signal him, over at the counter where she was examining a bolt of flannel cloth.

'If you will excuse me, Mistress Turner.' Mr Moore bowed again, then headed over to the young woman.

Rachel forced herself out of the store, her face burning. It's just the heat, she told herself. She should have brought a parasol to shade herself from the sun.

She had waited for weeks for Mr Moore to call again, after his astonishing rescue of Maria. But there had been no sign of him, either at their house or around the streets of the small colony. She supposed his ship had sailed again.

And now he was back, with a wife perhaps, or at least walking out with a woman younger and better dressed than her.

She tried to laugh at herself. What had she expected? That his impulsive speech so many years before had really been a promise?

And what if it had been? She had told him she wouldn't be any man's sea-wife. But what had she been to Surgeon White? He must know about that now. What man would take on another's child?

Well, plenty, she admitted, especially when the woman had a good house and income from her former lover. But not one she'd want. Not a man like Mr Moore, well-dressed and not a convict.

She glanced back, in case he and his lady friend had come out of the shop. But there was no sign of them.

She sighed and walked back up the hill. A crowd had gathered. Someone was being tied to the stake near Government House. Probably some poor fool who had sworn at his master — you got fifty lashes with the cat-o'-nine-tails for that, and 150 for taking a day off. That was enough to cripple or even kill you unless the flogger allowed you to take your punishment over a few weeks.

She heard the high-pitched song of the lash as the flogger swung it through the air, the first scream from the man at the stake. The crowd cheered. Floggings were the chief entertainment in Sydney Town, apart from getting drunk, and watching hangings. There'd be blood on the ground tomorrow.

It was a good thing she hadn't brought Andrew with her today. Rachel hurried down the dusty lane to home.

Mr Moore was on her doorstep five weeks later.

If I'd known I would have put on a clean apron, she thought, glancing down at the carrot stains from Andrew's dinner. She'd have put on her best cap too, the one Maria had trimmed with real lace ...

Behind her came the stamp of the hornpipe in the kitchen. Nanberry was back from his latest voyage, bringing her a bolt of blue cloth from the Cape that Maria had pounced upon with joy, planning the dresses she'd make for them both, and a carved elephant for Andrew. Nanberry had already been out bush for a week, returning with more honey and a fish so large she'd had to give half of it away. He'd sharpened the knives (Big Lon ground down half the blades if it was left to him), mended the broken shutter, shown Andrew how to swim and even persuaded Maria to join them in a picnic at the beach. Now he was dancing to amuse young Andrew, the child shrieking with joy every time Nanberry clapped his hands and turned around. She could hear Maria's laughter too.

It was so good to hear Maria laugh again.

'Mr Moore! May I help you?' He might need to see a surgeon, she thought suddenly. That would be why he was here. 'Surgeon White no longer lives here,' she added, 'but if you go to the hospital …'

'I have no need of a doctor.' He bowed. He wore the same dark suit as he had in the shop, and the same top hat. He didn't look like a sailor now. 'Good morning, Mistress Turner.'

She gave a small polite curtsey. She hesitated. 'Would you care to come in?'

The neighbours would talk if they saw her chatting with a man on her doorstep. It would be more discreet if he came inside. Maria and Nanberry were here, so she was chaperoned. Not that many would care in this colony of whores and convicts. But there were a few, like Mrs Johnson, whose opinion she valued. She put her chin up. And her own …

She took his hat and hung it on the peg next to Nanberry's, then led him into the parlour. It was the room that had been the Surgeon's study and still smelt a little of the spirit he'd used to preserve his specimens. But she and Maria had made cushions for the hard-backed chairs and Nanberry had made a frame for one of Maria's embroideries on the wall. It was too hot for a fire, so she had arranged a bottle of roses in the hearth.

'Please sit down, Mr Moore. I'll fetch tea.' She hoped there was some tea left. And that Nanberry hadn't eaten all the hearth cakes.

No, there were still some on the plate on the kitchen table, rich with currants and candied lemon peel. The Surgeon had sent the currants and lemon peel too. She emptied the dregs of sarsaparilla flowers, the Surgeon's favourite of the native herbs, from the teapot into the slops bucket. She then began hunting for the tea caddy.

Nanberry looked up, a giggling Andrew in his arms. 'Who is here?'

Rachel found she was blushing. 'Mr Thomas Moore. He's the man who rescued Maria. He's a ship's carpenter. I met him at church.' She didn't say it had been over three years earlier.

'He's a good man. I'll make the tea,' said Maria firmly. She had already heard the tale of how Mr Moore and Rachel had first met.

'Please, come and join us —'

'I think it's you he wants to see,' said Maria quietly. 'Nanberry and I will watch Andrew. You go into the parlour and sit down.'

Rachel nodded, flustered.

'You call me if he gives trouble,' muttered Nanberry.

She smiled at that, thinking of the big hunting spear in his room, up on the wall out of Andrew's reach. Nanberry was so young, and so protective. But he *would* protect her too, not that she thought she needed help with Mr Moore. She straightened her cap again as she went into the parlour.

Mr Moore looked too big for the chair, his hands thick and red after the Surgeon's long fingers, which were white from being scrubbed so often every day. He stood as she came in and sat only after she was seated.

'You'll be wondering why I'm here, Mistress Turner.'

'To ask how Maria is, perhaps?'

'I'm here to court you,' he said simply.

She stared. Whatever she had expected, it wasn't this. 'I beg your pardon?' she asked faintly.

'To court you. I think you know what that means. We sit and talk over a cup of your tea. We take a walk each afternoon. And at the end of it all, if we suit — and I think we will — I ask you to marry me. My intentions are honourable, Mistress Turner.'

He smiled, but she could tell there was tension there too. 'You said when we met that day that you would be no man's sea-wife. So here I am. I waited till I had all that I promised you. I've a shore job now — I'm a colonial carpenter, with a good brick house in three acres of orchard and garden up at the top of the Tank Stream. I've applied for a land grant too —'

'Sir, I'm sorry.' She had to stop his catalogue of assets. 'Why?'

'Why do I want to marry you?'

She nodded, though there were other questions too.

He considered. 'I saw you walking up that road and thought: That's the woman I want to marry.'

'That's all it took? One look at a pretty face?' At least she hoped she had been pretty, hoped she was still pretty now.

He smiled at that. 'You're beautiful,' he said. 'But it were more than that. I saw you stop to give something to children who had nothing — and you gave it with a smile, not the pursed lips of duty.

'You looked like a miracle, Mistress Turner. There was Sydney Town filled with red-faced drabs in dirty petticoats. There was you, all clean and shiny-haired, your skirts mended even if they were no fine lady's clothes. I thought: Here's a lass who is kind, who can work, who is proud of who she is and what she can be.'

'Mr Moore …' He knew nothing of her, she thought. Not about her years with Surgeon White, that Andrew was her son, not a child she had been looking after …

But before she could say anything else Maria appeared, holding a tray with the pot and cups and a jug of milk and the sugar bowl, with Nanberry behind holding the plate of hearth cakes.

'Mr Moore, you must remember my friend, Mrs Jackson, who you rescued so nobly. This is my ... my foster son, Nanberry White.' She had never used the term before, but it was true, she thought. Nanberry was her foster son now as much as he had been the Surgeon's.

Mr Moore stood up again. He bowed to Maria. 'I'm right glad to see you looking so well, Mrs Jackson.'

Maria curtseyed. 'If I am, it's thanks to you, sir.'

'It were my privilege. And Mr White.' He bowed again to Nanberry. Rachel was glad to see him polite to a man with dark skin. 'I hear your foster father was a good man. The Captain of the *Brilliant* spoke well of you too.'

Nanberry bowed in return, with the perfect formality he could assume when he liked. Mr Moore looked back at Rachel. 'And your son, Mistress Turner? I would very much like to see him again too.'

So he must know that Andrew was the Surgeon's son. Must know that she and the Surgeon had never been married; that she had given the Surgeon what she had told Mr Moore she would give no man without a ring.

She felt her knees tremble. She sat, quickly, as he pulled a small carved boat from his pocket. 'I made this myself, Mistress Turner. I hope your son likes it.'

He smiled, aware of her shock. 'There are no children's toys for sale yet in the colony. But there will be one day. One day I reckon you'll be able to buy anything here in Sydney Town that you can in London.'

'This place?' Maria shook her head.

'We have the best harbour in the world, Mrs Jackson. That's all a town needs to become a city. That and good grazing and whales in the water.'

A cry came from the kitchen — Andrew, feeling neglected.

He toddled in, one shoe off, his face smeared with jam. He glanced at the stranger then at Nanberry. 'Dance!' he commanded.

Nanberry looked at Rachel, then at Mr Moore. Nanberry took Andrew's hand. 'We'll dance in the kitchen,' he said. Maria gave another small curtsey and followed them out.

Mr Moore met Rachel's eyes. 'You can find many things in the stores of Sydney Town, gossip being one of them. It is still small enough here for everyone to know his neighbours' business.'

She tried to keep the flush from her cheeks. 'What do you know about me, then?'

He hesitated. 'Mistress Turner, your case at the Old Bailey made you famous for a time. A servant girl betrayed by her master, defended by a man in court.'

Her flush grew deeper. 'I wasn't guilty of the crime, but I wasn't innocent either. The Master gave me those gifts for a reason and I accepted them. And I lived with Surgeon White as his wife, with no wedding ring.'

'But you've lived with no man since. I've lived a long time without marrying, Mistress Turner, back and forth on whatever ships will pay me best. Maybe by now I don't think of marriage the way a young man might, back in England. I don't want a young innocent. I want ...'

He struggled to find the words.

'Someone to trust? To talk about your day with? To share your life with?' It was what she wanted, so desperately, she thought.

He grinned at her. Despite his many voyages, his teeth were still good. 'See? I knew we'd be well matched. You're highly thought of, Mistress Turner. A woman I would be proud to have as my wife.'

She still couldn't believe it. 'You could have anyone. Far younger than me,' she added frankly. 'I ... I saw you with a young lady in the store that day.'

He laughed. 'That's Mrs Marsden, the new clergyman's wife. I'm sure you'll meet her soon. I offered her an escort through the streets while her husband was away. As I said, I weren't coming to you till I had my shore job and my house.'

'You could set up in business back in England.'

'And be a workman all my life? Can you read, Mistress Turner?'

'I've taught myself a bit, the last few years. I'm no hand at writing though.'

'I can do neither, though I can do some figuring. But here I can make myself a gentleman. There's land grants and free labour from the convicts. There's mills hungry for wool back in England and we can send it to 'em. The colony needs ships and I can make 'em. By the time we've been ten years wed you'll have a diamond necklace, I promise you that. And I keep my promises.'

He does, she thought. At least he'd kept this one.

'And you haven't said no,' he added with satisfaction.

She hadn't, she realised. She had doubted he knew what he was doing. But it had never occurred to her to say no.

'There's no hurry,' he said gently. He looked like a man who was used to getting his own way. But it would be a good way and he would be kind to all about him.

He stood up. She had a feeling he wasn't a man to sit still long. 'How about we take young Andrew to see if this boat I've made will sail in the stream? It'd be a poor lookout if a boatbuilder made a toy boat that sank. We need to give it a trial, before I make a bigger one.'

It was a joke, she thought. He was laughing. To her surprise she found she was smiling too.

'I'll get my bonnet,' she said.

They married the next January, in the Reverend Johnson's new church. It hurt, a little, to leave the Surgeon's house, to see new folks move in there.

But Mr Moore's house was bigger, with rooms for Andrew and Maria and Nanberry too, as well as rooms off the kitchen for a maid and a man to do the heavy work. There were silk carpets from China and carved chests from India, bought on his travels; a set of fine porcelain dishes that he'd found in a foreign port and carried to Sydney Town in his sea chests. But best was the furniture he had made with his own hands in the last few months — the tables, the bedsteads, as well as the carved shelves he had made during many long days and nights at sea.

Yes, this man knew exactly what he was doing. He dreamt of it, he planned it and then he did it.

But more than that, he was honourable and generous. I have been lucky, she thought. Three men in my life and two have been kind. This last was the kindest of all.

Her life was so rich now. Rich in friends, in good deeds, a grand colony to build, her husband, and her son.

Chapter 54

ANDREW

SYDNEY COVE, JANUARY 1798

A hand on his arm woke him. Andrew saw his brother's face, grinning at him from above the bed. Sometimes visitors stared when he said that Nanberry was his brother, because Nanberry had black skin. But Nanberry was the best brother in the world.

'Wake up,' whispered Nanberry.

'Why?'

'Shh. Don't let anybody hear.'

Andrew sat up. Dawn was a grey haze behind the window shutters. 'It's still night.'

'No, it isn't. It's almost dawn. The best time of the day to go hunting.'

'Hunting!'

His brother grinned again. 'Would you like to hunt with me? Or stay and do lessons with Mama?'

'Go hunting,' said Andrew. He blinked at Nanberry's spear. 'Can I use that today?'

'One day. Not yet. A warrior has much to learn before he may use a spear.'

Andrew swung out of bed and reached for his boots.

'No boots,' said Nanberry softly. 'Animals hear boots. They smell them too.'

'My boots aren't smelly!' Papa Moore had bought them from an American whaler last week. Mama said no boy in the colony had boots as fine as these.

Papa Moore was the best man in the colony. He could make ships and carve a penny whistle and he let Andrew ride on his shoulders and pretend he was a horse. Most men in the colony were drunk most of the time. Like all Sydney Town children Andrew had learnt early how to tell when a man was angry drunk, and to stay clear of fists and kicks.

But Papa was never drunk. He laughed a lot too. Andrew hardly ever saw grown-up men laugh, unless they were drunk, except Nanberry.

Now Nanberry looked at him as though they shared a private joke. 'Your boots are smelly to animals.'

Nanberry waited while Andrew pulled on his shirt and trousers. He was proud of them. It wasn't so long ago he'd worn a little boy's smock. He followed Nanberry down the stairs as quietly as he could.

Nanberry paused in the kitchen and propped a piece of paper on the table. Andrew tried to read it, but there were too many big words.

'It says I have taken you for a walk,' said Nanberry. 'A friend wrote it for me yesterday.'

'Why don't you learn to write? Papa Moore is learning. Mama writes beautiful letters, now, all curly.'

'Anyone can do my writing and my reading. I know other things.'

It was cool outside, the breeze from the south still blowing, and fresh, the cook fires still smouldering under their banks of night ashes. They walked swiftly up past the headwaters of the Tank Stream, down a gully and over two hills.

A shadow moved from the trees towards them. Andrew stopped.

It was a native savage. A stranger. Mama warned him never to talk to strangers. The boy looked to be a couple of years older than him.

Andrew took it for granted that almost everyone around was guilty of some crime, except Papa and the Reverend Johnson and Mrs Johnson, and the Governor, Mr Hunter. Even most of the officers were what Papa called *thieves and bounders*.

Andrew wasn't sure what a bounder was. Maybe it meant they were good at jumping. Though there wasn't a law against jumping, was there?

Strange natives could kill you with their spears. At least this boy had no spear.

Nanberry took Andrew's hand, as though he knew that he was scared. 'This is your friend,' he said.

'I don't know him!'

'You will know him after today.' Nanberry knelt down to Andrew's level, as the native boy walked towards them. 'Andrew, I have to go away tomorrow on the *Reliance*. When I get back ...' He hesitated. 'I have to see my own people then.' He shook his head. 'I am a sailor and a warrior. There isn't time to show you the things you need to learn.'

'Papa Moore says I will have a tutor —'

'Not for these things.' The native boy had come up to them now. He stood listening, though Andrew thought he didn't understand the words Nanberry was saying. Most natives didn't know proper words, Maria said, only their own savage tongue.

'You were born in this land, Andrew. Your body is made of its earth, just as mine is. I remember that when I am travelling. You must remember it too.'

240

Andrew nodded. It didn't make sense. But so much adults said didn't make sense.

'Garudi learns things from his clan. Now you are his friend he will teach them to you.'

Andrew looked at the boy suspiciously. He was naked, like most of the savages. His hair was tangled. His feet looked as though they had never worn boots at all. How could a boy like this teach him anything?

The boy looked back, equally suspicious.

'Come,' said Nanberry. He spoke more words to Garudi, a long patter of words that sounded like o'possums' grunts, not real words at all.

The boys followed him into the shadows of the trees.

The horizon was pink now, out at the edge of the sky and sea. The day was warming up. Nanberry stopped and put his hand up for silence. He pointed to a pile of rocks.

Garudi grinned. Andrew looked at him with dislike. What was funny about a pile of rocks?

He looked at the rocks more closely. There were faint scratches …

Suddenly something moved between the rocks. Nanberry froze. So did Garudi; they were almost not breathing like they had become rocks too, or trees. Andrew tried to do the same.

Nanberry pounced. He held something up in triumph.

It was a goanna almost as long as Andrew, with great sharp claws and a snake head and skin like old grey lace. It wriggled a bit as Nanberry held it up, but not too much.

Garudi said something.

Nanberry spoke to Andrew. 'A good hunter doesn't run. He waits. Waits by a waterhole for the animals to drink. Waits where he sees o'possum scratches or where goanna claws have been. This *gan* has been asleep all night, when it was cold. He sleeps all winter too. But when the rock is warm in summer he comes out early. But he is still too asleep to try to fight me.'

Nanberry casually whacked the creature's head against the rock. The skull cracked, and Andrew stared as blood seeped through the skin.

Nanberry grinned. 'Now we make a fire.'

~⁂~

The remains of the goanna lay by the ashes of the fire, shreds of skin and bones, the skull and claws. Flies buzzed about it, sounding lazy in the heat.

Andrew felt sleepy too. He lay back against a tree, like Nanberry and Garudi. The goanna had tasted strange: food in a dream. It tasted like smoke, like dirt, like animal. He had never tasted meat that tasted of animal before. Vaguely he knew that lamb chops came from sheep, and salt beef from cattle. But to pluck the meat straight from the body ...

It had tasted good.

Nanberry's eyes slid open. 'Would you like the claws?'

'Why?'

'For a necklace. Or to wear on a string around your waist.'

Andrew considered. 'Do you think Mama would let me keep them?' he asked cautiously.

Nanberry laughed. 'No.' He looked at Andrew seriously. 'Some things women don't need to know.'

'What about Papa Moore?'

'He is from the land called England. He doesn't know these things either.'

'Papa Moore knows lots of things!'

'He does. But not these.'

Garudi was awake now. He looked at Andrew with what might have been contempt. He spoke again in the strange language. Andrew was starting to make out word shapes in it.

'What did he say?'

'He said you were a little caterpillar who doesn't know how to break out of its cocoon.'

'Is that bad?'

'Yes.'

'Well, he is a savage who doesn't know how to ... to brush his hair or wear clothes.'

Nanberry looked from boy to boy. At last he said, 'We'll go swimming. Come on.'

It was a cove several bays along from the houses. The cliffs seemed too steep, the boulders too piled up to get down. But Nanberry knew a way. The boys followed him.

Below the cliffs a tiny curve of sand edged the waves. Nanberry unbuckled his belt, took off his trousers and then his shirt. Garudi had already waded into the water and plunged under the lapping waves. Now his head burst into the sunlight again.

Only savages swam naked. Only savages swam, though Mama let him swim with Nanberry. He thrust his trousers down and pulled off his shirt. He ran to the highest boulder, then glanced at Nanberry for approval.

Nanberry nodded.

Andrew dived, just as Nanberry had shown him before Christmas, jumping up then swooping down. I am a dolphin, he thought. I am a whale. His head burst into the water, bubbles all around him. He let himself rise, his feet treading water, to find Garudi staring at him and Nanberry smiling on the shore.

He laughed for the first time that day. Garudi couldn't dive! Suddenly the day seemed full of light. He splashed Garudi, saw him grin through the water dripping down his face, dived under the water again and grabbed Garudi's legs. They came up kicking and splashing at each other, in the bright, clear water.

But Garudi was laughing too. Andrew thought: This means that we are friends.

Chapter 55

ANDREW

The kookaburras were calling. A splatter of pebbles against the shutters woke Andrew up. He opened them and peered down, in time to see Garudi vanish into the orchard.

He grinned. He never knew when Garudi might be able to come into the township. Sometimes it seemed his family spent long months in other places. But then there'd be the pebbles on the shutters before the colony was awake.

It had been two years since Nanberry had told him Garudi was his friend. They hadn't been friends, not really at first. But now they were. Garudi had shown him how to catch bandicoots in traps made from woven tussocks, and how to climb a tree and capture a bungu, which was the native name for an o'possum.

But fishing was best. Nanberry had shown them both how to spear fish the last time he had been back onshore. For some reason Garudi didn't have spears of his own, even if he was a black savage. Andrew wondered if Garudi's family thought he was too young.

Even the black savages had rules about what children could do, just like Mama and Papa Moore made rules. Mama and Papa made funny rules sometimes, like not jumping in mud puddles or throwing horse pies at the seagulls.

They gave reasons for other rules though, like not playing with the convict children in case he caught diseases or with the orphans who clustered by the taverns begging for pennies, in case a drunk man hurt him.

He and Garudi had to wait till Nanberry came back before they could use the spears again. Unless ...

Andrew hesitated, then grinned.

He wriggled out of his nightdress and into his trousers then stared down at his boots. Mama told him over and over he must wear boots, but you couldn't feel the mud squish between your toes in boots. Why did he have to wear boots, when almost every other child in the whole of New South Wales went barefoot? His feet felt like they had to lug a ball and chain around. But Mama said the boots showed he was a gentleman's son, and not a convict brat.

Finally he picked up his boots in his hand. He would hide them under a bush and put them on before he came home. Mama would never know he hadn't been wearing them.

He listened at Mama's bedroom door, but all he could hear were Papa Moore's snores.

He tiptoed down the stairs.

Andrew knew he had another father too, a gentleman, the man who sent them money and presents on every ship, and a letter to him, signed 'your loving father', which Mama would read to him, over and over till he knew it by heart.

Father sounded like a nice man. It was good to have two fathers. Mama said that many boys in the colony had no father to look after them at all.

He made his way over the smooth boards of the kitchen to Nanberry's room. In their old house Nanberry had slept in the room next to his but in Papa Moore's house he had to sleep down here, like Cook. He listened. Cook and the other servants were asleep too.

He reached for two of the spears Nanberry kept on his wall. He would have liked to take the giant hunting spear, but Nanberry had never let him touch that, or Garudi either. He took the two lighter fishing spears instead. Even they were longer than Andrew, of the hardest wood he had ever felt, so hard it didn't bend, with barbs halfway up made of fish bone, and more barbs at the tip. He lifted them reverently down.

He tiptoed out into the kitchen. He knew he'd get into trouble for missing out on his morning lesson with Mr Flitch. But it was worth it. What would Garudi say when he saw the spears?

He looked around the kitchen. There was fresh bread in the sack from yesterday's baking, and cheese, cold mutton chops and cold corncobs in the fly-proof safe hanging outside in the cool under the eaves. He helped himself to bread and cheese, then stuck the corncobs in his pocket. Garudi loved corn ...

The muddy path was cold under his feet as he ran between the houses. He could smell ripe peaches, stronger scented than the apples hanging on the trees. Houses gave way to huts, fields of corn tall now in midsummer, rows of cabbages. Then the fields were behind him. He ran down towards the cove that Nanberry had shown them, so long ago. It was their secret place now.

Garudi was sitting on the rock above the water, waiting for him. He wore what he usually did: nothing much, just a belt of twisted hair around his waist with a scrap of leather twisted between his legs and an armband of feathers and hair.

He grinned, his teeth very white in his dark face.

'Andrew!'

It was one of the few words of English Garudi knew. Andrew knew that Nanberry wanted him to teach Garudi English. But somehow words never seemed important when you were tracking wallabies or collecting mussels in the mud.

Garudi pointed at the spears, and did a little dance of joy. Andrew joined him, dancing too, holding the spears up above his head. It was as though they danced with the waves and the spray, like the fish swimming in the cool green water. There were many ways to talk to each other when you didn't have words, many ways to show that you were happy.

At last Andrew handed Garudi one of the spears. Garudi took it, solemn now. Andrew felt a thrill run through him. Mama would have pink kittens if she knew he was using a spear.

Andrew grinned. Mama said don't go down to the wharves — the sailors will kidnap you for a cabin boy. Don't go swimming if Nanberry isn't with you. But she had never told him not to go spearing fish with a native boy.

He tried to copy Garudi's stillness as he held the spear. That's what you had to do to spear a fish — stand quite still, so the fish didn't guess there was danger above.

The tiny waves swept in and out, pricked with foam. The water was clear enough to see down to the rocky bottom. But there were no fish.

Suddenly something swam into sight. A fish ... but too small. Not worth spearing ... too hard a target to hit too, he admitted. But big fish usually followed little fish ...

And there they were, a shoal of big 'uns, their scales sparkling silver and blue. Garudi moved a second before he did. Both spears flew into the water.

Andrew held his breath.

The water swirled, too thick with foam to see what had happened. Andrew waded into the water, his eyes half expecting to see his floating spear ...

But there were no spears to be seen. Just red speckled water, and then two fish, breathing in agony. Triumph filled him. He felt like leaping, roaring from the water. Instead he laughed. Garudi laughed too. Laughing was another way to talk when you had no words. They both bent to the water again.

The wounded fish were tiring now. The other fish had swum away in terror. The bloody water grew still. Andrew reached down, till his head was under the water too, and grabbed his spear as the dying fish twisted past. It took all his strength to stop the fish from wriggling off, taking the spear with it. But by the time he had lifted it from the water the fish was dead.

He pulled out the spear proudly, trying not to tear more of the flesh as the barbs came out. The fish was as long as his arm, with two rows of small sharp teeth. Its scales were already turning dull. Garudi's fish was smaller. Andrew wondered whether it was best to have caught the bigger fish, or have the skill to spear a smaller one.

It didn't matter.

His wet clothes turned the breeze from the sea cold. As there was no one to see him here, he took off his shirt and trousers, and laid them on a rock to dry; he was even more naked now than Garudi. He felt the sun on his skin as they crouched above the tiny fire Garudi made under the cliffs, piling on dried bark and shreds of driftwood, then touching the bark with a glowing coal held in a piece of bone till the first sparks flashed up into the air, followed by a flame.

The dry driftwood gave no smoke, so no one would see it from the town. The boys threaded their catch on green wattle branches, then propped the spits up on a rock to grill the fish above the fire. The scales smoked and blackened, easy to pull off to get to the white flesh below.

Later they lay on the sun-warmed rock, and watched a big ship come in — not another whaler, or a sealer. It flew the English flag, not an American one. Maybe it brought more convicts, Andrew thought idly. There might even be another present from his father and a letter and new things to buy in the stores, like the gingerbread and barley sugar he once found there.

What would it be like to sail on one of those big ships? Nanberry said sailing was exciting. Mama said that it was horrid. You starved and the journey went on for month after month, the waves making you sick, with smells and vomit.

But Mama had been a convict (though that had been a mistake, of course, because Mama never did anything wrong). It might be different when you were a sailor (though Mama made sure Nanberry took lots of dried fruit and portable soup, every time he went to sea) or a respected passenger like his father had been.

One day, he thought, when I've learnt my letters properly, I'll write to Father and ask him what it was like to sail here, then sail back to England.

Sand seemed to have crept into all the crevices of his body, even though the cove was mostly rock. The waves seeped out, showing a gentle slope of stone, covered in jagged oyster shells. Andrew would have liked to spear another fish, to take to Mama or maybe just for fun. But for some reason Garudi never took more than one and Andrew couldn't give Mama a fish with a great gash in its middle without telling her how he'd got it.

He had forgotten the corn. He pulled the cobs from his pocket. The two boys gnawed on them, then threw the leftovers into the waves and watched the cobs bob back and forth, before finally drifting out into the harbour.

Would the chewed corncobs float out across the harbour to the sea eventually? wondered Andrew. All the way to England, maybe, the mysterious land where gentlemen lived; the place the convict hulks came from, bringing their starving, white-faced loads.

It was late afternoon when he headed back, leaving Garudi clambering along the cliffs towards the south. He hid the spears under some rocks — someone would see them if he took them back now. He'd have to retrieve them tomorrow, before anyone was up. His face felt hot from too much wind and sun. His shirt was stiff with salt. His head ached a bit.

He should have worn his hat, but it was bad enough being burdened with shirt and trousers. Lucky Garudi, who could wear a twist of leather on a thong around his waist; who could spend the whole day spearing fish and wandering along the shore.

What does Garudi do at night? he wondered. There were lots of natives in Sydney Town these days, but mostly drunk like the white men, around the taverns. He wondered if Garudi's mama told him, 'No playing with the convict brats. Don't go near the taverns!' too.

Garudi *did* have a mama, didn't he? Garudi looked too happy to be like the orphans who sat begging by the taverns, or picked coves' pockets, and curled up in doorways to sleep.

He could smell dinner when he opened the door. Beef and onions — Papa's favourite. He wondered if there'd be jam pudding too. But he'd eaten too much fish to feel hungry.

He peered into the parlour. Mama sat in the big soft chair one of Papa's ships had brought last year, reading a sheet of paper covered in tiny writing, then written crossways too, to save paper and ink.

He waited for Mama to scold him. But instead she just sat there, looking at the paper in her hand.

'Mama? Is that from my father in England?'

She held the letter to her, not even asking where he'd been. What was wrong with her? 'Yes, it's from your father. But it's to me, not you.'

'Can I read it?'

'I ... I don't know.'

Andrew stared. Mama never sounded unsure.

'Father is all right, isn't he?'

'Yes,' she said absently. 'He's well. He's moved to a new house.'

'That's what he wrote to you about?'

'Yes. No.' She seemed to look at him for the first time. 'Andrew! Look at the state of you! Where have you been all day? You haven't been playing with the convict brats, have you?'

'No, Mama,' he said truthfully.

'Well. You go and wash now. It'll be dinner soon.'

Suddenly the smell of fatty meat made him feel sick. 'I'm not hungry.'

'Not hungry? After being out all day?' She laid her hand across his forehead. 'You've got a fever,' she said with sudden worry. 'Too much sun …' Her touch was gentle now. 'You go get into bed. I'll bring some supper up. Some toast and treacle, how is that? Your papa brought some treacle today.'

Papa … Father … Mama, all close and worried. His head thudded. Too much sun. He nodded and headed out the back to the washtub.

~ ❦ ~

The voices woke him. Or maybe it was the pain in his head, behind his eyes. The darkness swirled around him.

'… another letter from his father.'

'What does it say?'

'He is getting married.' There was a strange note in her voice.

Papa Moore's voice sounded strange too. 'Rachel … do you mind? Do you still love the man?'

Mama laughed, but it almost sounded like crying too. 'No. Of course not. I never loved him in the way that I love you. I … I admire you too, Thomas. You know how much.'

'Then what is it?' Papa's voice was gentle now.

'His father insists I put Andrew on the next ship to England. To live with him and his new wife. Thomas, he's only six years old!'

Papa's voice, heavy and trying to comfort. 'You always knew this day would come.'

'But not so soon! He's still too young! I can't let him go. I can't!'

'You must do what's best for him, Rachel. A fine home, a gentleman for a father, a stepmother who will treat him as her own —'

'But he is mine! Not hers!'

'I love the lad too. The last thing I want is to see you weeping. But think of the opportunities Andrew will have in England. A proper school.' There was silence, and then he added, 'He'll be an English gentleman, Rachel. Something I can never be.'

'You're a better man than any English gentleman. No! He won't go! Not yet!'

'Rachel ...' There was something in Papa's voice he had never heard. 'Andrew's father is a man of influence. If you refuse to send his son he can force you to do it. All it needs is a letter to the Governor.'

There was silence, except for what might have been a sob.

Andrew lay back on his pillow. His head seemed to burst with the news.

Go to England? Vanish on one of the big ships with flapping sails, creaking its way out across the harbour? Was there even such a place as England?

Leave Mama? Leave home? He couldn't! They wouldn't ...

'Mama?' He hadn't meant to call her, but the swirling darkness frightened him, and the pain in his head. 'Mama!'

'What is it?'

Mama appeared at the door, a candle in her hand.

'Mama ... is it true? Do I have to go to England?'

She caught her breath. 'Maybe. Some day. But not yet.'

'I don't want to go! Not ever!' He tried not to cry. Big boys never cried. 'People die on ships. Nanberry said so many sailors die sometimes they can hardly make it to harbour.'

'Nanberry shouldn't fill you with such tales.' She rubbed her forehead, as she usually did when she was upset. Her face looked strange, as though she was swimming under the sea. Like a fish, he thought. He felt so hot.

'I don't want to die on a ship. I don't want to leave you.' He could see the tears on her face in the candlelight. Or was it a candle? Maybe it was a sun ...

'Andrew, all we can do is pray. Have you heard of guardian angels?'

'Yes, Mama.' The Reverend Johnson had talked about them at church service. Mostly Andrew didn't listen at church, but he had that day.

'We will pray that your guardian angel will look after you.' She shut her eyes briefly. 'It is all that we can do.'

'Mama ...?'

'What is it, darling?'

'There is a sun in my bed. A hot sun. Do you think my angel put it there?'

'A sun? What are you talking about?'

She bent and touched his forehead. 'He's burning up! Fetch the doctor ... Mr Balmain! He'll come ...'

Chapter 56

RACHEL

She sat with her son as he burnt and muttered. Typhus, Mr Balmain had said. Mr Balmain had been no friend to Surgeon White, but she knew he'd help his son now.

Typhus came with each convict ship, blazing its way through the colony, then dying out until the next ship arrived. Typhus killed more than half the adults who caught it and nearly every child.

Her child. Her precious child. He couldn't die.

She bent her head, feeling the tears cold on her cheeks. How could she live without him? Day after day, year after year, when he was simply … not.

If only she could keep every day of his six years with her, like you stored butter in a well, days that she could take out and live again. But you never paid attention when you should. You spent the days cooking, washing, brushing your hair. Stupid things, when you could have been watching your son.

She knew there would never be another child. Not for her.

There was nothing she could do. Wash his face and chest to try to keep the fever down, bundle him in rugs when the chills came, reassure him when he screamed in his delirium. Try to coax him to drink some boiled water, to eat a spoonful of stewed apple.

And pray.

It was her fault. Don't play with the convict brats, she'd said, as if that was enough to keep him safe. But the whole colony was a land of convicts and their diseases.

She should have sent him to England last year, when his father had first written about Andrew joining him. There'd even been a woman passenger, one of the officers' wives, who'd have looked after him, especially with the golden sovereigns his father sent. Andrew should have been in England now, in that fine brick house on the hill, being raised a gentleman, not running wild with muddy feet.

Not lying here, dying.

Her fault. All her fault.

She bent her head. 'If he lives,' she prayed, 'I will let him go. I promise. No matter how much it hurts, I will let him go.'

She opened her eyes. Somehow she had hoped that her prayer might have made a difference. But Andrew still lay there in a feverish sleep, from which it looked like he might never wake.

He needed fresh water. She stood, leaving the candle burning by the dish of stewed apples, went out to the kitchen and dipped the bowl into the bucket by the door. It wasn't till she was headed back that she saw the thing on the table.

A fish. A giant fish. Had a friend of her husband's brought it? But they would have left it covered in a cloth to keep off the flies. And this fish had a great gash in its side. It had been speared, she thought, not caught with a net or hook.

It was a mystery. But she had no time to spare for mysteries now. Still she stopped to put the fish away in the fly-proof safe.

255

Chapter 57

ANDREW

He was cold, then he was hot. He shivered when he was hot and sweated when he was cold and monsters lurked at the edges of the room, even when his eyes were shut.

He had to go. To death, to England, into the monsters' jaws, it didn't matter. All that was Andrew was going to vanish as though it had never been.

A monster growled at him; a monster with the face of one of the small green birds, a monster with a beak that clacked and chirped ...

He opened his eyes, hoping the monster would vanish.

It did. He was all alone. Tears sprang to his eyes. No Mama. No Papa, no Father, no Maria or Nanberry. He was going to die; and if he lived he would be sent away.

Alone. Alone.

Tears made the room shimmer. Something moved on the windowsill.

He blinked, trying to see more clearly.

It was … fuzzy … its shape indistinct in the darkness, but sort of golden with the brightness of the moon behind it. Like a halo, he thought dazedly. But only angels have haloes.

An angel in his room.

The angel gave a tiny growl. It lifted up his bowl of stewed apples and bent its head.

The door opened. The bowl clattered onto the floor, spilling the stewed apples.

Chapter 58

RACHEL

She caught a glimpse of an o'possum as she came in the door. A big old o'possum, bending down to eat stewed apples, just as the Surgeon's o'possum had, so many years before. The bowl crashed onto the floor. The animal vanished in a blur of fur.

Could it be the same one? She supposed so. Kangaroos and emus were never seen in the town these days, but there were o'possums in plenty, feeding on the fruit trees and the roses. She had no doubt that the Surgeon's o'possum had done very well. And it had loved stewed apples …

'Mama!'

Andrew struggled to sit up. She ran and put her arms around him. 'What is it?'

'Mama!' His voice was weak but steady. 'Mama, I saw an angel!'

'A what?' She wondered if he was still delirious. But his face looked cooler now.

'An angel,' he whispered. 'By my bed.'

She looked down at the broken bowl, at the scatter of droppings on the floor. 'That was no ...' She looked at her son again. His face was thin, and there were black shadows under his eyes. But the fever had broken. He looked at her in wonder.

'Is it my guardian angel? Just like Reverend Johnson said?'

'Reverend Johnson didn't mean ...' Or did he? she thought dazedly. Perhaps angels could come in many forms. Even as o'possums ...

She looked at her son. 'Yes,' she said steadily. 'Maybe it was your angel. I'm sure you have an angel who'll look after you.'

'Even if I go to England?'

'Yes.' It tore her heart to say the words. 'Even in England. Your angel will look after you. Your angel will bring you home.' He nodded, already half asleep. She settled him down on the pillow, swept his hair from his forehead with her fingers, then sat by the bed and watched him. The moon slid across the sky and the o'possum crashed from branch to branch.

Her son. Her wonderful, dear son. But she had promised. She had to think of him, not herself. She had to let him go.

Chapter 59

RACHEL

She hugged him before he got into the ship's boat to be rowed out to the *Brilliant*. He didn't like being hugged in public, not by his mama. But this time he hugged her back, as though he'd never let her go.

At last Nanberry put his hand on her shoulder. Nanberry was a fine young man now, tall and broad-shouldered, his hair caught back in a sailor's braid. Even the gap in his teeth made him look like a sailor who had lost a tooth to scurvy.

She nodded. 'I love you,' she whispered to her son. 'Stay safe.' Then she stepped back.

It was a silly request. She knew it. The dangers he was facing weren't ones he could avoid: the enormous waves that crushed a ship, the ice floes that might wreck it. How many ships had already been lost on their way to the colony or back? Had anyone even bothered to keep count?

Dysentery, ship's fever … She shut her eyes, then opened them again quickly, so as not to lose a second of these last moments watching her son, trying to keep the memory of his warmth on her skin.

The tiny boat bobbed on the waves. The rowers heaved at the oars. She watched as the boat reached the ship, out in the harbour, and as they climbed the rope ladder.

At last two figures stood by the rail: one small with white skin, one tall with black. They waved at her. She waved back.

The ship's sails had already been hoisted. She saw the anchor raised, dripping seaweed, saw the taller figure run off to his duties on the ship. But the small one stayed by the rail. The sails billowed. The ship glided across the blue. Then it rounded a headland and was gone.

She thrust her fist into her mouth so as not to cry out. Her son was gone. She forced herself not to think of shipwreck, his tiny body washed up blue on the ice; not to think of him bullied at school as a *convict brat*; not sick and calling for her, impossibly far away across the oceans.

No. She had to think of the man he could become; an old man with a grey beard perhaps, but still the same green eyes, laughing with his grandchildren at his knee. He would be a gentleman. He would be happy. He would be safe. He would survive.

But the boy she had waved away — the seven-year-old, with scabby knees, who'd played around the rocks and coves of this beautiful, alien harbour — that boy was lost to her forever.

She turned at last to go home and found her husband behind her. He must have waited there to let them have their last minutes alone; he had wished to let her drink in the last sight of her son, to make memories of his face she could call up when the pain grew too great.

Thomas folded her in his arms. He didn't say, 'We will have other children.' He knew it wasn't likely to happen now.

Nor would it have made any difference to her feelings. One child couldn't replace another. Instead he said, 'He will come back to us. I know it.'

She nodded, feeling the comfort of his warmth.

Chapter 60

NANBERRY

Nanberry stood at the rail, Andrew's hand again in his. His brother was trying not to cry. Nanberry picked him up and hugged him, as he had so many times before. The boy felt smaller, somehow, out here beyond the land.

The ship had changed course now; the colony was lost to sight behind them in the massive harbour. The land was treed again, and here and there appeared the small spires of Gungai fires.

Sydney Town is tiny, thought Nanberry, clinging to the edge of a vast land. If the country shivered, if the wind blew strong, perhaps the whole colony might vanish, leaving the land to the black nations once again. Sometimes — just sometimes — he even hoped that might happen.

He put his brother down and smiled at him. 'Come on, my brother. I'll show you your bunk. It's in a cabin! And how about a slice of your mama's plum pudding? I'll tell you a secret.'

He bent down. 'Plum pudding is the best thing in the world to keep away seasickness. You won't be seasick, will you?'

'No.' The boy's voice was uncertain. He lifted up his chin. 'But I didn't cry, did I? Mama would have been more sad if I had cried. I am going to be brave. Like you.' He hesitated. 'Will you sleep in my cabin too?' He tried to make it sound as though he didn't care one way or the other.

'Of course.'

There was no of course about it — mostly Nanberry slept in a hammock, taking turns with whoever wasn't on watch. But there was no need for Andrew to know that. It was his job to keep the child happy. Keep him alive, through storms and freak waves, stop him falling overboard when he had to sit on the high toilet seat above the waves.

And after that ...

Nanberry gazed back as the land turned to pale blue haze on the horizon. When his brother was safe he would come home again. It was time to go bush, to listen to the trees, to watch for badagarang prints among the tussocks, to be a Cadigal for a while, instead of an Englishman. To take a wife. He would have children, and they would have children too. He was Nanberry, striding across the world.

Epilogue

CAPTAIN ANDREW WHITE

SYDNEY, 1823

He had forgotten the smell of gum trees.

Captain Andrew White of His Majesty's Royal Engineers, a hero of the Battle of Waterloo, stood at the rail as the ship glided across the smooth waters of the harbour. He had forgotten the way the land slipped a thousand tiny fingers towards the water, shining like the waves were scattered with diamonds.

England was behind him: years living in his father's house, years of boarding school with its cold baths, burnt porridge and floggings, years studying engineering at military college, the horror of Waterloo, a killing field where bodies and severed limbs lay among the mud.

He had survived.

Now he was coming home.

Yet how could a land be home when you hadn't seen it since you were seven? His early childhood seemed like a dream now.

Had he ever been that barefoot lad, running down to the harbour? And fishing with spears? Was it even real? There had been an angel too.

He smiled, and shook his head. A small boy's dreams.

And yet some of the most unlikely things had been real. A brother with black skin, who had taught him how to swim. Nanberry had been real: his mother spoke of him sometimes in her letters. She'd sent him a throwing stick one Christmas, a gift from Nanberry. Andrew smiled at the thought of using a native throwing stick in front of his fellow officers.

No, that part of his life was secret. A ghost life: the ex-convict mother; the black brother; the even worse secret — his parents hadn't been married. His father had advised that they let everyone think his first wife had died, that Andrew was his legitimate eldest son.

But the ghosts had kept whispering to him — the blue of the mountains, the smell of the smoke. Home, they whispered. This land is home.

The Scots called it your calf country — the land where you were born, that gave you life. You never forgot it, they said. Andrew gazed about him at the white-trunked trees around the harbour. Was this really home?

The sails flapped above him as the ship turned into another twist of harbour, the wooden hull creaking, the sailors yelling as they hauled at ropes. He stared. That couldn't be Sydney Cove!

He'd left a huddle of huts creeping up the hills. He'd come home to a city.

Where there had been cabbage-tree huts, there were stone warehouses, stout cottages, and wharves not with one poor vessel hired to ship convicts, but ship upon ship. Suddenly he could smell the oil: whale oil, seal oil, the stench of burning blubber. How many whaling ships must use this harbour now?

But there were other ships too. There was at least one other passenger ship — he could see ladies with bright parasols on the deck. Another that might be a convict hulk ...

It was ... big.

If only Father could see this, he thought. His father believed that nothing could come from New South Wales but dirt and squalor, that it was merely a huddle of captives at the bottom of the world.

But it was beautiful, thought Andrew, remembering the birds and playing in the waves. It was beautiful when I was a child. It's still beautiful now.

He stared as the shore grew near, as though he might see his mother's face among the crowds on the wharf. But that was impossible. She didn't even know he was coming. The first ship that could have brought her a letter was this one. She would be at her home in Liverpool, with his stepfather. His stepfather was magistrate now, one of the wealthiest men in the colony. But Nanberry ...

Andrew breathed deeply, trying to find the tang of gum leaves again. Home.

It was strange to feel solid ground under his feet. The world still shifted from side to side.

There was no chance of taking a carriage to Liverpool today, not till his luggage was brought ashore. He found a hotel not far from the wharves — a good one, with a bedroom to himself, a feather mattress and clean sheets. A fire burnt in the fireplace. He sniffed, the scent of gumwood suddenly almost unbearably lovely after the sour coal fires of England.

He went downstairs to the taproom and ordered dinner, then stepped out of the door and looked around.

Once again he was shocked at how … *substantial* everything was. The old huts and cottages had looked as though one big southerly could blow them away along with all the white people on the continent. These grand stone buildings and broad streets and solid warehouses would be a credit to any city in Europe. Even the streets in this part of town seemed to go in different directions from those he remembered, though of course they hadn't even been streets then. Just paths through the mud. This might have been a different town entirely from the place he'd known as a child.

At last he decided to go uphill, and south, to try to find the house where he'd been born.

The street sellers' cries rose around him as he walked along the footpath, 'Pies! Hot pies! Oyster pies!'; 'Who'll buy my lavender? Sweet lavender!'; 'Fisho! Fisho!'

They were the same cries you'd hear in any English city, and the same accents too. It was almost possible to forget that this was still a place of punishment … Then he saw them: a line of lags in convict grey, chains linking their ankles as they shuffled up the road.

A passing man saw him staring. 'Road gang, most like.'

'They look half starved.'

The man shrugged. 'Well, that's government work for you.' He tipped his hat politely, and walked on.

Andrew kept walking too. But it was impossible to find the house or even the street. Either it had vanished or his memory — a seven-year-old's memory — wasn't good enough to find it. Instead he walked down to the harbour, not to the wharves, but to one of the coves, a little way beyond. Suddenly he was a boy again. These were the rocks where he'd speared fish with Garudi. It hadn't been a dream, after all. The waves were the same, slapping against the rocks, the white spray.

But no Garudi. No black limbs outlined against the startling blue of the sky. How could he have forgotten this sky? What had become of Garudi? Is there even, he wondered, any way to find out?

He walked slowly back to the hotel. The dining room was full of men like himself: solid respectable men, ships' captains or merchants perhaps, with money for good food and lodging. There were no women — even the servers were men, pockmarked and brittle-toothed. Old lags, he supposed. But at least they had food here, not like the poor wretches working the roads.

Faces turned to look at him as he came in. He heard a mutter: 'Waterloo.' The news must have come from the ship already. Andrew was used to the awe that people showed to any Waterloo veteran now.

Every man who had survived the Battle of Waterloo was a hero. They had saved England — and all of Europe — from Napoleon. No man who had served at Waterloo had to pay for his own drink in any hotel in England. But in truth he recalled little about the actual battle.

Instead there were memories of small things: grimly focusing on scraps of paper in front of him, trying to sketch maps of what troops were moving where to send to the commanders; seeing a redcoat scream defiance as he charged at the French soldiers with his bayonet, only to realise that the Englishman's left arm was a bleeding stump ... and yet the man kept on, running a Frenchman through before he collapsed; the messenger boy who had brought news of one of the battle's shifting tides, standing there at attention till he fell dead, the blood soaking the back of his red jacket.

He forced his mind away. There would be no more battles for him. But he had come back to his mother a man of substance, with the prize money from Waterloo and the rank of captain. His stepfather might be wealthy, but Captain Andrew White needed no man's charity.

Supper was roast beef and greens. The beef was tough, but the slices generous. Fresh meat and vegetables were good after the months of shipboard salt-meat stew. He smiled at the memory of his father's parting words. 'Make sure you eat plenty of fruit, lad, and buy more, fresh and dried, at the Cape to see you through the rest of the voyage.'

Would he ever see his father again? His stepmother? His half-brother and -sisters? Had he really done the right thing, coming back here, to the end of the world?

'There's apple pie, sir, and cheese if you'd like it.'

'Both, please.'

The serving man nodded, and left behind a stink of rum and sour breath.

It was still early when he went up to bed, hardly dark. The hotel was lit with whale-oil lamps, not the beeswax candles a hotel like this might have back home.

No. Not home. This was home now. Or was it?

The bed was soft at least. The feather mattress had been well aired.

Slowly the noise of drunks singing and the street yells faded. It was hard to sleep in a bed that didn't sway. He watched the moon through the window: a window with real glass, not wooden shutters.

Rrrrhhrrr!

The shriek had him sitting upright, his heart pounding. What was it?

The noise came again. *Rhhhhtt! Skrrrikkk!*

Andrew shoved the window open and looked out.

Something small and furry ran along the hotel's back fence, then jumped up onto the scrap bin. The creature stood upright, then snarled again at its opponent, hidden in the shadows.

Shhhhkkkkttt!

Andrew laughed. A *bungu* in the moonlight. He had forgotten the word till now. All at once his memories felt real.

He'd hoped to leave at dawn. But it would take all day, it seemed, to get his trunks unloaded from the ship. He sent the porter to hire him a carriage. He'd rather hire a horse, but he didn't know where to go in this strangely big colony.

He needed to find a grave.

It was where his mother's letter had said it would be, under the trees of an orchard, overlooking the silver water of the river. Two wooden plaques marked the spot among the daisies in the grass — English daisies under English trees.

He bent down to read the words. *Bennelong, King of the Wangan*. The other plaque read: *Nanberry White, Chief of the Cadigal*.

Chief? King? He had never heard his brother use either of those terms. But he had been so young when he left. What use were the memories of a child?

He remembered the warmth of his brother's hand in his. He remembered the hornpipes and the laughter. He even remembered how to trap bandicoots and climb an o'possum tree. But the little he knew of the last years of his foster brother's life came from his mother's letters: written by a scribe in the early years, then by Rachel herself as her handwriting became more fluent.

Nanberry had stayed less and less in the room that was still kept for him, with a good English suit and hat so he could dine with them respectably. But at least once after every voyage — or before one — he would call in, always bringing gifts of honey, fish or o'possum fur to trim a cloak.

His brother had been in battles with other natives. Once he had been badly speared in the leg but rescued by his friends from the crew of the *Reliance*. He had even accompanied Matthew Flinders in the *Investigator*, on an expedition to map the coastline of the entire continent, but had left, sensibly, when the boat had looked as though it was going to break up in the next big wave ...

'You looking at the King's grave?' The woman's dress was filthy. She stank of rum. He wondered what her crime was, why she'd been sent out here, then realised that like him she might have been born here.

'The King?'

'Old Bennelong. Right old rum artist they say he were. A real savage.'

'Did you know him?'

'Me? Do I look that old? Nah, but people talk.'

Andrew doubted whether they talked much sense. His mother had written that Bennelong had 'gone bush' soon after he'd come back from England. She'd mentioned that in the last months of his life he had been 'sadly addicted to the drink'. Andrew wondered if Bennelong had used alcohol to blot out the pain from his many wounds. He'd known old soldiers who did that. Scars that ached before it rained. Memories that ached even more.

'This is my brother's grave.'

'Your brother?' She stared at him. 'You ain't a darky, are you?'

He supposed his tanned skin might have made him look half-caste. 'No. My foster brother. Nanberry White.'

'He the other savage buried here? An' you say he's your brother?'

'Yes. He is my brother.' He raised his hat — she was still a woman, even if tattered, stinking and ignorant — then walked back to the waiting carriage. He would have liked to sit by his brother's grave longer, but not with her. Besides, he didn't know who owned the land now. James Squire, who had buried both

Bennelong and Nanberry, and been a friend to both, had died the year before.

Nanberry had been in his forties when he died, old age for a sailor. It might have been from scurvy, or influenza … His mother didn't know why Nanberry died. It had only been two years ago. Andrew felt a pang. If he had come back to this country a little earlier he might have seen his brother again. That whole part of his past was locked to him now.

Andrew hoped Nanberry hadn't died alone.

He looked back at the grave among the trees and flowers, at the sparkling river and the gleam of cliffs. No, his brother had died with those he loved around him and in the land he loved as well.

Suddenly another word from the past came back to him. 'Babana,' he whispered. 'Brother. Goodbye, babana. Thank you for teaching me to see the land around me. It's stood me in good stead. Rest in peace.'

⟋⊚

His luggage still hadn't been delivered when he got back to the hotel. He was just about to scribble a note to his mother when at last the porter appeared, wheeling his trunks on a trolley.

He sent the man to find him a carriage. Instead he came back with a cart pulled by two draught horses. It looked like it was mostly used for carting barrels of ale, rather than a gentleman and his belongings, but at least it was clean. Andrew helped the driver and porter load his sea chests, then gave the porter a shilling for his trouble. He climbed up beside the driver.

'Where to?' The driver took a swig from a stone jar. Rum, by the smell of it, or something worse brewed from potatoes. He offered the jar to Andrew, who shook his head.

'Liverpool. Mr Moore's house. Do you know it?'

The driver nodded. 'Biggest house in the colony, I've heard, though I ain't never seen it. On the Georges River.' He looked at Andrew. 'Terrible long way out to Liverpool, matey.'

'I'll pay you for the journey back too.'

'Can't say fairer nor that.' The driver jerked his head back towards the hotel. 'They says you was at Waterloo. That true?'

'Yes,' said Andrew repressingly.

'Easy enough to say it. Don't mean you was there.'

Andrew pulled open his coat and showed the medal that he wore each day of his life now.

The driver dipped his hat in respect. 'Well done, sir. Sorry for doubtin' you.' He flicked the reins. The horses began to pull, slowly and reluctantly. It will be a long day for them, thought Andrew. They'd be yearning for their stable and their hay.

'Ye got business with Mr Moore?'

'Yes,' said Andrew shortly. An officer and gentleman didn't chat to carters. But the man didn't seem to know or care about such etiquette.

'What sort o' business then?'

'I'm his stepson.'

The man stared at him, his mouth agape.

'Ye pullin' me leg?'

'No.'

'Well, blow me down and cover me with cabbages. His stepson, eh? Never knew Mr Moore had no stepson. An' not one as fought at Waterloo! Nor no sons neither.'

'I left here when I was seven.'

The man stared at him. Andrew flushed. He had just more or less admitted, he realised, that he'd been a convict brat, son of a convict woman.

But the man just said, 'Mr Moore is a right good man. Last time the floods came down the Hawkesbury Mr Moore paid for feedin' the families from his own pocket. Mrs Moore, she helped the Governor's wife set up the orphanage and a school too. There ain't a couple o' better people in the colony, nor back in England neither, I'm thinkin'. Ye must be proud.'

His mother had mentioned things like that in her letters — the hungry families, the orphanage. But he'd had no idea their charity had been so great that even a carter knew of it, and admired them.

'Yes,' said Andrew quietly. 'I'm very proud.'

It was a long hot way to Liverpool, past fields of wheat and barley and small camps of natives, huddled and in rags, so different from the tall straight people he remembered. Convict gangs worked wearily, carrying rocks to mend the road. None of the lags even bothered to look up as they passed, except when the driver stopped to ask the way.

But there were good things to see as well. Neat farmhouses with bee skeps behind them, and big-eyed dairy cows; here an orchard of peach trees and ripening plums or a boy shepherding a small flock of sheep, heavy with wool; there bullockies with teams of sixteen or more, hauling loads of logs or sacks of what he supposed was grain.

'Nearly there, matey, I reckon,' said the driver at last.

Shadows thickened the afternoon. He'd have to give the man money to stay at a tavern and stable his horses for the night.

And suddenly they were there. He recognised it, even though he'd never seen it. The driveway opened off the road, lined with tall English trees. The big house was of pale sandstone. It rose up above its gardens. Roses, hedges of bright flowers, gravel that looked freshly raked. His father had left behind a convict woman and her brat. Now she lived in a finer house by far than he did back in England.

He felt his heart thud. It had been more than six months since he'd had a letter from his mother — there was no way to get mail aboard ship. Perhaps a letter from her had passed him, travelling to England while he sailed here.

So much could happen in six months.

All at once he felt more fear than he had ever felt in the bloody chaos of the Battle of Waterloo. At least his mother must still be alive — the carter would have mentioned it if she'd died. But she was scarcely a young woman any more. Would he even know her after twenty-three years?

Would she know him? He had sent her a small portrait of himself, after Waterloo. Would she recognise him from that? What would she think of her son now? Would they be strangers to each other, despite the letters, after all this time?

The cartwheels sounded loud on the gravel as they reached the grand front door. The carter pulled the reins.

Andrew paid the man, jumped down from the cart and climbed the stairs, then lifted his hand to knock as the driver began to unload his trunks.

Something shrieked above him.

It was an o'possum. He gazed up as a furry face glared down at him, the dark eyes wide in the light from the carriage lanterns. It had a baby clinging to the fur on its back, almost as big as it was.

Andrew grinned. He lifted the giant doorknocker and brought it down. The door opened almost at once. The servant inside must have heard the cartwheels on the gravel and been waiting.

'Good evening, sir.' The manservant's dress was impeccable, his accent almost as good. Andrew could see the hall behind him, the flicker of the candles in the chandelier, polished wood tables, Chinese silk carpets, oil paintings on the walls. And coming out of one of the rooms …

Her hair was more grey than brown, held up with silver combs. Her dress was green silk. Green jewels shone at her ears.

But she was still his mother.

He stared at her, as the manservant spoke again. 'Who should I say is calling, sir?'

She knew him. Her face looked as though she could see every day that he had lived, every day that he had been away. He heard the rustle of silk skirts as she ran along the hall.

'Andrew!' Her cheeks wet, wet even before she reached him. He was crying too as he lifted her off the ground, as he hugged her, hugged her.

He was home.

Behind him the o'possums yelled at each other in the trees.

Author's Notes

Note: All opinions on different races, religion, whaling and possums in this book are those of the characters who lived in the eighteenth century. The author does not share them.

The events in this book are as true as I can make them. The first decades of the colony were an extraordinary and fascinating time. But there comes a point where a historian and author has to say, 'I don't know.'

I have done my best to interpret actions and motives in this book, but many things still puzzle me. There are places where I may think I have interpreted correctly, but have failed.

It is impossible to truly understand either the English or Eora cultures of the 1780s and 90s. We are simply too far away to understand people whose reasons for doing things and customs were so different from ours.

So little of what happened was written down back then. The books, diaries and letters that remain from that time often contradict each other. In many places I've had to choose one account over another while knowing that neither may be quite true.

Neither the English nor the Eora understood each other. In most cases, perhaps, they didn't want to, though the Eora might have wanted English axes, or the English Eora canoes or spears.

I was about three when my mother first told me stories of the early colony (I played doling out the stores in my sandpit). Ten years ago I might have said I had read every document available from that time.

I had no idea, back then, how much material might still be in England, unpublished and unavailable until recently, such as the remarkable trial records of Rachel Turner or the school records of Andrew White. Records of ships' crews are still being found, as has been a letter dictated by Bennelong.

To me, now, Nanberry and Andrew White seem to be the first modern Australians, triumphantly accepting both sides of their heritage. They each took what they needed both from English culture and from the land of Australia. Both, I think, led fulfilled lives, despite the hardships around them. Like the possum — another great survivor and adaptor — they triumphed. But neither may have been like the boys and men I describe in this book. I know enough to say, 'I do not know.'

The people in this book

All history books are detective stories, and history writers must track down information and put it together exactly as a detective does. When I began this book I thought it would be a simple story of a doctor and his attempt to tame a possum. But more and more evidence — often extraordinary and from the most unexpected sources — kept adding to the tale. A small part of this research has become this book.

Surgeon White, Nanberry White, Rachel Turner, Andrew White, Mr Thomas Moore, Mr Balmain, Booroong, Colbee,

Balloonderry, Bennelong, Governor Phillip, Captain Waterhouse, Major Ross and many others were all real people. The only 'named' fictional characters are Maria, Yagali, Andrew's friend Garudi, Mr Flitch and Big Lon, although people very like them existed. (I did find information that suggested that a certain Aboriginal boy may have been Andrew's companion, but it was too tenuous a link to add that real name to the book.)

Even the most incredible parts of the story in this book are true: the auction of the women, the 'smallpox' plague that killed only Aboriginal people but spared the white settlers, the convicts left to starve while the captains stole their rations and the almost-murder of Governor Phillip. Surgeon White really did give the same name to the Cadigal boy he adopted and to his son. The foster son seems to have used the name Nanberry White, at least most of the time, and not 'Andrew'.

One of the problems of writing about real times and real people is that you have to accept what happened, even if it does sound extraordinary to us, reading about it so many years later — and even if you'd rather it wasn't true. The Bennelong in this book becomes a drunk. He is sometimes a brute and violent, often a figure of fun. That is the way he was portrayed by those writing at the time, not the way I wanted to write him. The same writers respected and admired Colbee, Arabanoo, Nanberry and, to a lesser extent, Balloonderry, so it is unlikely they laughed at Bennelong's boasts simply because he was of another race.

Yes, only one man — Captain Waterhouse — went back along the beach to rescue the wounded Governor. I can't understand why others didn't run to help him or why the marines didn't try to fire their muskets sooner, but that is what seems to have happened. Even more hard to accept is that no one at the time seemed to think it strange. Perhaps it all happened far more quickly than the way they spoke of it implies. Again, I don't know.

I would have liked to change many parts of this story: to have Surgeon White come back to Rachel, to realise that this country could be both beautiful and generous, or to have Andrew meet Nanberry again (which indeed he may have done, as nothing is recorded about what either did for most of the years of their lives). It would have been good to make Nanberry become a magistrate or for the captains of the Second and Third Fleets and the officers of the Rum Corps finally to be held to account for their crimes.

But it didn't happen that way.

The past isn't always comfortable to look at or as we would like it to be. That's why it is so important that we try to work out what really happened.

John White (1756/7–1832)

Much of this book is based on Surgeon White's *Journal of a Voyage to New South Wales* (1790). According to his journal, he severely disliked Australia, describing it as '... a country and place so forbidding and so hateful as only to merit execration and curses'.

Surgeon White was an extraordinary man, conscious of his status as a gentleman, pompous enough to fight a duel (before this book begins) with his Assistant Surgeon Balmain, probably because Balmain didn't show him enough respect, and a superb and dedicated scientist, botanist and zoologist. As Surgeon-General to the First Fleet and the settlement at Port Jackson, his advanced ideas on diet and medical care meant that many of those weak and starved wretches survived a remarkable journey across the world. No other ship or fleet in the next fifty years would achieve as much.

Surgeon White worked desperately to save each new influx of convicts to arrive in Sydney Town dying from disease, starvation and the terrible conditions of the Second Fleet and subsequent contingents from England. He acknowledged Rachel's son,

Andrew, as his child, supported him and his mother after he returned to England in 1794 and sent for Andrew to join him there when the boy was seven.

In 1796 he resigned from his job as a naval surgeon rather than be posted back to the colony — despite having Rachel, Andrew and Nanberry to go back to. But it is worth remembering that this man had lived through the worst years of the colony, including the time when perhaps nine out of ten of the Aboriginal people in the area died of what he thought was smallpox.

His failure to help more than two of them and the appalling death rate of the convicts unloaded from the ships must have made his job a form of helpless Hell. He did admit in later years that the colony might have become a far better place than the prison hole he remembered.

John White worked as a surgeon at Sheerness from 1799 and then at Chatham Dockyard from 1803. He married twice — his first wife died — and he had two daughters, or two daughters and another son (there are conflicting records). He retired on a half-pension in 1820 of £91 5s a year. He died at Worthing on 20 February 1832 aged seventy-five.

Did Surgeon White have a possum?

When I began to write this book I was sure that Surgeon White had a pet possum. But as I looked through the letters and diaries written at the time, I couldn't find a pet possum anywhere.

Where did I get the idea?

I don't know. Possibly from the stories my mother had told me about that time. Some legend passed on from her mother, and her mother's mother, back through generations of women who had passed on stories of our family — and an old family diary, from the early days in the colony, and often malicious gossip about prominent figures they had known too.

Surgeon White wrote two books mostly about the wildlife of

the colony, particularly the birds he deeply loved and whose study he obviously found a comfort after the horror of his work. There were references to possums in White's writings: 'o'possums' he had tried and failed to tame. By June 1798 he certainly was very familiar with 'o'possums' and compared other new animals to them. He knew they had a pouch with teats in which to carry their young.

In one of his references to possums Surgeon White wrote that he had often tried to breed them in England, and had bought many and had others given to him by friends. He certainly studied them in detail, but also admitted how little he knew.

Rachel Turner (1762–1838)

Rachel Turner was one of the first people to ever be defended in an English court of law. In this book she believes that she was the very first person to ever be defended, by the young and enthusiastic Mr Garrow.

But although Mr Garrow's defence of his clients would change the way English — and Australian and American — trials were held, the first few times he tried to defend his clients the judges were so furious at what they saw as contempt of court that he did his clients more harm than good.

Although almost certainly innocent, Rachel Turner was found guilty; her sentence of death was changed to seven years' transportation to celebrate the declaration that King George III was sane again. She was truly an incredible woman, transcending the deprivations of her early life to become one of the wealthiest women — and possibly the most loved — in the colony, successful far beyond her dreams. Ironically, she became far wealthier than she would have been if Surgeon White had married her, and almost certainly had a far more fulfilled life, living in her grand house by her beautiful river, helping to make the new colony successful, and beloved and admired by many people.

Andrew Douglas (Douglass) White (1793–1837)

Andrew White is probably Australia's first Australian-born returned soldier, a man who became a hero of Waterloo, and, at last, came home. He was accepted by Surgeon White's new family in England, and became one of the first students at the new Chatham House boarding school, graduating as an engineer, serving at the Battle of Waterloo and then probably working on siege fortifications in the Lowlands — either Belgium or Holland — before coming back to Australia, the land he seems to have regarded as home, and to his mother.

Almost every man who survived that nightmare battle against Napoleon and the French army under Marshal Ney seems to have been regarded as a hero, but if Andrew White worked as an engineer or sapper, supervising the digging of tunnels to get closer to the enemy, or to protect the English and their allies from shot and cavalry attacks, then he almost certainly was heroic. In the phrase of the time, 'A Waterloo veteran could ask a drink of any man in England, and never have to pay.' Any veteran of Waterloo was treated with the same respect in Australia. It is hard to convey to a modern audience how much the men who survived Waterloo were venerated and given special privileges, both official and unofficial. I suspect Andrew Douglas(s) White's life deserves a book of its own. I now have far too much information about it to record here.

Andrew sailed back to England in July 1824. He returned to Australia for good in 1833. He married Mary Anne Mackenzie in 1835.

Andrew White stayed in the Royal Engineers even once he had come to Australia, till he retired on half-pay and became a magistrate. There is no record of any children. On the other hand, I may simply not have found the record or it may have been lost or never officially recorded.

I did find a record that the daughter of an Andrew White who lived at the same time and the same place had married a man named Weir (coincidentally the maiden name of my mother-in-law). I continue to look for more evidence of what actually happened to Andrew after he came back to Australia. Records from that time are incomplete, inaccurate and often very difficult to track down. It would be yet another of the many coincidences that I found while writing this book to discover that I am distantly related to Andrew, Surgeon White, Rachel Turner and even Nanberry, by marriage.

Andrew, like his mother, had a most extraordinary life. Even with the help and recognition of his father, he would still have had the stigma of being the illegitimate son of a convict, and from Australia. He rose from his humble beginnings to become an engineer, an officer, a hero, and — I hope, though have no evidence — finally happy and fulfilled back home.

Nanberry (–1821)

(Nanbree, Nanberry Buckenau, Nanbaree and other variations of spelling also exist, but almost certainly refer to the same young man, although he is probably not the Nunberri who sailed on the *Blanche* on the Shoalhaven River.)

Most accounts of Indigenous Australians in the early colony focus on Bennelong, a man who in many ways had a tragic life, stranded between two cultures and at times earning contempt from both.

Nanberry has been almost forgotten, possibly because he was intelligent, good-natured and hard-working. Loud-mouthed drunks may often get noticed, while intelligent young men may not.

Nanberry was adopted by Surgeon White when he was about nine or ten, but he may have been younger, as Aboriginal boys would have been taller and more muscular than the half-starved colonial children Surgeon White was used to.

It must have been a terrifying time for the small boy; no wonder that he turned to his protector and decided to 'become English'. Perhaps nine out of ten of the Aboriginal people around Sydney Harbour died. All, or at least most, of the others fled inland, away from the disease — the only thing they could do in the face of such a savage death rate. Nanberry must have felt his old world had died too. Surgeon White had saved him from death, possibly starvation, and had given him a home and status as his own son.

White gave Nanberry the name 'Andrew Douglass Keble White' when he adopted him, but the boy seems to have insisted on using the name Nanberry or Nanberry Buckenau, even though he used his adoptive father's surname till his death. (He stopped using Balloonderry's name after his friend's death.)

Nanberry appears to have been a brilliant linguist, quickly learning English — and English customs — and being used as the colony's official translator, an impressive job for so young a boy. At one stage it seemed that he might even have forgotten his own language, having used English for so long instead.

The examples of what we might regard as rudeness from the adult warriors towards him need to be seen from their point of view. I doubt that the important men and women of our day would like to be told what to do by a nine-year-old boy, especially one who appeared to ignore or even have contempt for our culture.

Nanberry seems to have decided to stay English until after White went back to England, possibly leaving him with no protector in the colony, and certainly without the man who had treated him in many ways as a son. Suddenly, with almost no warning, White was gone from Nanberry's life. I think it's no coincidence that it was about that time he decided to be initiated as a Cadigal warrior, probably near what is now the Sydney Botanic Gardens.

But even when he lived with Surgeon White he still became 'brothers' with Balloonderry, a young man some years older than him, and he twice warned Balloonderry about attempts to capture him or attack his comrades.

It has been difficult to trace much of Nanberry's life, not just because most of the time he seemed to be quietly working and so didn't appear in letters or newspapers, but because he was known by the name White as well as Nanberry (with the various spelling variations) and possibly other names that he took and used at times after he formally became a warrior. At the time of his death Nanberry was still using the surname White, as well as Nanberry.

Nanberry died in 1821, cause unknown. The Reverend Charles Winton, Minister of the Field of Mars (now more or less the Sydney suburb of Ryde) from 1826 to 1828, referred to him as a chief. But this title was meaningless to the Cadigal, and possibly just meant that the English settlers felt Nanberry was a respected man, looked up to by his people.

Nanberry requested that he be buried in the same grave as Bennelong. This was possibly because Bennelong, too, was a friend of James Squire and it was a place where Nanberry knew his body would be buried with respect. Despite Bennelong's earlier contempt for Nanberry the two men later became friends or at least colleagues in rituals and clan payback wars.

Another Aboriginal man, known as Bidgee Bidgee, also asked to be buried at the same site in later years, but there seem to be no records to indicate whether he was. James Squire died in 1822.

The words in this book that are said to be on Nanberry's and Bennelong's grave may not have existed — there is only one reference to them and by the 1880s there seems to have been no actual marker to show where the grave was. The wooden plaques that may have existed could have rotted, or been removed — or perhaps were never there.

There is a photograph in the Mitchell Library of a grave that is said to contain Bennelong, his wife, and 'Nanbarry' (sic). The grave is somewhere in Ryde. It was well-marked after Nanberry died. A stone and plaque in Cleves Park, Ryde is said to mark the site of Bennelong's grave, but it is now known that the actual gravesite is elsewhere, though nearby. The location is still a secret. Wherever it is, it is probably Nanberry's grave too.

I've tried to track shipping and other records to find the ships Nanberry sailed on, but in many cases the records of ships' crews and sailing times and details are either not available, or were never made at the time. There were also at least two sailors called White, on different ships at the same time.

Once again, colonial records are sketchy, and often inaccurate.

Nanberry wasn't the first Indigenous man to go to sea — that was the man known by the white colony as 'Bundle' or 'Bondel', who was also an orphan and accompanied Captain William Hill of the New South Wales Corps to Norfolk Island in March 1791 on the *Supply*.

By about 1810 there were several Indigenous men who worked as sailors, on fishing boats or whaling and sealing boats, or on ships that took those astounding voyages across the ocean in such tiny (to our eyes) sailing boats. They braved the storms and freak waves of the Southern Ocean and the mountainous seas by the Cape, sailed past ice floes and through the doldrums, where you could die of thirst when there was no wind to fill your sails. They were respected and valued crew members and were paid regular wages and given regular rations, on the same basis as white sailors. Native Americans and African Americans were also known to be crew members on many ships (often American) that landed in Australia or whaled or caught seals in Australian waters.

A few factors relating to Nanberry's time as a sailor, however, do seem fairly certain. On 30 October 1793, Nanberry sailed as part of the crew of HMS *Reliance* to Norfolk Island. He is listed as part of the crew on HMS *Brilliant* in 1800 — the same ship that took his foster brother Andrew to England or at least to Cape Town, where he may have transferred to another ship. I doubt that the two young men being on the same ship was a coincidence — it was a very long way to send a seven-year-old child, especially back then, without someone to protect him. Who better than his foster brother, an experienced sailor?

In 1802 Nanberry sailed with the explorer Matthew Flinders on HMS *Investigator*, in the attempt to circumnavigate and map the whole of the Australian coast. Nanberry returned to Sydney, though, in the ship *Nelson* when the *Investigator* began to leak badly. Flinders referred to him as 'a good-natured lad'.

The places where Nanberry's name doesn't appear are, however, as interesting as those where it does. He doesn't seem to be on any list of 'natives' who were given charity blankets or who lined up to get a tobacco ration. He wasn't ever taken before a magistrate and accused of drunkenness. He's not in the records for either committing any crime or as being the victim of crime. Nor was he a police tracker, nor given a grant of land or a fishing boat, one of Governor Macquarie's attempts to defuse increasing Aboriginal anger and homelessness. Nanberry's name is not on the list that Governor Macquarie had made of all the 'natives' who promised in future to be friendly to the English.

There are records of him participating in battles with other warriors with whom he had close family ties. Including a battle where he and Bennelong speared a man called Cogy — 'the leader of the Cowpastures'. Nanberry also speared and killed a man named Colinjong. I think the life I've portrayed in this book is probably the most accurate one — that he worked as a sailor and, in between voyages, joined up with his clan, taking part in their battles.

In other words, Nanberry seems to have lived an independent, successful and hopefully happy life both as a Cadigal, in the bush away from the colony, and as a member of the English community.

While there is no record of his marriage, it is unlikely there would be, as most 'native' marriages weren't recorded. (Nor were a great many 'white' ones.) There is a record of a Sophy Buckenau, who was born about 1806, and was living at Kissing Point with her daughter, where Nanberry is known to have stayed. As she wouldn't have used the name 'Nanberry' or 'White' after his death she may have used the other name by which he was known. But that is still supposition.

In one of the amazing coincidences that occurred while I was writing this book (new information appeared at the most unlikely times and places), I met a young woman at a history conference who told me that Nanberry was one of her ancestors. She promised to ask her uncle to contact me with more details, but at the time of writing this I haven't heard from him.

If Nanberry is now known to be someone's ancestor, he would need to have had a wife, the sort of formal relationship where the father was known as well as the mother. The little we know of Nanberry doesn't indicate a man who wouldn't feel responsible for his children.

I suspect that if Nanberry knew of his descendants now, he would be proud. He was a man who seems to have kept his own heritage while successfully being part of the colonial world too: an extraordinary achievement by a remarkable man.

Wollarawarre Bennelong (1764–1813)

The discussions about the true character of the man known as Bennelong are too long to have here. (He actually had a much longer and more complex name, and titles used only on certain occasions.) Bennelong was often violent, especially to women, and a boaster. But he was also a man of resourcefulness, courage, curiosity, incredible kindness and extreme endurance. He was far more complex than the white observers — and possibly his own people — of the time gave him credit for. The truth about who this man was is, I think, one of the cases where we need to say, 'I don't know.'

Bennelong appears to have become addicted to alcohol after his return from England, possibly because of pain from wounds and a deeper personal pain.

Even from his first imprisonment in the colony he was portrayed by almost all the diarists and letter writers as a boaster and even a buffoon. But he showed extreme kindness and dedication to Balloonderry, and managed to survive physically and mentally a voyage to England where he was pretty much displayed as a curiosity. In short, he deserves far more than a few paragraphs of summary.

Bennelong died in 1813, long before Nanberry, and was buried in the orange orchard belonging to a brewer called James Squire, who had befriended him, and been granted land on the north shore of the Parramatta River in 1795. It was said that Bennelong often camped there. Bennelong's death is usually attributed to his many wounds from arguments and fights, as well as to alcoholism.

Although we know that Nanberry and Bennelong were buried in James Squire's orchard, the exact spot of the orchard and the grave has been the subject of debate. It was also possible that the grave was in Squire's garden instead. As mentioned earlier, Bennelong's — and so probably Nanberry's — grave has finally been located. At the time of writing the exact location was a secret, possibly, in part, so that the warriors can still rest in peace.

Thomas Moore (1762–1839)

Thomas Moore appears to have first arrived in New South Wales as ship's carpenter on William Raven's *Britannia*. This may have been in either 1791 or 1792 — various sources have different dates for both the ship's arrival and departure for the Cape to fetch more stores for the colony. It is likely that Moore made several voyages before he settled in Sydney and married Rachel Turner in 1797. (Their marriage seems to have been soon after he took up a job as colonial shipbuilder, so I imagine they had met before.) There were still few women compared to men in the colony and Rachel was relatively young, beautiful and had an income from Surgeon White. Despite having an illegitimate child she would have had a wide choice of possible husbands — though given the nature of the community not many of these would necessarily have appealed to her. She doesn't seem to have been impulsive, so either she saw very quickly that Moore was a man of integrity, hard work and kindness or she had met him before. The colony was a small place in 1792 and Moore may well have needed a doctor's help for himself or a friend. It is quite likely they did meet before Moore decided to settle in the colony and Rachel may well have been one of the reasons he chose to stay there.

Staying in the colony was an extremely good move for Moore financially. He was well-paid; his skills were in great demand, and there were enormous opportunities for a man with vision and intelligence. Thomas Moore had both.

He and Rachel Turner were married by the Reverend Johnson. Both made their mark on their marriage certificate — an X instead of a signature. Possibly neither could read or write, though it was common for people to be able to read a bit, but to not have had any practice in forming letters. (There are many accounts of 'illiterate' mothers teaching their children to write by copying passages from a book that they could, just, read.) It is likely that both were able to read at least simple documents and certainly Moore would have been able to follow plans and maps. It is probable that both learnt to write in later years, given the works they were involved in.

Thomas became a master boatbuilder, with a house and a three-acre orchard by the Tank Stream — a respectable position and evidence that he'd worked hard since he came to the colony. A three-acre orchard might have about a thousand fruit trees, all of which would have had to be raised from seedlings or cuttings or bought at very high prices in Cape Town, then watered by hand and fed manure. For the first years of his marriage he mostly rebuilt the often battered and aged government-owned ships that had made their way down to the colony. He also built and worked his own ship.

Thomas received another grant of land of 470 acres in 1799, with more convict labour to work it, but he still worked as a master boatbuilder. By 1807 he had 1,920 acres. He stopped working as a boatbuilder and moved to his property and new grand house, Moorebank, on the Georges River. His business interests grew more and more varied and he travelled twice to England, shipping sheep. He was appointed magistrate for Georges River and then in 1821 for the entire Cumberland County. Moore and Governor Macquarie worked together to found the town of Liverpool and Macquarie even stayed at the Moores' house and encouraged settlers to the area. Moore helped start the Bank of New South Wales (now Westpac), a savings bank in Liverpool, as well as a branch of the British and Foreign Bible Society, and helped in relief efforts when floods destroyed farmers' crops. He also contributed to building a church school, as well as the first Roman Catholic chapel and Presbyterian church, even though he was a devout Anglican, with daily prayers for his entire household.

He seems to have had no children apart from his stepson, Andrew. Rachel was about thirty-five when they married, and although a thirty-five-year-old today may have children, Rachel had been through many years of extreme physical hardship. It is quite likely that by then she wasn't able to get safely pregnant.

Thomas Moore, too, was an extraordinary man, one who took all the opportunities this land offered him, and one who gave selflessly to others too.

Colonial records and spelling

Back in the late 1700s gentlemen and ladies were taught to write, but correct spelling wasn't particularly important. Even well-educated men might spell someone's name three different ways on one page, and not think anything of it. (There were few well-educated women. Well-off girls were taught to read and write simple books, and music, drawing and dancing and often French. Females' 'small brains' weren't expected to manage much more.)

This makes it difficult to track down people in old records. Many of the records of that time no longer exist, or were never made at the time. Many marriages and births were never recorded. Some, like a few of my ancestors, deliberately lied about where they had come from and their convict pasts, or changed their names. And — like today — sometimes people deliberately made false records or just made mistakes.

The English

I have referred to the colonists as English in this book, rather than British, even though a few were Irish or Scottish or Welsh, Native American or African. This is because the culture, law and customs of the colony at that time were English. It wasn't until many more Irish and Welsh were transported — sometimes because of rebellion against the English — that they became a major influence on Australian culture. The later Highland clearances — whole villages turned out of their homes and their houses burnt so that absentee English landlords could use their clan lands — and increasing Scottish poverty again affected Australia at a later period than the one in which this book is set.

Aboriginal languages and lands

In these days of cars, bridges and harbour tunnels, it's hard to realise just how vast the area around Sydney Harbour must once have been. Groups like the Cadigal, Dharug and Guringai each had their own land. They were more than clans, but not separate nations as we think of nations now — they had much of their language and customs in common, and joined together for ceremonies or feasts, and certainly spread news of events like the arrival of the colonists at Botany Bay. They seemed to have been known as the 'Eora' or 'people' even before smallpox killed so many of them.

The 'Aboriginal' words I've used in this book were those written down by English people from 1788 to 1820. This means they are almost certainly not very accurate. But as with so many of the incidents in this book, I chose to rely on the written records of the time, balanced with what I know of Indigenous tradition and history.

The peoples of Indigenous Australia had no written phonetic language — a phonetic language has symbols for sounds, so you can sound out new words from what's written down; 'b', 'oo' and 'k' will be 'book' even if you don't know what a book is. The Indigenous nations did have many written symbols, but a symbol doesn't tell you how it's pronounced. The Indigenous nations had no written history either, although they had a very strong and accurate oral history tradition. But when the nations were destroyed by disease and occupation of their lands many of the oral histories died with their custodians.

Leaving your sick or dead behind

The incident where Nanberry and his family are left, ill and dying, sounds callous. But it was also a necessary form of survival, and not just in Aboriginal Australia at that time.

Nowadays we are so used to quarantine areas in hospitals and masks, gloves and suits to protect health workers from infection (although they may not always work) that we forget that even a few hundred years ago lepers wore bells to warn everyone to stay away from them. Sufferers of viruses, such as smallpox, and the plague were simply shut up alone in their homes to die or recover. Probably many more died from lack of water and care than the disease.

Nanberry's clan must have realised that this was a new and deadly illness. The only chance to stop it spreading was to leave the sick behind. There were isolation huts at the colony's hospital, so Surgeon White had places he could safely keep the sufferers. He, too, may well have had either a mild form of smallpox, or more likely, been inoculated with it so that he didn't expect to catch it again, and so wouldn't infect the colony.

Why didn't the colonists die of smallpox?

This is one of history's mysteries. It was a new disease to the Indigenous people, one they had no resistance to. Many in the colony would have already survived the disease, or its relative cowpox, been inoculated or were the children of those who had natural immunity. But it was to be expected that some of the children, at least, would have been sick. Smallpox outbreaks in England still caused many to die.

Many theories have been put forward. This is my own — which I formulated with no medical qualifications, but a lot of reading on the subject. It is possible that the disease wasn't smallpox at all, but a far more virulent form of cowpox than the English had ever seen.

Bad cases of cowpox can look like smallpox. (In the 1930s the cases were still sometimes confused, even by doctors in England.) Most English cowherds in those days carried cowpox and just about everyone in the colony would have had a chance to be infected by it at some stage. (There was even a herd of cows in the middle of London to provide fresh milk.)

The early colony did have cows and the children in the colony would have been exposed to cowpox too. Cowpox was usually a very mild disease, but it did give a fair immunity to smallpox.

None of the Indigenous nations would ever have had contact with cowpox — even the traders from Indonesia and Asia wouldn't have had cows. I wonder if the dreaded 'smallpox' wasn't cowpox, striking an unprotected group of people with incredible severity. But, as I said, that is just my own theory — and I am no medical expert.

Oyster shells

Nanberry comments in the book that the white-ghost women gather oysters but take only the shells, leaving the meat behind. The shells were collected in the early colony to be ground up to make lime. This was used to cement bricks to make walls, and create a 'limewash' to waterproof both brick and 'wattle-and-daub' houses. However, the oysters may well have been eaten by the women too — they were one of the native foods that prevented the colonists from starving even though supply ships hadn't come. The fact that enough shells were collected to make limewash meant that there were enormous quantities of oysters all around the harbour. (There still were in the 1960s and 70s.)

Early colonial houses

There are probably no houses left in Australia from the period 1788 to 1800 and, although there are a few that may have been built back then, there are also good arguments that those houses were either rebuilt or enormously modified later. This is mostly because the colony's first houses were made either from cabbage-tree logs — easy to cut down but quickly rotted — or 'wattle-and-daub' — walls made of the trunks of small trees with mud pushed in between them that also slowly succumbed to rot and rainstorms. Even the first brick houses didn't last long, as the bricks and their tile roofs soon crumbled — the earliest colonial bricks were very poorly made.

Our earliest long-lasting major colonial buildings — often of stone — were built in Governor Macquarie's time, mostly of sandstone, and it is these that Andrew White would have seen when he finally came back to Australia.

Colonial and Eora medicine

Much of British medicine at the time was as likely to kill you as cure you — amputation, bloodletting, purgatives, arsenic, large doses of wine. But as a navy surgeon John White would have been very experienced at dealing with severe wounds, crushed limbs, etc. He would also have understood how often careful nursing and care during an illness can mean that the patient recovers.

But White was also a visionary. He was the one who insisted on the convicts having fresh fruit and vegetables — in those days most people, including doctors, thought fresh fruit was actually harmful, especially for children. He also collected and trialled Indigenous remedies, finding some extremely successful.

Two of these were bloodwood sap and eucalyptus oil. Both were used in colonial times for a variety of illnesses, but it's now known that using eucalyptus oil medicinally can lead to liver problems, so I haven't given details of how either were used in case someone tries to follow the old practices.

Thanks to the hard work of Governor Phillip and Surgeon White, the early colonists were relatively disease free until the arrival of the Second Fleet. From then on each convict ship that arrived also brought more illness to the colony. The 'First Fleeters' suffered from scurvy, especially those who refused to eat vegetables, or whose teeth were too bad to chew them, as well as accidents, injuries, tooth problems and the dangers from child-bearing, but until the Second Fleet arrived Australia was regarded as an extremely healthy place to live — if you were white.

Sarsaparilla tea

This was made from *Indigofera australis*, an Australian native shrub. It only tasted very vaguely like real sarsaparilla, but Surgeon White had the flowers harvested in late winter and early spring, and dried for tea. European sarsaparilla was supposed to be good for the digestion and some illnesses, and Surgeon White may have hoped that the native version would be good for them too. I've tried making tea from *Indigofera australis* flowers. It's pretty tasteless, but didn't make me sick. Don't try it, though, in case it has long-term toxic effects.

The New South Wales Corps

The 'Rum Corps' was as bad as I have shown it to be in this book. It was made up of men with sometimes little or no military experience or training. (In those days you, or your family, paid money so you could become an army officer. In the navy, on the other hand, a man with no money could be promoted on merit, although even then having wealthy or influential friends or family was usually necessary too.)

All of the New South Wales Corps volunteered to come to what they would have regarded as literally the ends of the earth. It was a job that attracted criminals and men who could get no better work.

The Rum Corps put most of their energy into getting land and money for themselves and their friends — and making sure that the colonial government didn't interfere with them. But on the other hand, their efforts to get rich — their farms, their stores, their shipping ventures — also made the colony prosperous. Some of the Rum Corps members, too, were good men who didn't have the courage to stand up to their more criminal comrades — or had the good sense not to.

The possum

The possum in this book is a common brushtail possum (*Trichosurus vulpecula*), as that is the one best resembling the descriptions of Surgeon White.

Brushtail possums are one of the few bush creatures that have happily adapted to gardens — and love to live in roof and ceiling spaces too.

Brushtail possums spend a lot of their time in trees (or your ceiling) but will also feed on the ground, unlike other possums like ringtails and sugar gliders. They can use their front paws like small hands, and grip with their tail too.

Brushtails eat almost anything — though much of that food may not be good for them. (Like the food many humans choose to eat.) Possums will take food from garbage bins, eat the fruit or blossoms from your trees, and munch through everything left out on your bird table. Their favourite foods though — here, anyway — seem to be apple leaves and shoots, loquat fruit and flowers, young Sydney blue gum leaves and leaf tips. They also eat quite a few snails.

A friend once rang me to complain that a possum had just arrived at her dining table and eaten all the tabouli, but still looked hungry. What should she give it next?

In other words, possums are very, very adaptable — and delightful companions if you don't mind stroppy shrieks outside the window and thumps on the roof. But as Surgeon White found, possums can never be made into pets — just like any wild animal. You can be on familiar terms with the possums in your garden, but never try to pat them, or cuddle them, even if they were hand-raised orphans.

The early colony at Port Jackson

The First Fleet was the longest expedition of its size in history, eleven ships with 1,487 people travelling 15,063 miles. Why on earth did England send a fleet of convicts right around the world?

The British needed a base in the southern hemisphere to supply their ships so they could trade with India, China, Korea and Japan, and to buy furs from the northwest American coast. They also needed a supply base in case the war with Holland meant English ships could no longer be resupplied at Cape Town in South Africa. As well, it looked as though the French were preparing for a war to drive the English out of India.

The English also needed somewhere to send the large number of criminals accumulating in their prisons, partly because of poverty after many wars, but also because of the enormous social problems of the day, especially those caused by alcoholism. Gin was cheaper than food and streets of sleeping drunks were common in poor parts of big towns. (The wealthy drunks tended to sleep it off at home or their clubs.) By the standards of today, people then drank an incredible amount of alcohol — and died very young, looking very old.

Of the 1,487 people on the First Fleet, 759 were convicts, thirteen were convicts' kids, and 252 were marines and their wives and children. Two hundred and ten were Royal Navy seamen and 233 were merchant seamen who would leave the colony when their ships sailed away. These numbers are slightly inconsistent as there were births, deaths, discharges and deserters. Often records were inaccurate too.

Nearly all the convicts were thieves — pickpockets, sheep stealers, poachers — with only seven swindlers and four forgers. There were no murderers or rapists — or at least no one who'd been convicted of murder or rape. (There were murderers on the

Second Fleet.) Most were young — but not healthy. They had been starved in filthy, disease-racked prisons and hulks (decommissioned ships floating — barely — on the Thames) before leaving England, and most were in rags until they were given new clothes on board the ships of the First Fleet.

Many had been convicted of stealing small things like a handkerchief, a piece of cheese, a packet of snuff, twelve cucumber plants or a book, like William Francis, who stole *A Summary Account of the Flourishing State of the Island of Tobago* — probably to sell, not read!

But most had really stolen much more. In those days if you stole goods worth more than a guinea you had to be hanged. So if the judge or magistrate thought you had a chance to reform they found you guilty of stealing only a few of the things you'd taken, so you could be sent to the navy — or transported to a new land. The poor wretches transported for stealing a crust of bread make a good story, but those who were transported for stealing small things were probably guilty of much more and had been sentenced by a lenient magistrate to give them a second chance.

Once the First Fleet arrived, however, most of the criminals still didn't want to make an honest living. They preferred to steal instead of work. The marines sent with them sulked because they didn't get the alcohol that was part of their wages. They wouldn't even guard the convicts, police the colony, or act as magistrates. They saw themselves as only being there in case the French or 'natives' attacked.

And then the *Guardian*, the ship bringing new supplies to the colony, was wrecked.

By the time this book begins, life in the colony was dirty, dangerous and hard.

Many people were also very hungry — unless, of course, they worked their gardens, like the Reverend Johnson, and had lots of vegetables like corn and potatoes, or went fishing every second night like Surgeon White, or collected oysters or wild spinach.

There was lots of food if you knew where to find it — and members of the Indigenous nations around Sydney Town lived comfortably and were tall, strong and well muscled, unlike the usually puny and starved colonists. But as this book shows, life was soon a nightmare for the Indigenous people following the arrival of the English.

Did the colony starve?

It is important to see the 'starvation' of the colony in context. The official rations weren't enough to enable anyone to do a full week's hard physical labour. But there was lots of wild food, fish and game (though that wasn't always plentiful), as well as oysters and wild green vegetables, like the warrigal spinach and cress that grew almost faster than it could be picked. (One warrigal spinach plant will cover three metres in two weeks of hot, moist weather. We grow it on our property — or rather, it grows itself.)

Each man in the colony was given tools and land on which to grow vegetables, but not the skills or knowledge to help them do this. Few bothered to try, and even fewer did it properly. The early 'colonists' were, after all, thieves and criminals, often people who preferred an easy life of crime to working. The marines, too, reared as gentlemen, refused to dirty their hands in the garden, and were furious that they were not given the rations of meat, bread and particularly alcohol that were part of their wages. It is their angry letters home that form so much of our view of the colony's hunger.

The few in the colony who did die of hunger were either mad, like the man who saved three weeks of rations so he could walk to China, or had their rations stolen or cheated from them.

While there are many references to the hungry colony, there are also references to it being a healthy place to live. The wheat crops failed, but the corn/maize crops were excellent. Potato crops were disappointing, especially in dry weather, but fruit and nut trees and vines grew fast, as did vegetables like pumpkins and cabbages. At the most hungry time, the ration of fish was 4.5 kilos a week, more than enough protein even for a hard worker, with enough flour for a bread roll a day — plenty if you combined the rations with fresh corn and other vegetables and fruits.

In addition, most, or even all of the marines and officials, including Governor Phillip, had brought their own stocks of food and animals from the Cape of Good Hope. (This was a good thing as the colonists were sent from England with female sheep but no ram. As lambs were born it seems that one officer, at least, had the sense to buy a male sheep and bring it to the colony.)

There were hens, cows and goats. Most of the cows soon strayed, although the wild herds would be found again years later, but the goats remained — so many that they soon became a nuisance wandering into gardens. So there would have been milk and fresh goat's cheese, although little butter. As for any farming community of that time before fridges, cans and freezers, however, there were periods when certain foods weren't available — the hens didn't lay, the cow dried up, rain or drought spoilt the harvest.

Mostly the colony was hungry for familiar food — bread and potatoes — and the amazing amount of alcohol most people drank back then. Mothers even gave their children gin to stop them crying, and wine was given as a medicine to the sick. The absence of lots of alcohol was seen as an extraordinary deprivation.

The convicts had been given a generous allowance of new clothes on board the ships before leaving England. But as Maria observed, most of them wouldn't have been able to sew, even though they had been given needles and thread to keep their garments mended. A hundred years later, all girls were taught to sew in village or 'parochial' schools, to both mend and make their family's clothes. From then up till about 1970, most girls were taught at school how to make simple outfits, as well as how to knit jumpers and baby clothes. However, many of the women of the First, Second and Third Fleets may never have learnt how to use a needle and thread.

Alcoholism

Rum was both the currency and the comfort of the early colony, after Governor Phillip left. Enormous amounts were brewed and distilled illegally, or brought in and sold by the officers. Drunkenness was common back in England; it was even worse here. Crops like wheat and potatoes were often used for making alcohol instead of kept for food; family life in many cases didn't exist. It is difficult, today, to realise quite how much terror and social stagnation were due to alcoholism back then.

What happened next ...

The tiny colony clinging to the edge of a great land became a town, then a city. More colonies were founded; new — free — settlers arrived; gold was found and even more people arrived. Then 101 years after Andrew White sailed for England, the land became one nation — Australia.

But that is the subject of some of my other books.

References

This book relies on the English accounts of those who wrote about the happenings at the time. The English almost certainly misunderstood much of what happened. Some were prejudiced; some were liars; at other times their accounts leave tantalising questions. But they were there.

These early accounts may all be hard to read at first, but as you get used to the old-fashioned way of writing, they are fascinating voices from another time.

Collins, David, *An Account of the English Colony in New South Wales, with Remarks on the Dispositions, Customs, Manners, etc. of the Native Inhabitants of that Country*, Reed in association with the Royal Historical Society, Sydney, 1975 [first published 1798–1802].

Flinders, Matthew, *A Voyage to Terra Australis*, G & W Nicol, London, 1814, vol. 1.

Fowell, Newton, *Letter Received by John Fowell from Newton Fowell, 31 July 1790*, State Library of NSW, Mitchell Library, MLMSS 4895/1/21.

Howe, George (ed.), *The Sydney Gazette and New South Wales Advertiser*, Sydney, 1803–1842.

Tench, Watkin, *A Complete Account of the Settlement at Port Jackson, in New South Wales: Including an Accurate Description of the Colony; of the Natives; and of its Natural Productions*, G Nicol and J Sewell, London, 1793.

White, John, *Journal of a Voyage to New South Wales*, J Debrett, London, 1790.

Other great references

Australian Archaeological Survey Consultants Pty. Ltd., *The Waverley Council Area: an Aboriginal Perspective: a Report to the Waverley Council*, The Council, Sydney, 1995.

Australian Dictionary of Biography, Melbourne University Press, Melbourne, 1996.

Flood, Josephine, *Archaeology of the Dreamtime: the Story of Prehistoric Australia and its People*, Angus & Robertson, Sydney, rev. ed., 1995.

Harris, Alexander, *Settlers and Convicts, or, Recollections of Sixteen Years' Labour in the Australian Backwoods / by an Emigrant Mechanic*, Foreword by Manning Clark, Melbourne University Press, Melbourne, 1964 [first published 1847].

Holden, Robert, *Orphans of History: the Forgotten Children of the First Fleet*, Text Publishing, Melbourne, 2000.

Horton, David, *Aboriginal Australia: Wall Map*, Aboriginal Studies Press for AIATSIS, Canberra, rev. ed., 2000.

Horton, David (ed.), *The Encyclopaedia of Aboriginal Australia: Aboriginal and Torres Strait Islander History, Society and Culture*, Aboriginal Studies Press for AIATSIS, Canberra, 1994.

Tindale, Norman B., *Aboriginal Tribes of Australia: Their Terrain, Environmental Controls, Distribution, Limits and Proper Names*, Australian National University Press, Canberra, 1974.

Acknowledgements

Nanberry: Black Brother White wasn't an easy, or simple, book to write.

It began as the story of a possum, and the man — Surgeon White — who tried unsuccessfully to tame it. At that stage I had read all the early colonial diaries and letters, and thought I knew all the story to be found.

But as I wrote, more information arrived on my doorstep, a series of coincidences: the discovery of the transcript of Rachel's extraordinary trial, more letters rediscovered, another painting, lists of ship's crew and Charterhouse students. The book changed to a deeper one, with Rachel; and then another, that made Andrew White the hero, as I learned more about his life too. But slowly, gradually, yet another book emerged. It was Nanberry who was at the forefront now, the amazing child who not only survived 'smallpox' and the death of his family but also the possible death of his entire people. The book changed, layer by layer.

As always, this book has been a team effort. When you are trying to reconstruct the past, working with often contradictory material and place names that have vanished — and in some cases the places vanished too — it is easy to get lost, especially when material comes from so many disparate places. Kate O'Donnell and Kate Burnitt worked with their invariable meticulousness and insight, keeping every thread together; the vision of Liz Kemp and Lisa Berryman, as usual, helped me find the true heart of the book. Lisa is combination guardian, Godmother, sounding board and concept launcher for every historical novel I write.

I'd also like to give my great thanks to Steve Sheen, for his invaluable material on Andrew Douglass (Douglas) White, researched over many years; and for the unstinting generosity with which he shared it and allowed me to use it in this book. Many thanks as well to Hugh Grogan, for setting me on the right course to find the sappers of Waterloo, and — always — to Noël Pratt and Angela Marshall, not just for helping turn a mess of a manuscript into a book, but for their kindness, their depth and breadth of knowledge, and their dedication and insight, helping keep the balance and accuracy needed when writing about cultures that aren't my own. There are few friends like Angela who, when asked to read a manuscript, have the wide eclectic knowledge to send back a footnote: 'By the way, Nanberry probably wasn't the one who sailed up the Shoalhaven.'

When you write about the past the problems are often the bits that you don't *know* that you don't know. (That sentence makes sense if you read it twice.) Angela's watchfulness has meant that the obsessive rummaging in the past that leads to these books is done by two, not one, and in this, as so many books, her help is beyond words of gratitude.

Outlands Trilogy
In the Blood • Blood Moon • Flesh and Blood

School for Heroes
Lessons for a Werewolf Warrior
Dance of the Deadly Dinosaurs

Wacky Families Series
1. My Dog the Dinosaur • 2. My Mum the Pirate
3. My Dad the Dragon • 4. My Uncle Gus the Garden Gnome
5. My Uncle Wal the Werewolf • 6. My Gran the Gorilla
7. My Auntie Chook the Vampire Chicken
8. My Pa the Polar Bear

Phredde Series
1. A Phaery Named Phredde
2. Phredde and a Frog Named Bruce
3. Phredde and the Zombie Librarian
4. Phredde and the Temple of Gloom
5. Phredde and the Leopard-Skin Librarian
6. Phredde and the Purple Pyramid
7. Phredde and the Vampire Footy Team
8. Phredde and the Ghostly Underpants

Picture Books
Diary of a Wombat (with Bruce Whatley)
Pete the Sheep (with Bruce Whatley)
Josephine Wants to Dance (with Bruce Whatley)
The Shaggy Gully Times (with Bruce Whatley)
Emily and the Big Bad Bunyip (with Bruce Whatley)
Baby Wombat's Week (with Bruce Whatley)
Queen Victoria's Underpants (with Bruce Whatley)
The Tomorrow Book (with Sue deGennaro)
Christmas Wombat (with Bruce Whatley)

Jackie French is a full-time writer and wombat negotiator. Jackie writes fiction and non-fiction for all ages, and has columns in the print media. Jackie is regarded as one of Australia's most popular children's authors. She writes across all genres — from picture books, humour and history to science fiction.